THE MAN WITHIN THE TEMPLE

THE GOLDEN MAGE BOOK TWO

C.G. GARCIA

Fantastical Press

The characters and events portrayed in this book are fictitious.
Any similarity to real persons, living or dead, is coincidental
and not intended by the author.

www.CGGarciaAuthor.com
Cover Design by C.G. Garcia
Model Stock Photography by Janna Prosvirina

ISBN-10: 0692529136
ISBN-13: 978-0692529133
Second Paperback Edition

Dedicated to my family who are always supportive, even when I disappear into my writing cave for days at a time

ALSO BY C.G GARCIA

Fractured Multiverse
The Supreme Moment
Black Crimson (Blood Fire Chronicles Book One)
*coming soon

Old Souls Trilogy
Old Souls
The Ties That Bind the Soul
The Name Within His Soul *coming soon

The Golden Mage Trilogy
The Kingdom of Eternal Sorrow
The Man Within the Temple
The Last Stone Cast

CHAPTER ONE

Allison sat silently in Aidric's sitting room near one of the few windows his suite contained, staring out into the indoor garden, her eyes seeing nothing and her mind a million miles away. Patiently, she waited for Aidric to return from Diryan's chamber, not at all anxious for the conversation she knew would happen.

After leaving Master Kiryl, she had remained silent, lost in a despair so great that even Aidric's gentle prodding couldn't coax a word from her. For once, even his nearness didn't seem to affect her in the least. She had only been able to think about Master Kiryl's words, echoing through her mind like the sound of a gunshot reverberating down a darkened hall. After they were offered another meal by the Providencen priests—a meal she had barely touched—Aidric had built another portal, and they had returned. To what, she was no longer certain.

Looking troubled, Aidric had reluctantly left her alone in his quarters while he ran off to speak with King Diryan, promising that they would talk when he returned. She had merely nodded, and he had sighed in frustration as he had left. Allison hated herself for shutting him out like that, but it was the only way she knew how to cope with the terrible weight that had been forced on her that even now was threatening to crush her.

In her childhood when her stepfather had beaten her, her only solace had been to lock herself within her mind, away from the pain, the anger, and the utter hopelessness she had felt. She had trained herself so well to lock herself away when the pain became too great that now it was second nature.

Alone with only her thoughts, Allison had finally allowed the chaos of everything Kiryl had told them to swirl around freely in her mind as she tried to make sense of it all. Kiryl had spoken of truths, but she had no idea what he had meant. It had all sounded like a bunch of new age mumbo-jumbo to her, something one of those televangelists would rave about. She doubted even Aidric knew what the Seer had meant, and that troubled her more than she cared to admit to herself.

Then, there was her suspicion that Kiryl knew something dire concerning her, and for reasons unknown, had allowed her to know he knew and maddeningly chose not to reveal anything to her. Inwardly, Allison fumed over his silence, but what could she do about it? It wasn't very likely that she would be visiting him again anytime soon, and even if she did, it was equally unlikely that she would even be allowed to speak with him again.

"I have never known you to be so silent," Aidric suddenly said behind her.

Allison had not even heard him come into the room. Slowly she raised her head to look up at him. His face was drawn and his posture wilted as though he was on his last dregs of strength. She knew building that portal home had stretched him thin, although he would never admit it to her.

Her earlier guilt came rushing back. *It's because of me he's ready to collapse.*

"You must be tired," she said, purposely ignoring his unspoken question. Now wasn't the time to be selfish. "Why don't you go rest? I'll be okay here on my own for the rest of the day. It'll give me a chance to read some more."

"You can't be rid of me so easily," Aidric said with a lopsided grin as he pulled up a chair and joined her. "I'm not so tired that I cannot sit and talk with you awhile because Allison, we *do* need to talk."

"I know." Allison refused to meet his eyes. She knew she would cry if she did.

"I took you to see the Providencen priests in hopes of laying to rest any fears, any questions you had regarding who you are," he began softly, staring at her with eyes that were full of conflicting emotions. "I never realized the extent of what they would reveal to you. Had I known, then perhaps I wouldn't have been so quick to bring you to them."

His lips twisted into something like disgust. "I did exactly as they wanted. You shouldn't have had the burden of another prophecy to shoulder so soon."

"Why?" she asked more sharply than she had intended, raising her eyes to his. "Isn't it better that I know the truth?" *At least some of it,* she thought bitterly, remembering Kiryl's knowing expression.

"Your silence when I left you here disturbs me, more so now than your silence directly after we left Master Kiryl," Aidric said. "Since your arrival to this world, you've always been full of questions, curiosity, even doubts, but now, there's—nothing." The look in his eyes was indecipherable. "It shouldn't have been this way."

"But it is," Allison said quietly, turning her eyes back to the garden. "It's funny, the games fate can play with you. You live your whole life thinking your life is your own and whatever comes of it is what you decide to make of it. Then out of the blue, fate comes along with a mocking grin and flings something like this into your lap, expecting what? For you to just cheerfully deal with it?"

"Allison..."

"I had thought the Golden Mage business was bad enough," she continued as though Aidric hadn't spoken, "and I *was* determined to deal with it and get on with whatever life I could make here. Then suddenly I'm not just some legendary mage destined to either save or destroy a kingdom I never knew existed until a few days ago, but also a mage destined to determine whether the people of this reality have a fighting chance to survive or not. There aren't enough words to even express how monumentally terrifying it is to know that the survival of a whole world is partially up to *me*, someone who doesn't really understand any of it."

Allison turned her eyes back to Aidric. He was looking at her grimly, the air of reassurance she had grown so accustomed to receiving from him conspicuously absent.

"Everything Master Kiryl told me made no sense at all! He told me to seek out truths—truths about *what*? And how, if I understand nothing?"

Aidric ran a hand through his hair in frustration

as he replied, "That's why we often don't seek out the help of the Order of the Providence. It seems they delight in speaking in riddles. Diryan especially abhors the thought of having to consult with them. If they would only speak in common terms that any layman could understand, then perhaps half the problems brought to them would not have ended in disaster. Perhaps these 'truths' Kiryl spoke of are merely representations of your acceptance of the destiny Seni has given you. It would seem so to me."

"I suppose you're right," she said thoughtfully. "Maybe I'm just trying to make something out of nothing. Lord knows I tend to do that often enough! Still, there's something that he was hinting towards but never actually said that's been bothering me."

"Aside from the obvious, you mean?" he offered, flashing her a weak smile.

"Funny," Allison retorted, but smiling despite herself. Over the last few days, she seemed to have developed a weakness for Aidric's smiles.

He shrugged. "I tried."

"You can try to cheer me up later," she promised, and then said more soberly, "For now, I'd like your opinion on my suspicions. I just couldn't shake the feeling that he was keeping something important from me—something that I desperately needed to know. It even seemed as if he *wanted* me to know he was keeping something from me. I could see it in his eyes when he looked at me."

"That doesn't surprise me a bit," Aidric said with a look of disgust. "If it's not riddles, then it's secrets. I have my own suspicions that the Seers enjoy watching us stumble along, helping us only when their own hides are endangered. Seni knows that they need a little amusement to liven up the drudgery of their lives. It's probably unfair of me to say such things of them. Deep down, their intentions are probably for the best. They are, after all, messengers of Seni, but one does wonder—"

He shrugged. "The Providencen priests, in a way, are like stern teachers, and the whole world, their novices. Their aid will only take you so far, and the rest is for you to stumble through."

"Not a very encouraging prospect in my case," Allison said dryly.

"Indeed," Aidric said thoughtfully, and then he abruptly sprung up from his chair with a burst of renewed energy that came from God-only-knew where. He held out his hand to her and said, "Come. If you are to venture into uncertain lands, then we both shall stumble through them together. That I pledge you."

"But—but where are we going?" Allison asked in bewilderment as she accepted his hand, and he pulled her onto her feet. "Shouldn't you be resting after casting so many draining spells today?"

"I have rested enough sitting here with you," Aidric said cheerfully. "Besides, I was never one to stay still for longer than a moment as you will soon discover only too well. Let's leave all our troubles and all thoughts of legends, prophecies, and duties behind for the remainder of the day. You have yet to see the kingdom that lies beyond these walls, and I don't know when we'll have another opportunity such as this to escape. The village of Ell is near enough for a day-long outing."

"But don't you have other duties to attend to today besides me?" Allison asked worriedly. "You're the Mage-general. Surely you—"

"Let me worry about that, milady," he cut in. "Let's just say that I'm taking the day off that I should've had the day you graced us with your presence. Now, no more protests. Shall we be off to the stables?"

"I can't ride," Allison warned as they left his rooms.

"Then it's high time you learned, isn't it?" Aidric said with a boyish grin.

"But in this?" she said with a raised eyebrow, fingering her flimsy apprentice uniform with uncertainty.

"Would you rather breeches?"

"Yes!" she said eagerly. *Anything but this weird nightgown!*

Aidric looked at her askance as if she had said something very amusing. "I was merely jesting."

"Well, why can't I wear breeches?" Allison demanded, stopping in mid-step and folding her arms against her chest stubbornly.

"It's not proper," he explained, as if to a very small child. Somehow, she found his tone more amusing than annoying. "You would scandalize the whole kingdom if you appeared before the public eye sporting breeches."

"I don't see how that would make much more difference now since my just being here is scandal enough for them, it seems," she retorted, "but if it'll cause you any grief, then I won't do it."

"Ladies ride well enough in skirts," Aidric offered.

"Well said for someone who's never had to ride in a skirt," she noted dryly.

"I stand rebuked," he said with a chuckle as he held the huge door of the Mage Hall open, waving his hand before her in an invitation to pass, "but I still remember my manners."

Allison smiled as she walked outside and immediately squinted as she was confronted by the bright sunlight, brighter than any sunlight on Earth. Blinking rapidly to clear the flashing spectrum from her vision, she shaded her eyes with her hand and gazed up briefly into the sky, marveling at the sight of the two suns. She supposed that she looked foolish gawking up at the sky, but this was the first time she truly was able to soak in her surroundings, and be damned with appearances! She was going to make the most of it!

The pungent scent of freshly cut grass reached her nostrils as she glanced all around at the expanse of the perfectly manicured grounds of the palace, drinking in the beauty, and at the same time wondering how they managed to keep a lawn so immense cut and free of weeds. *Because I don't think they have a lawnmower to help them along,* she thought with a grin.

Beyond, to the south, Allison could vaguely make out the shapes and shadows of a forest along the horizon. A strange sensation washed over her as she stared at the forest, not threatening, but something that seemed to beckon her from deep within the foliage.

"That's the forest you found me in," she spoke up suddenly, positive she was correct, "the Forest of Illusions, and that's where the Mage-field is located, isn't it?"

"How do you know that?" Aidric asked, his expression surprised, as he walked up behind her.

"I think I can—feel it," she replied with a slight frown, struggling to explain to him something she didn't fully understand herself. "I can't really explain it. It's like something in that forest is—" She struggled to find the word. "—calling me," she finished helplessly, "but that isn't exactly right."

"Yes," Aidric said distantly, his forehead creased as though he was deep in thought. "It's something all mages feel after they have Bonded with the magic there. In a sense, a mage has left a part of their essence there in the Field after the Bonding, and what you are feeling now is the result of it, though I cannot fathom why *you* are able to sense the Mage-field when you have yet to Bond with it."

"When I die, the energy released during that transition from life to death goes to that Mage-field," she stated vacantly, tonelessly, as if she was in a trance.

"*What?*" Aidric choked out in disbelief.

Allison shook her head a little and then looked at him questionably when she saw how agitated he was. "I'm sorry. I was woolgathering. Did you say something?" she asked.

"What did you just say?" he demanded.

She eyed him oddly. "I asked if *you* had said something. I guess I wasn't the only one woolgathering."

"No, no—before that," he said a little impatiently. "You said something about when you die, the energy released goes to the Mage-field. Where in Seni's name did you hear that?"

"I did?" Allison said, frowning. "But I don't remember saying—"

"Never mind," Aidric interrupted, running his hand through his hair, a gesture she was beginning to recognize as one he did when he was exasperated. "Something tells me we should just let that one be. I pledged that we would escape this madness for at least today, and damn it, we shall!"

Still frowning, Allison took the arm he offered and allowed him to lead her over to the stables, which were located at the south end of the palace grounds. The smell of hay was everywhere, causing her to suddenly erupt into a sneezing fit.

"Damn it all, I would be allergic," she said, rubbing her nose in annoyance.

"To horses?" Aidric asked incredulously.

"No, to hay, silly," she chided. "I hope you brought a lot of handkerchiefs with you because I'll be sneezing the whole trip."

"No need," he said and placed a hand over her nose.

"What are you doing?" she demanded, shying away from his hand in alarm.

"Ridding you of your allergy, so hold still."

Her nose instantly began to tingle, and a few seconds later, Allison felt the warmth associated with healing that she had grown so accustomed to feeling spreading up through her nasal cavity. When he removed his hand, the itching and sneezing had stopped.

"You never cease to amaze me," she said wondrously, rubbing her nose as if not quite sure to believe that the allergy was gone.

"And that's only because you amaze so easily," he teased.

Aidric introduced her to the Stablemaster, Ahern, a tall, dark-skinned man with a pleasant face. To Allison's surprise, he didn't show even an inkling of fear towards her, only a mild curiosity.

He bowed politely to her and said, "A pleasure, m'lady. I saw you at the celebration, though even then I couldn't believe my eyes. 'Tis not every day you get t' see a legend." He then turned to Aidric and said, "I'll have Shadow saddled up for you, m'lord."

"The Lady Allison is to be given a horse of her own," Aidric said. "She has no knowledge of horses—so she claims—so have you any suggestions?"

Ahern scratched his chin thoughtfully and replied, "I can give the lady the filly from Tilly's line if that be fitting, m'lord? 'Tis a gentle and easily managed mount."

Aidric nodded and Ahern disappeared into the stable. She could hear him ordering stableboys to bring saddles and tack for their horses.

"I like him," Allison commented as they waited.

"He seems like a pretty straightforward man, and he treated me as if I was normal."

"Indeed, he is," Aidric said, smiling down at her. "He has been the Stablemaster for the king for twenty years now, and I trust that he'll be so for twenty more. Never have we possessed horses of such strength and beauty such as Ahern has bred for us through the years. If I didn't know any better, I could swear that he can hold a conversation with his horses in their own language. His control of them is nothing short of miraculous. That's his gift from Seni."

"You really don't have to give me a horse," Allison insisted abruptly. "I'm sure other people'll need one more than I do, and I can always just borrow one when I need to ride."

"Nonsense," Aidric scoffed. "We have plenty of horses here that are in need of masters to give them their much needed exercise. The horse, if she pleases you, is yours."

Ahern soon returned with their horses, Aidric's a large, midnight black stallion that was true to its name and hers, a smaller, cream-colored filly, its silky mane almost a perfect match to the color of her own hair. Allison stepped up to her horse and slowly ran her hands over its sheer coat in admiration.

"She's beautiful," she breathed as she lovingly stroked its nose while the horse sniffed at her hand

and then her hair. "I don't know much about horses, but even I can tell that. I think I'll call her Destiny."

Ahern gave her a toothy grin and said, "Aye, that she is, m'lady, and a fine name at that. Shall I fetch you a stool t' help you mount?"

"No thank you," Allison said, grabbing onto the pummel and placing her foot securely into the stirrup. "I think I can manage."

"Allison, maybe I should assist—" Aidric began then stopped when he saw that she had already managed to mount and was fussily arranging her skirts about her.

"Stupid skirts," she muttered as she cast her eyes on Aidric's amused face.

"You will scandalize the kingdom yet," he said with a chuckle as he mounted Shadow with a flourish.

"What did I do wrong now?"

He raised an eyebrow and answered, "For one thing, Allison, a lady shouldn't sit astride a horse as you are now doing."

"In this case, I don't much care for what's proper," Allison retorted. "If I sit the other way, I'm bound to fall off if the horse decided to take an unexpected gallop. If the people don't like it, then they simply don't have to look. If you won't let me ride with breeches, then at least I can have *some* semblance of comfort riding like this." She smiled wryly at his dumbfounded expression, and added, "Now, are you simply going to sit there lecturing me on proper womanly etiquette, or are you going to teach me how to ride her?"

"Just when I believe that I'm starting to know you well, I always find that it's otherwise," he noted with the barest ghost of a smile.

Then before she could think of a proper retort, Aidric launched into a full explanation of the proper methods of signaling the horse to go where she wanted with reins and knees. Soon, after absorbing his instructions and practicing them a little in the open fields surrounding the stables until Allison felt reasonably comfortable having reigns in her hands, they were off to the west, to the village of Ell.

CHAPTER TWO

F or the first leg of the trip, they rode in a comfortable silence. Aidric's eyes were a bit distant, lost in
his musings, while Allison split her concentration between her riding and taking in the landscape around
her.

It was so peaceful here as opposed to the everyday
clamor of a major city that Allison had grown accustomed to ever since she and her mother had moved to
California. Here, there wasn't the ever-present buzz of
traffic zooming along a multitude of freeways, no
horns blasting, no car alarms, nor was there sirens
screaming by every few minutes to remind you just
how terrible the world around you could be. Here,
there was only peace—the serenity that only being in
true nature, untouched by the hands of mankind,
could exude.

It was then that Allison realized why the air had smelled strange when she had first arrived in the Forest Of Illusions. It wasn't really because of the odor of nature around her—although that had been a very small part of it—but the fact that the air was completely *clean*. Here, the pollutants of man-made chemicals and the exhaust fumes of perhaps billions of cars had never touched the air. Here, there wasn't even a word for smog or acid rain.

For the first time since this whole nightmare had begun, she felt truly relaxed, her mind unburdened for at least a little while from her problems and newfound responsibilities as her eyes absorbed the beauty of the land around her with an almost childlike sense of wonder. They were surrounded by a vast landscape of rolling hills, the grass a vivid green and flourishing. A few trees, different from those monstrosities she had seen in the Forest of Illusions and more familiar, dotted the landscape here and there. They resembled maples down to everything except the hue of the leaves, which were a yellowish-orange color that seemed fitting on a tree in late autumn, though Queen Ileanna had told her that they were well into spring, their world having four distinct seasons pretty much identical to Earth's.

Strange birds were constantly flying overhead, as well as periodically emerging from the trees. Allison squinted up at them, somewhat blinded by the suns, but nevertheless saw that they were much larger than the birds she was accustomed to seeing. She judged their wingspan to be at least six feet, but that was not what really drew her attention to them. It was the fact that their feathers were stark white and appeared to shimmer like diamonds in the rays of the suns.

Allison urged her horse to pick up its pace slightly so that she was even with Shadow and asked Aidric the name of the bird.

"Those are snowbirds," he replied bemusedly, his mind still lost in whatever it was he had been mulling over. "Well named since their feathers glisten as a snow-covered embankment does in the suns."

She nodded and left him to his musings, falling back a bit, and continuing her observations of the land. Every so often, their horses would startle an animal that looked every bit like a cottontail deer from her world that had been hiding in the high grasses near the wagon path they traveled. Seeing another familiar animal besides the horses they rode gave her a great sense of relief, making her newly upended world start to right itself, if only a little bit.

Allison sighed and closed her eyes and mind against thoughts of the alienness of her new world, determined to simply enjoy the feel of the cool breeze flowing across her face and through her hair and the lulling pace of her horse. It was no wonder Aidric had suggested that they ride in an attempt to bring her out of her crushing depression. With the steady rhythm of a horse trotting underneath you and the wind whipping through your hair, what better way to raise your spirits?

In fact, she had lost herself so completely to those relaxing thoughts that she didn't hear Aidric's horse fall back a little to trot beside her until his voice broke through the slight trance she had not realized that she had fallen under.

"I trust you are enjoying this little excursion?" he asked.

She opened her eyes lazily and turned her head to meet his steady gaze. Dressed in his Mage-general's uniform and the wind blowing his hair in untidy wisps across his face, Allison thought he had never looked more handsome than he did now. To her chagrin, she felt her cheeks begin to burn. Allison hoped that Aidric would think she was flushed because of the sunlight and wind.

"It makes me regret that I've never gone horse-back riding before this," she replied steadily, proud that her voice didn't betray her emotions. "Why is it that you always know how to cheer me up?"

Aidric chuckled. "Perhaps it's because when you brood, you remind me so much of myself. In fact, if

Selwyn had seen you after we returned from the Cala-mon Mountains, he would have said as much."

"You know," Allison began thoughtfully, "I just realized that I really don't know that much about you. I hadn't thought you to be someone who broods much, and yet, Raya said the same thing to me."

"Seni help me, I cringe to think about what else that woman has told you of me," Aidric said with a grimace. "What is it about me that you wish to know?"

"Oh, I don't know—your family to begin with. You've never mentioned them. Do you have any siblings?"

Aidric fell silent suddenly, the look in his eyes hesitant, and Allison feared that she had hit a sore spot for him just like he had when he had pumped her for information about her stepdad.

"If you would rather not—" she began hastily.

But Aidric shook his head and said, "Shall we make a bargain? I'll tell you anything you wish of me on any subject you ask—if you'll extend me the same courtesy."

"Fair enough," she agreed.

"My family lived in Sersia," he said, "one of the kingdoms bordering Lamia to the west. My parents were farmers, and although it was common for farm-ers to have many children so that they could help in the fields, I was an only child. My mother nearly died in childbed, and as a result of the complications, she became barren. They both died when I was but a lad of eight during an epidemic of the black fever in my village."

"I'm sorry," Allison said softly, wanting to say more, but everything that came to mind sounded artificial and trite so she just left it at that.

Aidric nodded his acceptance and continued, "I knew that I had the ability to become a mage, so it was then that I came to Lamia. Lord Othos, then Diryan's Mage-general, took me under his wing when he discovered just how powerful a mage I had the potential of becoming. He and Diryan were as close as brothers, thus I spent much time in the company of the king and queen. Lord Othos and Diryan became my unofficial adoptive fathers, and Ileanna, my adoptive mother. Now that Othos has passed through Aidius's Gates into the Thrones, they, along with Selwyn and Raya, are my family now. Although, for the sake of politics, none know that I hold such a strong bond with the king and queen. Not even Selwyn and Raya know how deeply that connection runs—we try not to behave too casually around others—though I believe they are beginning to suspect."

"So why are you telling *me?*" Allison asked, startled.

He shrugged. "I just felt that you should know. I

don't know why. A touch of Foresight, perhaps."

"Well, that explains a lot of things I had been wondering about," Allison said with a smile. "It seemed as if King Diryan treated you a little differently, more informally, than everyone else. Now I know why. Since they don't have any children, does that make you their heir? Are you a prince in your own right?"

A strange look flickered across his eyes before he barked a laugh. "I would sooner be the ruler of the Thrones above than sit on the throne of Lamia! Only one of the royal blood *and* one who possesses no mage abilities can assume the throne of Lamia. That law goes back to the story Kiryl told you concerning the war that divided Natia.

"After seeing what power could do in the hands of a greedy monarch, first with Rhan and Reznik, then a couple of centuries later with the Marzinan mage-king, Adok, the Senini of Jadwiga forbade any with mage abilities to take the throne after the premature death of the Jagwigan mage-king, Ladonis. It was because of the threat King Adok posed to Jadwiga that King Ladonis sacrificed his own life to create the Shield that now protects Lamia.

"Lamia evolved from what was once Jadwiga. In fact, the citizens changed the name of their kingdom to Lamia, which in the Natian tongue means 'eternal sorrow,' to remind future generations of the calamities they suffered at the hands of wars through the ages. He was the last mage to ever sit the throne of this land. Luckily, Ladonis left no heirs, thus the throne was indisputably given to the House of Lasha, cousins to Ladonis that did not have so much as a spark of mage potential in their blood."

"Then why have the king and queen not had any children yet?" Allison asked. "Queen Ileanna must be close to the end of her childbearing years, unless she is younger than I think she is, or in your world, women never lose that ability."

"You are quite right," Aidric replied and then paused as if he wanted to say more but wasn't sure if he should. Just when she thought that he wasn't going to elaborate, he suddenly fixed her with an intent gaze and said, "I don't know why, but I feel that you should know this truth. She had a child many years ago, a son that was healthy and perfect in every aspect except one crucial point that is considered a great gift in another but a curse to the House of Lasha—he was to be a mage. Now, there is also a second law of succession in Lamia, one that isn't a law of man, but of Seni, again originating with the Jadwigans and upheld presently by the Brothers in Divinity."

"Who are they?"

"The whole of our orders of priests, not just in

Lamia, but throughout all nations of Seni's World. They are the priests of our temples, the wandering friars, the monks who, like the Providencen priests, lead a life of seclusion, and the marshals of the laws of Seni. The Order of the Providence and the Horae are sects of the Brothers in Divinity, as are the Domni and the Senini. Should anyone break a law set down by Seni, then it's they, not the king of their lands, who must be answered to.

"Thus, as it's one of Seni's laws that a mage cannot sit on the throne of Lamia, should a prince or princess be born with mage abilities, it's thought to be a treason against Seni and carries a penalty of death."

"They don't execute the *child* do they?" Allison asked incredulously, her eyes widening in horror.

"No, the child, of course, is an innocent in the affair, but since the bloodline of the royal line of Lamia is supposedly free of the mage potential, then the spouse who is not of the blood is at fault, thus executed for treason. In the case of Diryan and Ileanna, the one who would have been accused was—"

"Ileanna," Allison finished with a sinking feeling in her stomach. "Some of the histories of Lamia I read named King Diryan as prince."

Aidric nodded grimly. "By some miraculous twist of fate, Diryan and Ileanna were in Sersia when she went into labor. Diryan had been negotiating a new alliance agreement with the king of Sersia, and Ileanna had insisted that she wanted to go along. Naturally, he protested because of her condition, but Ileanna was afraid that she would bear her child while Diryan was away and put her foot down. As it turned out, Ileanna had friends near the Sersian palace in the village of Ari, and while visiting them, her labor began. Her lady-friend delivered the child, and when they suddenly realized that the child would be a mage, you can well imagine the anguish—and the fear."

"How could they tell that the baby would be a mage? Do they glow or something?"

"Every mageborn bears this mark of Seni upon them," Aidric said, lifting his hair from his neck and turning his head so that she saw the red, circular mark about the size of a quarter just at the nape of his neck.

Allison felt all the color suddenly drain from her face as she stared in utter disbelief at the mark he bore, one identical to the birthmark she possessed in exactly the same place.

"Allison, what is it?" Aidric asked in alarm.

"I have that mark, too," she whispered, watching his eyes widen with surprise as she lifted up her own hair to show him her birthmark.

"That you have it shouldn't surprise me, but yet it does," he admitted. "I never thought to check. You say you knew nothing of Seni before you came here, yet He has given you His mark. I find that most puzzling."

"And something I'd rather not think about right now," Allison said firmly. "You were saying about the child?" she prompted.

Aidric stared at her for a few more moments before nodding reluctantly. "Yes, the child—Ileanna was not born of nobility. She was a peasant living in Avidon when Diryan met her. His father had been against the marriage from the start, but Diryan defied him and married her anyway. Although they later put aside their differences and his father grudgingly accepted Ileanna, he always said that she would bring Diryan nothing but grief. Diryan thought of this when his son was born, thinking perhaps that his father had somehow cursed them.

"However, Diryan was determined that Ileanna wouldn't suffer because of his father's ill wishes. They took Ileanna's friends into confidence, swearing them to secrecy in the name of Seni, an oath that would damn one's soul if ever it should be broken, and left the child with them to raise. They returned to Lamia with the story that the queen had had a difficult time in childbed, and despite the aid of a healer, had given birth to a stillborn infant.

"Over the years, they visited their son whenever

they could do so safely, mostly when Diryan had affairs of diplomacy in Sersia. The boy knew the conditions of his birth and why he wasn't allowed to live with his real parents. Diryan always held the hope that somehow his son would be able to return to Lamia, to succeed him on the throne, but sadly, when the boy was barely seventeen, he was accidentally killed during a tavern scuffle. Ileanna swore that she would never bear another child. The risk of producing another mageborn offspring was too great."

"Is this what you meant when you told me that the king had lost much to Seni?" Allison asked quietly.

His smile was infinitely sad. "Yes, and he *still* could lose Ileanna to this decree of Seni if any should learn of what occurred in Sersia, so I ask you not to breathe a word of what I've revealed to you today to anyone, not even Raya."

"I promise," Allison said firmly and then added, "I feel so terrible for them. Ileanna is always so kind to me, and I enjoy her company immensely. The king has treated me fairly considering the circumstances of my identity. Something that devastating shouldn't have happened to people like them."

"I know, but the worst seems to happen to the best of us. Present company included. Now, I do believe that it's your turn to speak of your family, but you must be swift about it for Ell lies only a few depths away, beyond that last hill."

Allison squirmed uncomfortably. "Oh, well, you already know most of the important things about my family—my stepfather's a religious fanatic, and my mother had a mental breakdown because of it." She turned away and concentrated on the landscape before her. "I had a horrible childhood, as did my sister, Katherine. If my stepdad wasn't beating scripture into me, then he was punishing me for my 'sins.' If I sneezed during services, I was punished. If I refused to read my bible, our holy book—and I often did—I was punished. Even if I dared to look him in the eyes when he was lecturing me for some supposed misdoing, I was punished severely for my 'insolence.' The fact that my mother and I were forced to leave Kat behind when she finally managed to leave her husband and his cult was always heavy on my conscious, and now that I'm here with no hope of ever setting foot in my world again, it hurts even more."

"You shouldn't punish yourself so harshly," Aidric said gently. "You didn't know that this fate would befall you."

"I know," she replied with a sigh, "but I still can't help feeling that I should've done more for her. In fact, the very day I was brought to this world, Kat had snuck away from home and had been begging me to find some way for her to live with me. I don't know how your laws are enforced here, but in my world, we go to court and plead our cases before a single individual known as the "judge.' That judge ruled that my stepdad, Kat's biological father, would have sole custody of her until she turned eighteen. Letting her stay with me could have landed me in jail for kidnapping, but I guess now I'll never know, will I? I'll never know how she's doing, or what becomes of her life. It's hard."

Allison felt tears begin to swell up in her eyes, and she squeezed her eyes shut tightly in order to keep them at bay. *Now is not the time to start crying, you idiot! I'm sure you'll make a good first impression riding into Ell with your face all red and swollen from crying...*

Forcing herself to smile for her sake as much as Aidric's she said, "I sure am trying my damnedest to get myself into a foul mood again, aren't I?"

"Like me, you have a gift for doing exactly that," he agreed, his eyes shining with amusement. "I would lecture you as Selwyn does me, but who am I to say anything? Now, no more talk of cruelties and childhoods. We are almost to the edge of Ell, and I doubt very much that you would wish for prying ears and wagging tongues to spread your personal business all over the kingdom, would you?"

"They aren't that bad, are they?"

"Believe me, little cat, you would *not* want to find

out from personal experience."

"Point taken," Allison said with a laugh, feeling the cloud of gloom that had fallen on her start to lift.

They both fell silent as they approached the outskirts of Ell. Aidric had called it a village, but to Allison's eye, village was not the right word to describe it. Ell was a fairly large town, but by no means a large metropolis or anything close to one. Farmhouses, a few large estates, and an infinite amount of open pastures filled with rows of crops or antar, and other animals resembling sheep and goats made up the outside vicinity of the village. In the heart of the town, after navigating a series of narrow, winding streets paved with cobblestones, lay the town's many shops.

The moment they entered the business district, Allison felt as if she had suddenly stepped into the past. What she saw before her was the perfect setting of a medieval town. Merchant shops lined both sides of the wide, cobblestone street they entered on, selling every kind of good imaginable—everything from fruits, meats, and bread to clothing, jewelry, and trinkets of every sort.

The buildings were constructed of stone, granite, or wood, depending on the prosperity of the merchant, yet all of their roofs were thatched. Allison had no doubt that the entire district would turn to ash in a matter of minutes if even so much as a spark touched one of those roofs.

Dozens of people, both nobles and peasants milled about. Among them were several minstrels singing at various stations among the shops and booths in hopes of earning a bit of coin. Several dancers and mummers, their costumes a bright assortment of colors and styles, also entertained the crowds, busking for whatever coin they could squeeze out of the villagers. It was a scene straight out of a history book or period movie.

"Shall we dismount and walk around a bit?" Aidric asked.

"Oh, yes," Allison agreed eagerly, following his lead to a public stable located between a cloth merchant's shop and a tavern.

She carefully dismounted and stood quietly off to the side as Aidric greeted what she guessed to be the Stablemaster and handed him a couple of silver coins he pulled from a small leather pouch hanging off his belt. The Stablemaster barked at two young boys, his sons no doubt based on the resemblance, to take the reins of their horses. They both stared at her with wide eyes, but said nothing as they quickly led their horses into a couple of stalls and set to work grooming them. Allison had the oddest feeling that the boys knew nothing of the Prophecy of the Golden Mage and stared at her only because they thought her coloring was weird.

Aidric offered her his arm and she gratefully accepted it as they headed out into the crowded street. She received a lot of sidelong glances and a few people nervously averted their eyes when she looked at them, but otherwise most of the people nodded or even bowed respectfully towards them as they passed, due to Aidric's status, she was sure. What was she to them but a nightmare turned to flesh?

Ignoring the people milling around her, Allison eyed all the shops around her, stepping up to several to inspect their merchandise. At a jeweler's shop, she admired a gold necklace with a centerpiece of small diamonds and sapphires, and to her chagrin, Aidric promptly bought it with little haggling, though she had vehemently protested.

Aidric dismissed her protests with a wave of his hand and said, "I have little to spend my earnings on. Accept it as a gift from me to symbolize the start of our friendship." He crossed his arms against his chest. "I'll take offense if you turn my gift down."

Allison laughed as he feigned a pout that made him look like a little boy disappointed because his mother wouldn't allow him to keep the huge tarantula he had just found for a pet. How could she say no to such a look?

Thus she allowed him to secure it around her neck

and were on their way again. At her request, they stopped to listen to a quartet of minstrels performing a lively song at a street corner. It didn't escape her notice that the crowd around the minstrels gradually began to thin out when they had arrived, and the people standing nearest her did their best to inch away from her as inconspicuously as was possible. She suspected that the only reason they didn't openly stare or run away in terror was because the Mage-general of Lamia accompanied her, and they didn't want to face his infamous temper.

Although it had stung, she chose to ignore the people's behavior and gave no outward sign that she had even taken notice of it. She knew better than to think that Aidric had not. Behind the laughter in his eyes was a fire she hoped she would never have focused on her. She was enjoying herself too much to let a few locals and their superstitious fears lower her spirits.

By the time Aidric suggested that they should head back to the palace, hardly anyone gave her a second glance. *Maybe Aidric is right*, she mused as they strolled over to the stables to reclaim their horses. *Once everyone gets used to seeing me around and find that I'm not going to fry them all to a crisp if they so much as blink in my direction, then maybe they'll stop seeing me as the "Golden Mage" and only see me as myself.*

CHAPTER THREE

Inside the confines of his study, Roderick paced, fuming over the last report his Lamian spy had given him. "Fools, I am surrounded by nothing but fools!" he growled as waves of rage crashed through his body so that he literally shook with the effort to contain it. Killing his entire entourage would *not* make matters any better for him, after all.

He was not in the best of moods these days ever since the troops he had sent to Idona came trotting back with their tails between their legs and words of defeat on their lips, not to mention the report that his mage, Kion, had been taken down by—surprise, surprise—Aidric. In a fit of uncontrolled rage, Roderick had killed the commander who had reported to him. Now he immensely regretted his hasty actions. Gion had been a good commander, well respected by his men, and he would be very difficult to replace.

"Shall I never be rid of the bastard!" Roderick raged to the Thrones as he plopped down unceremoniously into the huge, leather chair behind the ruins of his desk. In a fit of temper, he had set it aflame and then a moment later was frantically dousing the flames, all the while cursing Aidric, Lamia, Seni, everyone down to his own grandmother.

Aidric has taken the girl out of the palace—but where? he mused, recounting all the spy had reported in his mind. The spy had said that Aidric had visited Diryan early this morning, looking frazzled and worried. They had conversed privately inside Diryan's study under spell silence to the irritation of Diryan's councilors, it seems. After Aidric emerged from the room still looking deeply troubled, apparently he had gone back to his rooms, retrieved the girl, and word was that they had left on horseback.

What has him so worried? Had the wench Foreseen something, some plan of mine that I've yet even to contemplate? Or... He worried at the thought. *Has he taken her to those damned Seers? Damn, damn,* damn! *I need answers!*

Unfortunately, those answers had been denied him. All efforts he had made into prying into the girl's personal life had so far come to nothing. His spy had failed in retrieving the information from the girl's mind, though, Roderick admitted reluctantly to himself, through no fault of the spy's. The wards around her mind were of such power that the spy had not even been able to penetrate the outermost of the shields. Aidric had done his work well.

Be damned with her training! Roderick thought suddenly, a plan starting to form in his mind. *I'll train her myself. Aidric must be disposed of as soon as possible and the Golden Mage under my control. I have waited long enough—perhaps too long—for the conquest of Lamia. The Lamian Mage-field will be mine, and the golden-haired wench along with it!*

Hastily, he rummaged in his desk drawer in search of a blank sheet of parchment which hadn't been scorched earlier. Once he found a suitable piece, he scribbled a message onto the parchment. He picked up a piece of sealing wax, melted the end of it with a little exertion of power, and spread it onto the rolled parchment. He then pressed his personal seal into the hot wax and set it aside to cool.

With that accomplished, he sent to his chieftain, *"Toryn, I have need of you in my chambers."*

"Highness," Toryn acknowledged simply, and within a couple of depths he was knocking at Roderick's door.

"Enter," Roderick said gruffly.

Toryn stepped through the door, humbly keeping

his head bowed as he approached his king. Dressed in a uniform of Roderick's colors of black and gold, to any other's eyes, he presented a very formidable figure, looking more like an assassin than a chieftain. He bowed deeply and stood waiting in silence for Roderick to speak. Roderick lifted the sealed parchment and handed it over to him. Toryn took it wordlessly and looked at Roderick expectantly.

"You will leave immediately for Bar'taiver," he commanded.

Toryn raised an eyebrow but nodded his assent. It wasn't often that Roderick asked him to deliver messages personally.

"I dare not trust a messenger with a message as vital as this," Roderick added in a response to Toryn's unspoken question. "It seems that the reliability of my men has been questionable as of late, thus I entrust this task unto you who has never failed me. The dawn of my attempt to lay siege to Lamia is fast approaching, and the success of my conquest depends upon the deliverance of my message to the mage, Mordant."

Toryn bowed again and said, "It will be done, Your Highness. By your leave."

As Roderick nodded his dismissal and watched Toryn exit, he couldn't help feeling a tinge of excitement.

So it begins, he thought smugly. There was no turning back now.

***

Allison groaned in protest as a pair of hands gently shook her awake. She cracked open an eyelid, saw that it was Aidric, and quickly shut it again.

"Go away," she muttered wearily, drawing the blankets over her head.

After returning from their afternoon excursion to Ell, Aidric had suggested that they ride on to the Forest of Illusions so that he could introduce her to the Mage-field. Feeling exhilarated from her pleasant visit, Allison had immediately agreed. Besides, a nice ride through the forest seemed an enjoyable ending to a day that had begun so miserably.

Her first experience with the Mage-field had been an uncanny one. The moment they had ridden past the palace and she had fixed her sight on the distant forest, she had once again felt that peculiar sense that something was beckoning her. The feeling had intensified the closer they had come to the actual site of the Mage-field.

At first glance, the clearing that had suddenly appeared before them as they rode through the forest had looked exactly like the one she had found herself lying face-down in after the portal had spit her out into this world. The only thing that had made it seem out of the ordinary was the fact that her horse had whinnied and had begun to dance around nervously when she had tried to urge it forward.

Aidric had laughed and explained that only the Bonded could trek across the clearing. Then before he could protest, she had slid from Destiny's back and had ventured a few steps into the clearing. Immediately she had felt her body from her head down to her toes begin to tingle as if thousands of pins were pressing against her almost to the point of piercing the skin. She had shrieked in alarm and scrambled back to her horse where a very pale Aidric stood gaping at her in a strange mixture of relief and disbelief.

When she had asked him what was wrong, he had said grimly that it was fortunate that she somehow had already Bonded to the Mage-field—by Seni's will, he suspected—or else, she would have been consumed by the sheer magical power that didn't "know" her through the Bonding. She had blanched at the terrible fate her carelessness had almost delivered upon her. Curiosity, it seemed, had almost literally killed the cat.

Then Aidric had instructed her on how she could actually see the brilliant energy of the Mage-field as no non-mage could using her mage senses. He had said that in order to see the energy, she had to "see" it with her mind.

At his instruction, Allison had closed her eyes and imagined the grassy clearing filled with energy. Within moments, the darkness behind her lids had been filled with the most brilliant golden light that seemed to have come from heaven, itself, and she knew that she was seeing the infamous Mage-field for the first time, a vision she would never forget as long as she lived. It had even been more beautiful than the world of light within a portal, almost as though she had been seeing the physical manifestation of a human soul.

By the time they had returned to the palace, it had been sand-marks past the time the last sun had disappeared behind the horizon, so she had not been exactly early to bed. Furthermore, to make matters worse, she had not slept well that night. Her dreams had been filled with visions of burning cities, of dead bodies littering the streets, and people running and screaming in blind terror from a shadow that seemed to devour the heavens with a darkness of the vilest nature.

"Oh, I think not," she heard Aidric say cheerfully as her blankets were yanked from over her head. "Must I douse you with icy water to get you out of bed, little cat?"

"Try it," she threatened, opening her eyes to glare up at him, "and you won't be able to sit comfortably for a week. How in God's name can you be so cheerful so early?"

"A virtue of mine," he replied, grinning down at her. "Now up. Your lessons await you in the sitting room, and so shall I."

With a sigh, Allison dragged herself out of bed and headed for the suite's single bathroom, all the while muttering to herself. She nearly dozed off while she soaked in the marble tub that the palace servants already had filled and steaming. She didn't know how she was ever going to manage to concentrate on what Aidric taught her as exhausted as she felt. *Damn it all, if I'm ever going to get some sleep, I have to tell Aidric about those godawful dreams—about my part in them.*

After changing into her apprentice uniform and hastily running a brush through her damp hair, Allison hurried off to meet Aidric in the sitting room. She had always wondered why his sitting room was so large with so little furniture and the ceiling so high. It seemed like such a waste of space. Now she had her answer.

Aidric sat cross-legged in the center of the room on a few cushions, his eyes closed as if he was meditating. For one uncomfortable moment, he reminded her of Master Kiryl. A few feet across from him were another assortment of cushions that she assumed were for her.

Noiselessly, she made her way over to the cushions and took her seat. Aidric immediately opened his eyes and smiled at her. "Ah, awake and ready at last," he teased. "I feared you had fallen asleep in the bathing tub."

"I almost did," she admitted.

"You didn't sleep well." It was more of a statement than a question.

"No…"

"These dreams of yours, those which you refuse to speak of, are the cause, aren't they?" he asked, staring into her eyes intently, his eyes daring her to deny it.

Allison cast her eyes down onto her hands in her lap, still hesitant to talk about her dreams despite her determined thoughts earlier. Was it really the right time to bring them up?

"If your mind is elsewhere," Aidric said, "then your lessons won't go as well as I would have them. You'll find me a most stern teacher, but even more so if I think you aren't giving me your absolute best effort."

"You sound like an old math teacher I once had," Allison said lightly, and was surprised when he didn't even crack a smile.

"I'm quite serious, Allison," he said firmly. "During lessons, we are not friends but teacher and student.

Understand, it must be so, or we'll accomplished nothing." His features softened a bit. "However, now I listen as a friend and not a teacher. I know these dreams have been plaguing you for some time now. Perhaps I have even shared some of them."

Allison started at that. "How is that possible?"

"Some of them are Foresight dreams," he explained. "One in particular, I'm certain you have had. A village is in flames. You don't recognize it since you have never been there, but it's the village of Avidon. Burning bodies litter the streets, the screams of suffering souls echo through the air, and in the center of all this chaos is a single figure, the face hidden in shadow. It's this person that has wrought all the destruction, and you know who it is."

"Me," she whispered, her mind suddenly overwhelmed with conflicting emotions of fear, disgust, and shame.

"It's only one of many paths you could take," Aidric said softly. "Only one, Allison, and I don't believe that particular dream will ever come to pass. Dreams, Allison. They are only dreams if you so will them to be."

"But if you're having them too—" Allison insisted bitterly.

"That doesn't mean that it's a certainty. Any with the gift of Foresight have been having that same dream for centuries. There are also many others we have had—dreams of victories in many battles, led by that same figure in shadow. Seni sends us these dreams only as a warning that one or the other can come to pass. It's for us to choose which. The future is not set in stone."

"Then why haven't I had anything but those horrible nightmares ever since I learned who I was?" Allison demanded stubbornly. "Not one of them has been positive in any way."

"What can I say that will make you believe otherwise," he said, shaking his head.

"Probably nothing," she replied with a grimace. "I can't help thinking the way I do. I was raised to think the worst about everything, especially when it had anything to do with me. It's so ingrained that I'm not sure it's even possible to break the habit anymore. You can blame my stepfather for that."

"I shall," Aidric grumbled, "but anger will get us nowhere. I ask you to at least try to ignore the dreams for now. We'll deal with them and your Foresight ability at a later time."

Allison nodded, a bit relieved that he wasn't going to press the matter. "Whatever you think is best. At the very least, I don't have to worry about telling you about them anymore. That's one less distraction."

He nodded, satisfied, and said, "Good. I guess as

good of place as any to start is shielding. So far, the shields I have placed in your mind have prevented you from using your abilities." He smiled at her wryly. "Well, at least *most* of the time. Today, I'm going to teach you how to do this shielding yourself. You must maintain stable control of your abilities at all times if you are to learn to use them properly in spells and such. In time, it'll become as natural as breathing to you. Now, I want you to clear your mind of all thoughts, and place your concentration to the frontal lobe of your brain."

Allison nodded and closed her eyes, doing her best to clear her mind of her troubles and any stray thoughts and concentrating on placing her attention where Aidric had instructed.

"Picture the shield in your mind," she heard Aidric's say. "Picture it as a complex set of corridors, each with a sturdy door at the end. Beyond some of those doors is the energy of the Mage-field and the ability to draw energy from the minds of others beyond the rest. Imagine that you can feel both forces pressing against the doors, wanting to enter freely, but unable to until the doors are opened, in this case, by my will alone."

Allison struggled to obey. The way Aidric explained the images seemed rather easy to duplicate, but actually doing it was a different story. Stray thoughts kept creeping into her mind just when she had the visualization as she wanted it, thus forcing her to have to start reconstructing the image all over again.

When she finally built and held the image, she said, "I see it."

"Now, focus on the doors," he commanded. "Go over every aspect of them, their shape, height, length, and width until you are confident that you can build them again exactly as they are should they suddenly be taken away."

Feeling silly, she did as he asked, studying the image of the doors in her mind until she was certain she could have reconstructed them exactly as they were, even with a splitting headache. She nodded for him to continue.

"Now, I'm going to remove my shields. The doors will vanish in your visualization, and it's your task to rebuild them again. I warn you that when the doors are removed, the various energies will surge forward until you slam the doors shut on them again, and they will continue to surge until *you* not *I* cut off the flow."

Then before she could even chew on that remark, the doors in her mind vanished just as Aidric had promised, and after that—was chaos. A brilliant light immediately surged through the opened doorways, filling her mind until the power seemed to scorch her brain. Fire ran down every nerve in her body from head to toe, feeling as if it was eating at her flesh in an attempt to escape. The light was immediately followed by volumes of sound that began to whirl around in her mind in a garbled cacophony of madness as the voices had that first day in the forest.

Allison lost all aspect of where she was and what she was supposed to be doing. Her eyes flew open, staring at nothing and everything, and her hands instinctually came up to her ears in a futile attempt to block out the stream of sound that rushed into her mind.

"Make it stop!" she cried.

"The doors, Allison," she heard a maddeningly calm voice say somewhere within the chaos. "Only when you rebuild the doors will the madness that consumes you cease."

The word "doors" immediately brought memories of a web of corridors to surface, and with that, the task Aidric had set for her. Desperately, Allison clung onto that memory and tried to bring the vision she had once held back. She could feel beads of sweat streaming down her face and back with the effort of trying to ignore the pain the light and sounds were causing her and the impossible task of concentrating on solely the vision she was reconstructing.

However, as quickly as she visualized the maze of

corridors, her concentration faltered under the pressure of the wild energies driving against her, causing her to fall back into the turmoil within her mind, and the mental picture crumbled away. She tried it several times with no more luck than the first.

"I can't do it—I *can't*! For God's sake, make it stop!" Allison pleaded. "Make it stop, *please!*"

"You can, and you will," Aidric's voice said sternly.

"Damn you, you bastard!" she screamed. "Damn you into the lowest hell!"

"The doors," he said simply, unperturbed by her curses.

Oddly, rather than infuriate her further, his calmness gave her mind something to latch onto, a foundation on stand on.

Gritting her teeth with a new determination, Allison brought the vision back and fought with every last inch of willpower she had left in her to construct a door in every opened corridor and slamming it shut against the current of power flowing into her channels. When the last door was in place and closed, the brilliant light disappeared in a flash and the only sounds that reached her ears was her own ragged breathing and the pounding of her heart.

Allison felt herself slump forward, too weak to stop herself or to even care if she fell flat on her face.

However, Aidric was there to prevent her fall. He drew her against him until her head rested on his chest. She gratefully collapsed against him and allowed her tears to flow freely.

"Damn you," she whispered hoarsely.

To her surprise, he chuckled and embraced her more tightly. "Believe me, little cat, I cursed Othos more profoundly and inventively than you cursed me when I set up my first shields. You did well."

"Don't you *ever* put me through something like that again!" Allison spat out angrily. "I nearly went mad!"

"Never again," Aidric promised her, unperturbed by her tone. "That's the worst and most difficult lesson that a mage must learn, but once you learn it, it need not ever be repeated unless you take down those shields yourself, which isn't likely to happen."

Allison lifted up her head and looked up at him with eyes that were accusing. "Why didn't you tell me that it would be so terrible?" she demanded.

"Telling you would have served no purpose other than frightening you, which would have made the experience worse for you."

"I don't see how it could've been worse," she muttered under her breath as she pulled away from him and began to hastily wipe at her eyes. "I hope that you weren't planning on teaching me anything else today because after that nightmare, I refuse to learn anything else."

"Yes, I think you've accomplished enough for one day," he said, "but tomorrow, be prepared to work most of the day on your magecraft."

"I can hardly wait," Allison replied dryly as Aidric helped her up onto unsteady legs. "You know, I could really learn to hate you before all of this is over."

"Every mentor's fear," he said softly.

CHAPTER FOUR

K ing Diryan frowned at the letter before him, reading and rereading the words until they blurred and began to run together, but still, no matter how much he wished them to change, they ultimately reported a message that he preferred not to have seen.

Seni help me, what I most feared has happened. Evil has joined with evil, and it's Lamia who is at the center of their ambitions.

"Voytek!" he called.

The last syllable had scarcely left his lips before the boy entered his study and presented himself before him.

"What does His Majesty wish of me?" he asked eagerly.

Suppressing a smile at the lad's eagerness, Diryan

ordered, "Go find Lord Ion, lad, and inform him that I wish for him to assemble my councilors immediately and meet me in the Council Room. Make haste!"

Before Diryan could blink, Voytek was scurrying out the door. *Seni bless the soul who sent that boy to me,* he thought as he rose from his chair and left his study. A couple of his guards posted at the entrance to his chambers immediately fell into step behind him as he strode down the hall, down the stairs, and into the Council Room.

"Allow no one to enter this room except the Seneschal, my councilors, and my scribe. Even if the Mage-general comes storming up to you with Seni, Himself, demanding admittance, you are not to admit them, understand?"

"Yes, Your Highness," they replied in unison.

Diryan scarcely had time to take his seat at the head of the table before the door swung open, and Lord Ion and his five councilors noisily filed into the room. Voytek followed not far behind, out of breath, and his face a shade of red to match his hair.

They all bowed to Diryan, and he dismissed them impatiently and waved them to their seats.

"What we discuss today in this room must not, under no circumstance, be discussed with any member of the Circle unless I deem otherwise under penalty of imprisonment and loss of rank." They all nodded and then fixed their eyes on him expectantly. "Today, I received a most disturbing report from one of my spies in Bar'taiver. It seems our good neighbor, King Roderick, has sent his chieftain to visit the mage, Mordant, whom we all know to be one of the most vile mages under the Thrones.

"Seni knows why King Al'nar has allowed such a foul creature to roam free after all the havoc he is reputed to have caused in that kingdom, but no matter the reason, he is there and at this very moment negotiating a pact with Roderick. Now, what that pact is, my spy was not able to learn, but whatever it is, I would be willing to bet my life that Lamia is a part of it.

"He wants Lamia's Mage-field, and he will do everything he can to win it. Attacking Kemos and Idona is only the beginning of his tyrannies. How long will it be before he is at our borders again attempting to bring down the Shield? Or that he asks for more than I can give, and the price of refusing his demands is the lives of an ally kingdom and the betrayal of a centuries-old promise? War has not been declared yet but is most assuredly eminent, gentlemen, and I have called you here today to hear your thoughts on the matter before I announce my final decision to the Circle and then to the kingdom."

"Shouldn't we wait, 'Highness, until more information is known about Roderick's intentions?" Lord Ion asked. "To act this prematurely could in the long run prove to be fatal, not only to the troops we send out, but to the citizens of Lamia as well."

"We can't afford to wait, Lord Seneschal," Lord Osrik, the eldest member of the Council said firmly. "Would you have Roderick standing at our border with his monster in tow pounding on our Shield with the Dark Powers before you deem we have information enough? Or, for that matter, holding an ally village for ransom? Roderick certainly will not give us the luxury of time. I say we should strike now while we are still one step ahead of Roderick."

"I agree," Lord Liam added. "Seni knows what the twisted bastard plans to do next, and if we wait for more information to surface, it may be too late to counter him."

"But at what cost?" Ion demanded. "We all know that war with Mihr is in the near future, and Roderick is in the process of negotiating a pact between a man who would be right at home in all the hells of Ter-ob. But that's *all* we know. I propose that we send more spies into Mihr and try to learn more of what Roderick plans and what part Mordant will play in them. I fear ignorance in this instance will most assuredly lead to our downfall."

"And in the meantime, while these spies are digging up your information, what do you propose we do? Sit on our arses and hope that Roderick does nothing?" Lord Ambrus spat out. "I, for one, would rather we double the number of troops along the Kemosian and Na'aran borders if we are to not attack Mihr openly just yet. That way we'll not be caught off-guard if another situation such as the near disaster in Idona arises."

"I have no problem with strengthening our defenses along the borders," the Seneschal said. "It should be done immediately, of course. I only object to any declaration of war against Mihr at this time. Perhaps it's what Roderick wants us to do."

"I disagree," Lord Claudium said. "Roderick was never one to fight directly. His methods were always deceitful at best, and downright blasphemous at the worst. He hanged a *Domnae*, after all! How can we possibly predict what the bloody bastard will do next? Our only defense is to prepare ourselves for the worst. The surprise attack on Idona has taught us that. Had we not been Forewarned, then perhaps the issues we are now discussing would be more serious, more desperate."

"And you, Talus," Diryan interjected, fixing his eyes on the youngest of his councilors, a man just shy of thirty, "have you nothing to say?"

"I do, my king," Lord Talus said quietly, a quality that would have been a flaw in any other councilor but was a mark of power in him, "but I believe all the major arguments have been raised—all, that is, except for one, though it has been hinted upon. The Golden Mage—where does she fit into the picture?"

Everyone began muttering at once, but it was clear that the Golden Mage had not been far from their minds. They just had not had the nerve or the tact Talus possessed to have raised the point at the right moment.

"Seni wouldn't have delivered her into our hands at this time of unrest unless she was meant to have a hand in its outcome," Talus asserted gravely.

"What do you propose we do? Appoint her to this Council?" Claudium sneered.

Unperturbed, Talus replied, "Of course not. Do you think me a fool? I only suggest that a strict eye be kept on her at all times. From her performance at the festival, it's clear that Seni has chosen her as his primary vessel, and we would do good to pay mind to her dreams and thoughts. We must not make the mistake of discounting her because she hasn't yet reached adept status."

"He has a point," Osrik admitted reluctantly. "To ignore her *would* be dangerous. Can we trust in the

Mage-general, alone, to maintain control of her? Perhaps we should confine her to the palace and not allow her the freedom of the villages. After all, can we be so certain of her loyalty?"

Diryan narrowed his eyes dangerously. "I shall not even bother to tell you where to stick that suggestion," he said. "Understand this, all of you. Allison McNeal is *not* our prisoner. By what right have we to judge her, to interfere? The will of Seni has brought her to our kingdom, and it's our place to accept it as such without question or doubt. Never again speak of imprisonment in my presence. We must allow fate to run its course."

"Even if that fate leads to our destruction?" Ambrus demanded.

"Who are we to interfere?" Diryan repeated stonily.

His councilors fell uncharacteristically silent, glancing at one another as if assuring themselves that the others were as ruffled as they. Ambrus and Claudium glared openly at Talus, no doubt blaming the unpleasant turn their discussion had taken on him. Talus merely stared back, an eyebrow raised ever so slightly. Diryan envied the lad his composure. Yes, Talus had been a good choice, despite his councilors' protests.

Well, at least he had gotten through to them, made them face the brutal reality of the mysterious maiden that now resided in Aidric's suite. It was time to revert back to the primary issue.

"Yes, I shall send more troops to the borders," Diryan stated into the silence, "but the Seneschal speaks wisely in his insistence for more information. I don't know what Roderick schemes to do, but whatever it is, we shall be ready for any ill he throws our way, for we have a weapon at our disposal Roderick never anticipated. Perhaps, in the end, that weapon is what will save us all."

"And perhaps it won't," Ion said softly.

The atmosphere in the room was grim when Diryan finally adjourned. He began to wonder if he would ever live to see his people living without the threat of war again.

CHAPTER FIVE

"Mind if I join you?"

Allison raised her head from the book she was reading and smiled, recognizing the voice of her friend.

"Of course," she replied, closing her book. "Any company these days is always welcome."

Raya grimaced as she plopped down onto the bench alongside Allison. "I swear, you and Aidric are two kindred souls," she said. "Always so pessimistic and forever brooding. What will it take to liven up your spirits a bit more?"

"Other than the obvious, you can start by making my mage powers disappear."

"Lessons are not going well, I presume?" Raya asked, flashing her a sympathetic look.

"I abhor those damn lessons," Allison admitted.

"I still have nightmares of that first lesson. Aidric is pushing me so hard, but that really isn't the problem. He warned me that he would be a stern teacher from the very beginning, and I understand why he's being so hard on me. I expected no less out of him. It's the fact that Aidric is a different person while he instructs me, and it's a person that I'm learning to despise. Let's just say that the tension in that suite is a bit thicker than when he first brought me to live there."

"Mage lessons are difficult in the beginning, but things will start looking brighter," Raya assured her. "Tempers flare and friendships tend to take a turn for the worst during those first few quarter-moons. Lady Kiara was my mentor, and for the first couple of moons I lived with her, I thought she was the vilest woman that ever lived and made sure I let her know she was every chance I could get. Remember that I was still the 'barbarian' back then, and I had no qualms about cursing people to my heart's content. Aidric most assuredly can tell you that I had a tongue that would make a harlot blush. My people believe in speaking freely, no matter who we offended! Yet, Lady Kiara understood the trials I was undergoing and took no offense of the crude names I was constantly throwing in her face. Now I think of her as the mother I never had."

Raya had been orphaned at an early age, though

she never disclosed to Allison how young she actually had been or the circumstances of her parents' death. It had been a difficult time for Raya, living off whatever she could scavenge in the streets of her village, until she learned the significance of the circular birthmark on the back of her neck. She knew of Lamia only through vaguely remembered tales her mother had spun, though at the time, she had thought the kingdom only myth. At age thirteen, Raya had left her village for good and made the long journey to Lamia with only a small, nicked hunting knife and a loin cloth to cover her nudity. She had avoided villages altogether, heeding a lifetime of Hrefnan council that the outkingdoms were hostile lands.

As fate would have it, a couple of days into Sersia, Raya had stumbled upon a caravan of merchants. Curious, she had shadowed them for a quarter-moon, careful to keep just out of sight but not so far away that she could hear nothing of their conversation. After a couple of days, she had deduced that they were Lamians after realizing that a couple of the men bore the mark of a mage. Only two kingdoms in the region held Mage-fields within their borders—Lamia and Sarim. Those of the caravan were too pale to be Sarens, for those of Sarim sported skin that was a deep bronze, more rust-colored than brown, really.

Raya had picked up several Lamian words from

her eavesdropping, and luckily, never once had the Lamians become aware of their little shadow. Thus, when she arrived at the Lamian border station, half-naked, dirty, and looking more like a thief than anything, what saved her from being arrested by the borderguards was the mark of the mageborn and four uttered words in heavily accented Lamian: "Hrefna. Become mage. Learn."

After undergoing a heavy mind-probing by Lord Othos to assure them that she was not one of Roderick's lackeys, Raya had been given to Lady Kiara, and the rest, as they say, is history. Now, as Allison regarded the younger girl, who was by far years older than she in experience, she couldn't help feeling that had she been in Raya's situation, she would have died in the streets of her friend's village.

She didn't have half of Raya's strong will—not by a long shot—especially when it came to her mage lessons. There had been times during the last quartermoon that she had thought that living under her stepfather's hand was preferable to her mage lessons. A scary thought, that.

"I had no idea that learning magecraft would be so hard," Allison complained. "Aidric made it look so easy—a wave of his hand and *poof!* Someone was paralyzed, healed, or a portal stood before you. I had no idea that so much went on within his mind when he did those things."

"He's already teaching you spells after only a quarter-moon of lessons?" Raya asked, surprised.

"No, just the mind-mage stuff," Allison replied with a shrug. "I've gotten that part down pretty well. I can read people's minds, probe, cast fairly simple, but sturdy, shields on others as well as myself, levitate small objects, and of course thought-speak as well as anyone. Of all of that, mastering thought-speech was easiest. Later on today, Aidric is going to teach me how to channel power from the Mage-field, and I can tell you that after the way I felt after I accidentally channeled all that power in my sleep, I'm not looking forward to it."

"You've learned quickly. It took me a little over a moon to master what you have mastered thus far."

There was a hint of awe in Raya's voice, and Allison didn't know if she should have been flattered by what was obviously meant to be a compliment or irritated. Too many people had treated her as if she were a living goddess, and she was at her wits end over it. She didn't want one of her new best friends to start treating her as one, either.

Allison shrugged uncomfortably and said, "I'm just a fast learner, nothing more. It has nothing to do with—*who* I am."

Raya nodded, her eyes softening in understanding. "I'm sorry, Allie. I know how sensitive you are about the Golden Mage business. In your place, I know I would be."

Allison winced inwardly when she heard Raya use the nickname Kat had always used. Raya had just begun using the name a couple of days earlier, and it depressed her to hear it spoken, though she didn't have the heart to ask Raya not to use it. Her use of the nickname was, after all, a sign that they were truly close friends, just as Aidric had taken to calling her "little cat."

"Where is His Highness, by the way?" Raya's voice cut into her thoughts.

"What? Oh—he's in another one of those meetings with the Circle," Allison answered.

"Ah, that's why I couldn't find Sel. This is the third meeting in a row, which is very unusual. Something big must be blowing in the wind. No doubt that Roderick is involved in this somehow. He always is these days. Has Aidric spoken anything to you of it?"

Allison laughed. "You would think they were plotting the destruction of the world in there with all their secrecy. Aidric says that the king forbade any discussion of whatever it is that has them so worried outside the Circle." She made a face and added, "Aidric says that I should be a member of the Circle because of who I am. He's been trying to sway King Diryan to induct me in, but so far the king has refused. Truth told, I'm relieved. If there's anything I abhor more than mage lessons, it's politics."

"I agree, but I still wish that I knew what was being said behind those doors. It would almost be worth suffering through those long, dull meetings to have access to that kind of intelligence. If King Diryan is planning on declaring open war on Mihr, which I suspect he is, then I would most certainly want to know a little beforehand so that I can properly prepare myself for what will undeniably be a *long* war."

Allison went cold inside at the thought. *My God, there might be a war. What will I do if they send Aidric and Raya off to the battlefield? Heaven help me, what will I do if they send* me?

"You're sure there's going to be a war?" Allison asked, afraid to hear the answer.

"A few moons ago, I could've told you that a war with Mihr was avoidable," she replied, "but now, with everything Roderick's been doing along the borders of Kemos and Na'ar, the only way this conflict'll be resolved is through warfare. Roderick isn't the negotiating type, and he cares nothing about the lives he's destroying while he's striving to fulfill his ambitions."

Allison opened her mouth to speak, then quickly closed it when she suddenly felt eyes boring into her back. Reflexively, she glanced over her shoulder, straining to see through the bushes at her back, but there was no one in the immediate vicinity of them. A sense of *déjà vu* washed over her and she shivered, feeling a chill that had nothing to do with the weather.

Raya hadn't missed the change in her expression and asked worriedly, "Allie, what is it?"

God, just like Kat—

"Allison?"

She blinked, and seemed to see Raya for the first time. "Dear God, it's happening again," she whispered.

"What is?" Raya asked with a concerned frown.

"The eyes watching me, eyes that are there but not there. I feel their gaze burning into my back, just like before that portal appeared in front of me and brought me to this world."

Raya looked at her askance and then scanned the area around them. "I see no one except Galen," she said with a shrug, "and he's not even looking in this direction. Perhaps all you felt was someone staring at you from afar. Aidric told me that your empathic senses are exceedingly receptive. Although you've been here among us long enough for everyone to grow accustomed to your presence, there are still some fools who insist upon staring at you as if they've never seen a woman before."

"You're probably right," Allison said dubiously, not ready to dismiss her feelings totally, "but I still say that this felt a lot different from the casual stares I get in the palace."

"Perhaps it's Seni, Himself, watching over you," Raya joked with a grin, but Allison shivered, not finding it funny at all.

"I hope not," she said seriously. "It's bad enough that I've drawn the attention of the whole kingdom on me. I sure wouldn't want the attentions of a *deity* along with it!"

A shadow suddenly fell over them, and Allison's head jerked up, her heart beginning to race as she looked up into a face that was vaguely familiar to her, though she couldn't remember where she had seen him. As her eyes locked with his, he instantly froze, staring back at her with more fear than she had ever seen on anyone's face when they had looked at her. She opened her mouth to speak—a greeting, words of concern, she didn't know—but Raya beat her to it.

"Oh—hello, Galen," Raya said cheerfully, unaware that anything was amiss between them.

Upon hearing his name, Allison suddenly remembered where she had seen the man.

Of course—he's a member of the Circle. I saw him that first day during my presentation. A mind-mage, I think.

"You know Allison, of course," Raya continued

conversationally.

Galen tore his eyes away from hers and blinked dumbly down at Raya. He shook his head a little as if trying to drag himself from his thoughts and seemed to really see Raya for the first time.

"I'm sorry, milady, but I must make haste," he muttered and continued on his way towards the arch leading to the garden and Mage Hall entrance without so much as another glance.

Raya glanced peculiarly at his retreating back and commented, "I don't understand. He's usually really friendly. I've never known him to be so rude. The meeting must have gone badly."

Allison barely registered Raya's words, her attention on the retreating figure that was hurrying away as if a pack of rabid hounds were nipping at his heels. Somehow, she *knew* that it had been his eyes that had been watching her earlier—watching and waiting.

***

Hurrying through the arched doorway separating the courtyard from the indoor garden, Galen nervously glanced over his shoulder at the two figures sitting on the bench almost fully obscured through the thickness of the bushes. They appeared to have returned to the conversation he had interrupted as he had passed them by, but he wasn't all that certain that the hell-spawn was not still watching him. Even now, he could still feel her eyes boring into his back, blazing like two green mage-flames as he hurried away from the two women.

She knows, he thought, feeling sweat starting to bead on his forehead. *Blessed Thrones, she knows that I was watching her. I mustn't be so careless in the future. I can't very well serve my kingdom dead should she learn my true intentions!*

Galen hadn't meant to spy on her in the court-yard. He had merely been returning to the Mage Hall after the Circle's meeting with the king and his councilors and had spotted her on the bench talking to that barbarian mage. Despite his better judgment, he couldn't resist seizing this opportunity to send a Probe of Inquiry over to her to eavesdrop on their conversation and her thoughts.

Unfortunately, the moment his probe had touched her mind, she had suddenly stiffened and began to anxiously look about her. He had frantically pulled back his mind-probe before she could realize what it was that disturbed her, all the while cursing his stupidity.

It was all he could do to suppress the fear that was rapidly building up in him as he forced himself to walk past them. He hadn't intended to stop, but when the hellspawn had raised her eyes to his, his whole body had instantly frozen, inadvertently caught in the trap of a viper's deadly stare. If Raya had not spoken to him, he believed he would have lost control of himself and either started yelling or attacking.

That would have been a disaster since the Golden Mage had done nothing as of yet that proved her to be the hellspawn that she was. She was still hiding behind that façade of innocence, and the fact that her warning on the night of the celebration had saved the Idonans from certain death did nothing to help prove his cause. Had he named her a hellspawn in public as her gaze had almost caused him to do, a hangman's noose surely would have found its way around his neck before the day was finished—if the Mage-general's hands did not do the deed first.

But I'll not make that deadly mistake twice, he vowed as he headed for his rooms. *Those who walk in Seni's grace are surely more cunning than the minions of the dark god, Arioch, and in the end, it's I who'll open the eyes of the kingdom so that they may see the Golden Mage for the hellspawn that she is.*

Had anyone been present in the Mage Hall to see the peculiar glint in Galen's eyes, they would have thought that they were looking into the eyes of a madman.

CHAPTER SIX

Sitting comfortably on her assortment of cushions on the floor of Aidric's sitting room, Allison curiously watched Aidric as he set his wards of protection all around the room to prevent any stray magic from escaping beyond the walls. No matter how much she detested her mage powers, she always enjoyed watching Aidric use his. As long as it was someone else who was casting the spells, she found magic fascinating.

"How well do you know Galen?" she asked abruptly, breaking the silence.

Aidric turned to her and raised an eyebrow. "Oh, so you are speaking to me once again. You mean the mind-mage, Galen, of the Circle, I presume?"

"Yes." She chose to simply ignore his comment.

"Why the sudden interest in him? Have you a fancy for him?"

"Of course not," Allison snapped, a little more forcefully than she had intended. She immediately regretted the bite in her words. "I'm sorry," she apologized with a heavy sigh. "I didn't mean to sound so harsh. I had a very upsetting incident today, and I shouldn't take out my frustrations on you."

"It had something to do with Galen?" Aidric guessed as he walked over to his set of cushions and gracefully seated himself onto them. If she lived to be a thousand years, she knew she would never achieve that type of effortless grace. He made her feel like a three-footed cow whenever they were together.

"I thought so earlier, but now I'm not so sure," she said, troubled.

Allison described her feelings of unease while in the courtyard, and the sensation that someone was watching her. She relayed the sense of *déjà vu* those eyes had made her feel, then Galen's uncharacteristic behavior and her suspicions that it had been the mind-mage's eyes that had been watching her. Aidric listened to her words silently, and at first he said nothing. For a long moment, she feared he wouldn't say anything, or worse, accuse her of being silly.

Then he shrugged as Raya had and said, "I've never known Galen to wish ill on anyone, but I've never known your feelings to be wrong, either. Galen has the Foresight gift, so perhaps he has also had dreams of the figure in shadow. Perhaps he's just wary of you, but if it's made you uncomfortable, then I'll speak to him the next time I see him."

"No," she said quickly. "I don't want to stir up any trouble. Maybe I should just forget about it. I've been so paranoid these days that I'm probably just jumping at my own shadow, but I appreciate your offer. We haven't been on the best of terms these days, and I admit that I'm mostly to blame for it."

"Mostly?" he echoed, raising an eyebrow.

Allison glared at him, and then chuckled at his exaggerated stern expression. She never could stay angry with Aidric for long. "All right, *milord*, I'll take all the blame. Shall we call a truce?"

"A truce," he agreed as he reached over for her hand and brought it up to his lips for a light kiss.

She smiled, hoping that she was not blushing, as he released her hand. "Well, at least we'll be able to breathe a little easier in here," she said lightly.

"For now," he said with a wry grin. "We'll have to see after your lessons are over."

"That completely depends on how much of a drill sergeant you're going to be today," she replied, smiling.

"In that case, I think we're in trouble. Shall we begin?"

"I'll pretend I didn't hear that," Allison said dryly,

"but yes, let's get this over with."

"You're enthusiasm for magic just amazes me," Aidric said sarcastically, shaking his head with mock incredulity. "Truly, I don't believe I've ever had a pupil that was more eager to learn."

"As long as we understand each other," Allison said with a serious nod, though the faint smile that touched her lips ruined the effect.

"I believe you've been spending too much time in the company of a certain barbarian woman who'll remain nameless. I fear you are beginning to pick up her habits."

"Don't blame me," Allison warned. "You were the one who introduced us. Besides, according to Raya, I'm beginning to pick up all *your* bad habits!"

"Oh?" Aidric remarked, raising that eloquent eyebrow once again. "And what might those be?"

Allison smiled and shook her head playfully. "Trust me, you probably don't want to know."

"With her tongue, you are probably right. Now, shall we begin—"

"Aren't you just a teeny bit curious to know what she has to say about you?" Allison interrupted quickly.

Aidric laughed, catching her off guard as he reached over to hug her affectionately, something he hadn't done in a long while. Everything she had been about to say instantly melted from her mind at his touch.

"I know what you're trying to do, little cat," he said with amusement as he released her, pulling away a bit until she was drowning in his amazing eyes.

"Do?" she echoed dumbly.

"As much as I enjoy our conversations, this isn't the time to have one of them. Even if you manage to distract me long past the last sundown, you'll still have your lesson, and I'll be no less the sterner for it. You might as well get this lesson over with now. Then, I promise we can talk. That is, if you haven't decided to strangle me."

Allison forced herself to tear her eyes away from him. Only then was she able to regain enough composure to reply, "Something tells me that I should just strangle you now and save myself the trouble of suffering through the lesson since I know I'll probably strangle you afterwards, anyway."

"Don't temp me, milady," Aidric teased, "else I just may allow you to do it. It would save me the torment of the Circle meeting I have in the morning! Now, our tongues have wagged enough. I'll start today's lesson by explaining the concept of channeling and why only mages can do this."

The teasing was instantly gone from his eyes and demeanor, replaced by a stony seriousness that transformed him into the man she had told Raya she despised. Allison sighed, resigned to spending a long afternoon once again with the Drill Sergeant.

"The body is," Aidric continued, ignoring her sigh, "in a sense, a shell containing the energy of life. Channeling on a much smaller scale is occurring daily with the functions of the body, the transferring of energy from one place to another to be used as the body deems fit. The same is done when a mage draws energy from the Mage-field.

"The body becomes the channel as your nerves are the channel for energy going from the brain to other parts of your body. The Mage-field energy is drawn into your body through those visualized corridors in your mind. It's there that the energy must begin to be shaped into what you desire. Next, the energy must be sent through the body to the point of release, which, in most cases, is your hands, although it can occur at numerous other places, but those tend to not be pleasant experiences.

"Next comes the most crucial part of the channeling, the spell. Now, there are three categories of spells. Those that require only hand gestures to complete, the sculpting of the energy, if you will, are the first type. The second are those which solely require the incantations in the Ti'ar language, and the last are the spells that require the utterance of incantations in the Ti'ar language as well as hand gestures."

"Why are incantations spoken for some spells and not others?" Allison asked with a frown.

"With the spells that almost all mages can cast, the minor spells such as a paralysis spell or a glamour, their powers of concentration alone are enough to manipulate the flow of energy being channeled through their bodies into the spells they desire. Now, the more difficult spells, such as the Portal spell, cannot be controlled with only the mind and hand gestures. The energies being channeled are too great, and a third factor must be added to fully bend the power to your will, that of the incantation.

"Sound travels in waves of energy, thus can be used to manipulate the natural flow of the energy of the Mage-field. The articulation of the ancient words spoken changes the frequency of the sound waves slightly, providing the right vibrations to manipulate the energy as the spell requires. That's why these spells are so draining. Much of your personal energy and concentration goes into making sure that all goes as planned."

"You've lost me," Allison said, his words whirling chaotically around in her mind and threatening to give her a headache.

"You don't need to understand it completely,"

Aidric assured her. "I, myself, don't completely comprehend the hows and whys of it. I don't believe that even the High Priest fully understands the exact physics of magic. We only know that it *works*, and for me, that's more than enough. Don't worry. I'll teach you the spells that require incantations at a much later date. You must first master the Ti'ar language. Remind me to give you the lesson book after we are done here."

"Why is it necessary that I learn this language?" Allison asked in puzzlement. "Can't I just memorize the incantations? Do I really need to know exactly what I'm saying?"

"No, you must understand the incantations," Aidric said firmly. "It's vital to the spell that you know the meaning of each word spoken. Remember that your mind plays a large part in the shaping of spells, and the incantations used in a spell aid in the mental picture you must draw up to shape the spell before the energy is released at your fingertips. However, as I said, you need not worry about that aspect at this moment. I'll explain everything more thoroughly when the time comes. Today, you'll only practice channeling."

"Is this going to be as bad as shielding?" Allison asked anxiously.

"No, but it's still difficult," he replied sympathetically. "However, once you master it, you'll never forget. Now, bring up your mental picture of the corridors and doors."

When this is all over, I'm going to be eating, dreaming, and breathing corridors and doors, Allison thought irritably as she brought up the mental picture with minimal effort. She didn't even have to close her eyes to achieve it, and considering how her first lesson had gone, she considered that no small feat.

Nothing existed for her any longer except for her maze of corridors. Aidric's voice was but an echo that resonated up and down her corridors as he instructed her.

"You feel the power of the Mage-field pushing against the doors you've constructed, begging to be released. You'll release some of that power, but not as it would have it. The rate of the flow must be controlled. Slowly open one of your doors that holds back the power of the Mage-field, and when the power lurches forward, meld your mind with it until you and the power are one. Then slowly move the power down from your mind to the palms of your hands. You will feel a slight tingling as the power moves through you. It won't be nearly as intense as the time when you so recklessly entered the Mage-field, so don't be alarmed.

"If the power escapes your grasp, *do not panic*. You need only close the door you have opened, and the flow of power will cease. When the power is in your palms, close the door. For now, you'll only practice channeling the power successfully to your palms until you can do it without being in the semi-trance you are now in. Now go."

Feeling her stomach knot up with trepidation, Allison slowly "opened" one of her doors and nearly cried out when the flow of power beyond eagerly sprang forward more quickly than she had anticipated, like a starved lion springing for its prey. Immediately, she slammed the door shut against the current and outwardly shuddered. The picture vanished, and she was once again staring at Aidric's impassive face.

He said nothing, only stared expressionlessly at her, his demeanor expectant. She swallowed with some difficulty and tried to still the rapid beating of her heart before she made another attempt. This time she was more prepared, knowing what to expect of the power when she unleashed it.

As the power leapt forward, Allison concentrated on melding her mind with the power just as Aidric had taught her earlier when she was learning to read minds.

"In order to read minds," he had explained, *"you must first match the energy of your mind with the energy of the person's mind you wish to read. Your mind must be utterly blank and open for reception. In a sense, in order to meld your mind with another's, you must become that mind, but you must take care*

that you retain just a bit of your own self-awareness lest you wish to be trapped in the mind of your subject for the rest of your days. Believe me, it's happened before."

Allison remembered that warning now as she cautiously allowed her mind and the personality of the Mage-field to become one. She was fairly surprised at the ease with which she did it.

Carefully, she maneuvered the flow of power down through her body until she felt its heat in the palms of her hands, growing hotter when the power had been stilled. It felt almost as though someone had lit a cigarette lighter underneath the skin of her palms. Hastily, she closed the door on the power, and the burning in her palms immediately ceased. A slight tingling bordering on pain shot along her nerves throughout her body.

Rubbing her palms, Allison said, "That burned. Was it supposed to burn?"

"When you hold power too long in your hands, yes," Aidric answered with a hint of amusement. "It begins to build up to levels that your body cannot tolerate. That's why when you're channeling, the power must leave the body as swiftly as possible and never be allowed to be static for more than a few depths at a time."

"When I cut off the power, I felt a tingling throughout my body. Was that supposed to happen?"

she asked worriedly.

"It's quite normal," he assured her. "You just channeled a fair amount of power. Did you think it would just disappear when you cut off the initial flow? It had to go somewhere, and since you didn't cast it from your hands, your body simply absorbed it. It's quite harmless at these low levels, but if you ever channel more power than your body can safely absorb and you don't immediately rid yourself of it, then the power *will* consume you. Channeling is never to be taken lightly. Extreme caution must always be used. Now, show me you can channel as easily as you can breathe, and we'll go on to the next step."

Allison channeled several more times under Aidric's critical eye until she was pretty sure that she could do it in her sleep with no problem and he had nodded his approval. Her shoulders sagged wearily, and her head was beginning to ache. She hoped that Aidric would end the lesson soon.

"I think you're ready to begin shaping the power you've channeled into something useful," he informed her, dashing her hopes. "It's not exactly a spell, but it's a good exercise for you to prepare you for when I assign you the task of casting your first spell. This time I want you to direct the energy to your left palm only, and when the power you've channeled reaches your palm, allow it to rise from within and form it into a small sphere of light simply by willing it so in your mind. It should continue to glow until you have stopped channeling, then vanish as quickly as it appeared. That will be your last task for the day, but we'll not stop until you've mastered it, even if it takes the rest of the day and night to do it."

"I was afraid you'd say that," she muttered, sighing tiredly, but determined to show him that she didn't need as much time as he had given her.

For the next couple of sand-marks, Allison practiced creating the ball of light in her hands, perfecting the speed in which she could make it appear as well as dimming and increasing its illumination. When Aidric finally motioned for her to stop, she was more than ready to go collapse onto her bed and sleep for a quarter-moon.

However, fate had other plans for her.

As she stiffly picked herself up from the pillows, Aidric suddenly stilled, and his eyes glazed over as if he had suddenly lost himself in thought. *What is it now?* she thought, frowning, and was about to ask him just that when sense abruptly came back into his eyes.

He fixed her with troubled eyes. "I know you must be tired," he began cautiously as though afraid of having his head bitten off, "but Diryan summons you to his study. I'm afraid you must go at once." He held his hands out in a gesture of helplessness and added,

"Had I known this would happen, I wouldn't have worked you so hard on your lessons. Forgive me."

He looked so stricken that Allison began to feel guilty even though she knew she should be angry, at him for working her so vigorously and mercilessly in the first place, and at King Diryan for his wretched timing. *Damn it all!* she grumbled to herself. *Will they never give me any peace?*

"You couldn't have known," she assured him with a weary sigh. "Well, so much for my plans of immediately collapsing onto my bed. Do you know what this is all about?"

Aidric frowned, her question seeming to trouble him even more. He slowly shook his head.

"No, but whatever the reason, Diryan was insistent that you make haste—and that you go alone."

Allison raised an eyebrow at that, but didn't comment on it. "Then, I guess I should get going," she said bravely, though inside her stomach was beginning to knot with anxiety.

He nodded. "I'll be here when you return."

CHAPTER SEVEN

A s Allison walked down the dim corridor of the Mage Hall towards the indoor garden, the hollow echoes of her footsteps on the marble floors the only sound around her, she suddenly felt more alone and vulnerable than she ever had in her life. She had grown so accustomed to having Aidric at her side through every trial and unknown she had ever faced in this strange world that now, as she was on her way to face yet another of those unknowns, she suddenly felt naked without him.

What does the king want? she worried, unconsciously biting her lip in her uneasiness. *And why did he ask for me to go alone? I had thought there were no secrets between them, at least none concerning me. Why doesn't the king want Aidric there?*

Abruptly, she stopped as a terrible thought suddenly occurred to her. *My God, what if he's decided that I'm just too dangerous to be allowed to live and doesn't want Aidric to know that he plans to sentence me to death? Or worse—to the dungeons for the rest of my life? I'll run away before that happens!*

Allison laughed bitterly at that thought. *Yeah, right, Allison, and go where? Considering that you could even get past those bloodhounds at the border, which is, in itself, near to impossible, what would you do then? Where could you go? You've never even been past the border, and who knows what lies beyond? Plus, you're the only one in this godforsaken world that has blonde hair! Unless you find some way to dye it permanently, you'll just be shit out of luck won't you? You're stuck, whether you like it or not, and you might as well face up to it. Your fate is in their hands now, and there's nothing you can do to change that.*

Scowling, Allison forced her feet to move and headed to the king's chambers with a kind of resignation. Whatever it was the king wanted with her, whether it was to condemn her or for some other reason, she knew she wouldn't like what he had to say. She had enough control of her Foresight to sense that much about the meeting as she made her way across the courtyard, through a pair of doors, and up the stairs to the hall that led to King Diryan's rooms.

At the door to his chambers, she was immediately

halted by a pair of guards that for all their differences, could have been twins with their identical manners and identical expressions of coldness and suspicion on their hardened faces. If she had met them under different circumstances, she would have even thought them handsome.

Both were probably in their early thirties at the oldest, well-muscled, and had auburn hair that fell in waves to their shoulders in identical styles, but while one had blue eyes that uncomfortably reminded her of Master Kiryl, the other's eyes were a deep brown, a color which would have softened any other's features but accomplished quite the opposite for this man.

Allison felt her skin begin to crawl as they eyed her up and down with steely eyes that seemed to see more than she thought they had a right to see. She fidgeted under their scrutiny and averted her eyes, hating that she let them cow her so easily.

The guard nearest to her leaned over to his companion and whispered something in his ear. The other man nodded, stepped forward, and firmly grabbed her arm as though he expected her to bolt any second. She had an angry suspicion that they had read her mind and knew of her fears regarding the reasons behind the summoning.

"His Majesty has been expecting you," the guard holding her arm growled in a voice that sounded as if it had no use for laughter.

Suddenly, neither one of them seemed very appealing anymore.

With a guard on either side of her, Allison was ushered into King Diryan's chambers and led into a room that Ileanna had pointed out as the king's study on her first visit here. They walked her to the center of the room as if she was a prisoner being led to face the king for judgment. The guard holding her arm released her and stepped back with his companion to take up positions on either side of the door.

Allison blinked in surprise when she saw that the king was not alone. The Seneschal and a raven-haired, olive-skinned man stood on either side of the king, both regarding her with equal expressions of emptiness, while the king wore a very open, troubled expression that did nothing to ease the edginess of her nerves.

The Seneschal, she had half-expected to be present—seldom did she ever see him not by the king's side—but the other, she didn't recall ever having seen him here, whether during court or outside. He was dressed strangely, in a gray tunic of simple design that seemed to say volumes for its simplicity in a kingdom where clothing was never simple. On his breast lay a large insignia of a golden-hilted sword slashing through a silver lightning bolt. She was certain that she had never seen anyone bearing such a symbol.

Though trembling inside, Allison faced the king and the other two men with outward calm and gracefully curtsied in humble respect. Then folding her hands in front of her in a show of meekness, she silently waited for the king to speak as Aidric had told her was the proper etiquette when summoned before the king, struggling to keep her legs or hands from trembling.

"Guards, you may leave us," Diryan said into the silence. She sensed that the guards were bowing behind her, and although she expected it, she nearly jumped out of her skin when the door banged shut behind her.

"You look unsettled, milady," the king remarked.

Allison bowed her head and said, "I would humbly ask Your Majesty to forgive my unseemly appearance, but I had just completed one of my mage lessons when I was summoned here."

With considerable effort, she suppressed a triumphant smile as she saw identical looks of surprise flash across Diryan and Lord Ion's eyes.

Didn't expect a response like that out of me did you? she thought smugly. *I didn't sit there day by day in court just idly twiddling my thumbs in boredom as everyone else seemed to be doing.*

In fact, she hadn't been nodding off, either. She

had made sure that she paid close attention to how everyone addressed the king and their superiors, as well as studying the speech and manners of those who stood before the king. Allison knew that if she was ever going to get into the good graces of the Circle and King Diryan's councilors, she would do best not to offend anyone with her ignorance of their ways. Maybe then, they would stop their damned staring!

Immediately recovering from his surprise, Diryan nodded his pardons and then stated formally, "Allison McNeal, you have been Summoned to appear before the High Priest of the Brothers in Divinity in response to the question of your loyalties to our lord, Seni. Domnae Eban and his guards will be your escorts to Kal. You will leave immediately—within the sand-mark—as soon as the supplies for the journey are readied and your horse saddled."

Domnae?

The cool calm Allison had been struggling to maintain instantly shattered at his words, and she didn't even bother to hide the shock and dismay she felt at this newest turn of events.

Dear God, he's sending me away with this strange man, she thought frantically, eyeing the dark-haired man, who had thus far remained silent, with rising fear. *He's sending me to those—those people who would kill Ileanna if they knew the truth of her son!*

"But—but, Your Majesty," Allison stammered, the last bit of her cool composure shattering, "what about my mage lessons, and shouldn't I inform Aidric of this?"

Lord Ion eyed her disapprovingly for her outburst. She knew she had spoken out of turn, but at the moment, Allison didn't in the least bit care what he thought of her.

Frowning, Diryan answered, "Your mage lessons must be postponed for the moment, I fear. I would not have it so, but in matters which involve Seni, my wishes fall under those of the Brothers in Divinity. As for the Mage-general, yes, he needs to be informed, and I see no harm in you bearing the message yourself. However, you must—"

"*No*," the man whom Diryan had called Domnae Eban interrupted sternly, fixing her with a gaze so cold that it would have even cowed Master Kiryl. "She will *not* be allowed to converse with any henceforth except those of my order under penalty of charges of heresy. I would have none whispering information to her. She will come to us with only the answers she holds now within her soul."

Allison suddenly found it difficult to breathe, and with horror, she realized that she was on a verge of another panic attack. *NO!* she screamed inwardly as the room began to swim around her. *I will* not *let this happen! I've struggled too hard to rid myself of these attacks, and I won't have a relapse of them now!*

Reflexively, she reached out to Aidric with her mind, getting as far as calling out his name before she realized what she was doing and cut off her thought with sudden fear. *Oh God, oh God, what have I done?*

Trembling in fear and from the effort of trying to draw breath around the hand of terror that tightly squeezed her throat, Allison fell to her knees to the startlement of the men, and cried, "Forgive me—p-please forgive me—I didn't mean—it just slipped—"

From the expression on his face, Diryan understood exactly what she was struggling to say despite her garbled words, and the cold anger that filled his eyes was enough to make her cringe, even as she gasped for breath.

"What has the child done?" Domnae Eban demanded, stepping towards her.

The Domnae put his hand under her chin and roughly lifted it up, forcing her eyes to meet his hard gaze of green flames. He towered over her as she reluctantly looked up at him, longing to lower her eyes but not daring to do so.

I can't breathe—

"Answer!" Domnae Eban commanded.

Allison opened her mouth, desperately trying to find her voice, but at that moment, the door suddenly swung open and the blue-eyed guard who had brought her into the room hesitantly entered the room. If he was surprised at the scene he saw before him, his expression nor voice as he addressed the king gave no indication.

"Your Highness, pardon my intrusion, but the Mage-general is at your door demanding that he be admitted, and I fear that he will—"

"Like bloody hell I shall!" came Aidric's voice a split-second before he stalked into the room, his face red with rage, and stopped short when he saw Allison on her knees before Domnae Eban. "What is the meaning of this?"

Not bothering to wait for an answer, he hurried over to Allison, and knelt down beside her, ignoring the Domnae completely. She looked up at him gratefully and struggled to speak, but that only had her gasping for more breath. By then, her heart was beating so fast that she thought that it would soon burst.

"She's having another one of her attacks," Aidric said angrily to no one in particular, his eyes never once leaving hers. "Couldn't you see that she couldn't breathe?"

As before, Allison felt immediate warmth fill her body, and instantly, she began to breathe more easily, the hand of panic around her throat melting away with the warmth. Truth told, just having Aidric so near did more for her than the healing ever could have.

"I didn't mean to call you," she whispered miserably when she found her voice again. "He forbade me, but I swear it just slipped—"

"I'm glad you did, else they may have let you strangle on your own fear here," Aidric said with a gentle expression, though his words were razor sharp.

Aidric looked up at the Domnae then, and to her shock, his eyes instantly glazed over with recognition and the blackest fury Allison had ever seen reflected in a man's eyes. Not even her stepfather's eyes had ever held half as much rage at his worst. Her skin began to tingle as she felt the power within Aidric rise dangerously, and for one terrible moment, Allison feared that he was going to strike out at Eban.

Then, in the blink of an eye, the moment was gone. Aidric shook himself a little, and the inferno in his eyes died down into a roaring flame. Allison slowly released the breath she had not realized she was holding.

Aidric nodded up at Eban and said coldly, "Ah, *Domnae* Eban, we meet again. Fancy seeing you in Lamia when you *swore* you would not set foot on Lamian soil again even if Seni, Himself, were to order you. Would you mind explaining to me just what you were doing to my *ward*?"

Aidric's voice was steady, but Allison clearly heard

the bite underneath, and she had not missed the emphasis he had placed on Eban's title as though meant as a mockery to him. It was painfully clear that there was no love lost between the two men, yet Domnae Eban didn't seem the least bit affected by Aidric's open contempt of him. In fact, it seemed to only amuse him.

"Things change, *Mage-general*," Eban replied just as coolly, "and as for the child, I need not explain my actions to you. Unless she proves otherwise, she is no longer your concern but the concern of the Brothers in Divinity."

"She has been Summoned?" Aidric asked in disbelief.

Allison did not in the least bit like the way Aidric had said "summoned," as if the word itself said volumes more other than its simple meaning. Also, was it just her imagination, or did Domane Eban look just a wee bit smug at Aidric's question?

She glanced over at King Diryan and Lord Ion to see what they thought of this exchange, and immediately looked away, troubled by what she saw in their expressions. Diryan still looked angry, but now it was mixed with uneasiness. Lord Ion simply glared at her, contempt etched into every inch of his body. He didn't bother trying to conceal it from her. She wasn't surprised to see that the guard had inconspicuously made his way out of the room sometime earlier. She envied him.

"Why so surprised, Mage-general?" Domnae Eban answered. "By proclaiming herself the Golden Mage, she has thus announced that she is not of this realm. Being not of this realm, she has not made her Oaths to Seni. If you have instructed her correctly in obedience to Seni, then she has nothing to fear of us or our questions, doesn't she?"

Grinding his teeth in anger, Aidric stood up until he was face-to-face with Eban, violence in his eyes, and appearing as if he was indeed going to strike him. The tension in the room was stifling. Lord Ion stepped forward as if to step between them, but changed his mind in mid-stride, apparently because of something he saw when he looked at the two men. Her skin began to tingle more insistently.

"Aidric don't," Allison pleaded within his mind, climbing unsteadily to her feet so that she was standing between them. *"This is my fault. I shouldn't have called you here. Please don't do something you'll only regret later!"*

At first, it appeared as if he hadn't heard her. His eyes never moved away from Eban's stare, nor did his stance shift out of its guarded position. Then, just when Allison feared that he wasn't going to back down, Aidric balled his hands into tight fists and slowly backed away, the violence in his eyes beginning to die down with every step. Her relief was almost overwhelming. Aidric tore his eyes away from Domnae Eban and fixed them onto her. They were the eyes of a stranger. He nodded stiffly towards her and then fixed his eyes onto Eban again.

"So be it," Aidric said calmly, maybe a bit *too* calmly, and with his next words, Allison knew why, "but I shall accompany her."

"Out of the question," Eban snapped coldly, his mask of civility gone. "I shall not have you influencing her in any way. You have done enough ill as it already stands. She goes alone, and that's the end of it. You forget, *Mage-general*, it is *I* who commands in this matter."

Aidric took a threatening step forward, and Allison hastily stepped up to him to prevent his advance. He blinked down at her in surprise as if he had forgotten that she was standing there between them.

She shook her head resignedly and said softly, "Aidric, I'll go with him. I've already caused you enough trouble. I don't want to cause any more."

"Well, at least one of you is speaking sensibly," Eban observed coldly, earning him an angry glare from her.

"And you're not making it any better by provoking him," she spat at him before she could think.

Lord Ion looked as though he was trying to prove

that his mouth could drop completely to the floor, and King Diryan appeared as if he couldn't settle on an expression. Allison thought she saw a shadow of a smile flicker on Aidric's lips for a beat and likely did.

Domnae Eban merely narrowed his eyes at her and said, "You are in need of learning respect for your spiritual lords, child. I'm beginning to wonder if the Mage-general has bothered to instruct you at all in regards to Seni, but we shall see." He glanced over at Diryan and said a little more civilly, "We waste time on this foolishness. King Diryan, is all ready for the journey?"

Diryan shifted his eyes to Lord Ion, who was still staring at the three of them as if he still couldn't quite believe what had just happened, and asked his silent question. Ion nodded, and his eyes took on the faraway look of someone who was thought-speaking.

"All is ready, My Lord King," Ion said a moment later. "Her horse has already been loaded with her traveling packs."

"Good," Domnae Eban said firmly. "Then we shall be on our way. I would ask, King Diryan, for your guards to escort her to the stables until she is under the eyes of my own guards."

"I shall escort her myself," Aidric said firmly, his eyes daring the older man to challenge him.

To her relief, Eban just flashed him a pained look

and said simply, "Let us go then."

As they headed towards the stables, Allison warily sent to Aidric, *"Why do I feel as if I've been charged with a crime, and I'm off to the dungeons?"*

Careful not to look at her—Eban had warned them not to speak to one another—Aidric replied, *"Because that's not far from the truth, little cat. When someone is Summoned, it's because they have been suspected of some form of heresy against Seni."*

"But, I've done nothing!" she cried.

"You haven't sworn an oath to serve Seni, and you are well over the maximum age in which a child must swear oaths or face charges. Thus, in their eyes, you have *committed a heresy against Seni. They'll hold you indefinitely until you swear that oath, so it's better that you do just that. However, I warn you that they know when someone is speaking falsehoods to them, and for your sake, always speak the truth."*

Domnae Eban eyed them suspiciously, and Allison was afraid that he knew they had been thought-speaking. She did her best to meet his accusative gaze evenly as if proving she had nothing to hide.

When his eyes turned away from her an eternity later, she asked, *"Aidric, why do both of you have daggers in your eyes when you look at each other?"*

"It's a long story," Aidric answered somewhat hesitantly, *"but what it boils down to is this. When I finished my mage training, the High Priest Summoned me to the Temple of*

Seni because of the strength of my mage and healing powers. He wanted me to join the Domni, the mage-priests of the Brothers in Divinity, and Eban was assigned to persuade me. He did everything but proclaim me a follower of the dark god, Arioch, to coax me into swearing oaths to the Domni, but as you know, I chose to swear oaths to the Horae in service to Lamia. Ever since, he has been bitter that I chose the path of the warrior instead of the path he had laid out for me, himself. He made my life a living hell that last quarter-moon I spent in the Temple, and let's just say I have yet to completely forgive him for it—if ever I can."

Allison fell silent, not sure how to feel about it. His story explained why they said each other's title so mockingly, but she found herself wondering what Eban had done to Aidric that last quarter-moon he had spent under Eban's eye for the contempt to run so deep. She knew that Aidric had purposely left out the details, and although her curiosity ate at her, she didn't have the courage to ask.

He's told me so many secrets about himself and those he loves already, she reasoned, *so maybe in time, he'll confide this secret to me, too.*

When they reached the stables, the second sun was already disappearing behind the horizon. Night was fast approaching, and her weary bones reminded her that she'd had very little sleep as of late and that she had been cheated from her much earned sleep by her untimely summons. From the way Domnae Eban had carried on about wasting time and his desire to reach Kal as quickly as possible, Allison feared that he meant for them to ride all night.

She wasn't sure at all of how far Kal lay beyond the Lamian border. Now she wished she had paid more attention to the maps she had seen of the region in her readings. It could be a very long ride, indeed.

Muttering curses under her breath, she allowed Aidric to lead her over to Destiny. Only when Aidric had helped her mount the filly and she was securely in the saddle, reins in hand, did the fear of what lay before her flow freely through her again. Allison felt tears beginning to swell up in her eyes, and although she tried to restrain them, a few still managed to fall.

Seeing her tears, Aidric frowned with concern and reached for her trembling hand, squeezing it reassuringly. Feeling his hand in hers only made her want to cry harder. Lord knew when she would see Aidric again, and the thought of being separated from him, even if it was only for a few days, was suddenly unbearable.

"I don't want to go," Allison whispered, hoping that Domnae Eban had not heard her speak.

However, the way her luck had been going lately, she was not at all surprised when she heard Eban bark, "I said *no* speaking!"

"Don't let that bastard intimidate you, little cat, Aidric said in her mind. *Remember that you aren't alone. Your thought-speaking ability is a strong one, and no doubt you can reach me even from the Temple City. If they mistreat you in any way, I want you to promise me that you'll bespeak me, and I'll ride Shadow to foundering if needs be to fetch you."*

"I promise, and thank you for telling me about the thought-speech. I feel much better knowing that I can talk to you whenever I like without anyone finding out."

Before Aidric could say anything else, Eban rode over to them and said crossly, "All right *Mage-general*, you have seen her to her horse. Your presence here only delays us, and we have much riding yet before we reach Kal."

Aidric deliberately took her hand slowly and made a great show of planting a parting kiss on it while Eban began to turn an interesting shade of purple.

"May Seni guide and protect you, milady," Aidric said sincerely as he gave Destiny a slap to get her going before Domane Eban's face could explode.

"Take care," she called back as, staring hard at Aidric before turning around, she followed Eban out of the stable, only to be immediately surrounded by the Domnae's guards as if she truly was a dangerous criminal on the way to the gallows.

Allison dared not glance back at Aidric lest she start to cry again, but she could sense that he was still gazing after her. When they reached the edge of the palace grounds, she heard Aidric's voice whisper in the back of her mind, *"Remember, I'll always be here for you."*

CHAPTER EIGHT

Sitting behind his desk and longing to be in his bed, Diryan rubbed at his temples and tried to block out the voice of his Seneschal, who was ranting and raving as if he had suddenly gone mad about the scene that had just transpired. *Seni help me, if he goes on any longer about this whole mess, I'll stuff his own cape down his throat to silence him before I go mad!*

"—and I just cannot believe the Mage-general had the audacity to burst into here *unannounced* and speak in such a vile manner to a Domnae! A *Domnae!*" Ion was saying.

"I can," Diryan muttered under his breath.

"The High Priest will condemn us for certain when he has wind of this!" Ion continued, almost in the same breath.

Damnation, does he never stop for breath?

"Were he not so important to Lamia, I would suggest that you—"

"Enough!" Diryan boomed, lifting his head up to fix Ion with a glare that would have melted an iceberg. The Seneschal blinked back at him in surprise, his mouth still opened on what he was about to say. He looked so foolish standing there with his mouth open and his eyes bulging in shock that it was all Diryan could do to prevent himself from laughing in the poor fool's face. He also feared that if he began to laugh now, he would never stop.

Instead, he said in a somewhat calmer voice, "Peace, Ion! Can you not put a leash on your tongue for at least a depth? I'm well aware of what the Mage-general has done without you ranting on and on about it like a fool. At the moment, we have much more to lose sleep over than the wrath of an insulted Domnae."

But Ion was no longer staring at the king but had shifted his gaze to the door, and the look on his face said that he was ready to chew iron and spit out nails. The king's eyes shifted to the door, and sure enough, Aidric stood at the threshold, calmly meeting Ion glare for glare.

"Ion, leave us," Diryan said sternly.

"But—Majesty, I—"

"Now!" the king practically snarled, feeling the

heat rising to his head. He seldom lost his temper, but after a day such as he had been having, it was a wonder how he had ever managed to keep a reign on it for so long.

Ion made a strangled sound and was immediately bowing his leave and scurrying out the door, nearly bowling Aidric over in his haste, as if Arioch, himself, was on his heels.

"Close the door, Aidric," Diryan commanded in a voice that was eerily calm.

Nodding, Aidric silently obeyed and then purposely walked up to the very edge of Diryan's desk, fixing him with those damned eyes that could make a man forgive him anything. However, this time Diryan wasn't going to let him off the hook so easily.

"What in the six hells were you *thinking*, Aidric?" the king raged, slamming a fist down angrily onto the mass of documents littering his desk, causing some of them to scatter onto the floor. "Are you determined to bloody well bring down the wrath of the High Priest on us all?"

"No," Aidric replied simply, maddeningly, the intensity of his stare never wavering a bit under Diryan's rage.

Diryan grunted, clenching his teeth against the retort he desperately wanted to spat out at the young man. He rose from his chair and began to pace the length of the small room. Aidric remained where he stood.

"We'll all be lucky if we aren't condemned as followers of the Dark God after what has happened today!" Diryan lectured. "You knew that Domnae Eban was doing his damnedest to provoke you, and still you allowed him that nudge."

"I couldn't help it," Aidric said softly, his back to the king.

Diryan ceased his pacing. "Is that all you have to say?" he demanded in disbelief. "After what that man can do to this kingdom?"

"What would you have me say, Diryan?" Aidric asked stiffly, turning around to face his king. "Would you have me tell you why I loathe even the whisper of his name?"

"Yes," Diryan said, his voice instantly losing its vehemence.

"Well, that I'll never tell!" Aidric declared fiercely, turning sharply away from Diryan. "On my soul, that secret I'll take to the grave!"

An uncomfortable silence fell over the room. Diryan shifted his feet uneasily as he stared at Aidric's back, which was stiffened with tension and anger. His own anger had melted away the moment he saw the look in Aidric's eyes when he had declared that he would never reveal what Eban had done to him those many years past, a look that contained no sanity.

Lad, lad, why won't you tell me what happened?

"Do you know," Aidric spoke up suddenly into the silence, "how difficult it was for me to allow that bastard to cart off the woman that I care so deeply about?"

Diryan said nothing. What could he say?

Aidric went on as if he hadn't expected an answer. "You asked me if I realized what my meddling in this affair could do to the kingdom. That was the *only* reason why I bit back all I desired to say and restrained myself from all I have dreamed of doing to him. That reason and only that reason, alone, is why I allowed him to take Allison."

"Lad, I——" Diryan began uncomfortably.

"You need not say anything," Aidric interrupted. "What is said, is said, and what is done, is done." Aidric finally turned around to look grimly at his king. "I've done what I pledged to do when I swore my oaths to the Horae. I've put my kingdom before myself and others, but in this instance, I hope that I haven't made a mistake in doing so." Then faster than Diryan could blink, that frightening rage appeared in Aidric's eyes as he said quietly, "But know this, Diryan. If that bastard hurts her in any way, no oath to this kingdom or even to Seni, Himself, will stop me from carrying out all I have promised him. That, I pledge you."

Once again, like many times beforehand, when it should have been Aidric leaving his study feeling guilty, it was Diryan who bore the guilt on his shoulders in the end. As they both left his study, each lost in his own troubling thoughts, neither one noticed the figure emerge from behind a group of large, potted plants, staring at the two retreating backs with a look of triumph.

***

"I trust you have a very good reason as to why you demanded that I drop everything and come to this cursed kingdom with all haste without so much as an explanation why," Mordant said irritably as Roderick and he sat over plates of steaming food—roasted mutton and ang, roots, tubers, freshly baked bread, and sweetcakes—and goblets of Roderick's finest mitis wine.

Roderick smiled amicably at the silver-haired mage while inside he fumed in annoyance over the pompous bastard's complaining. Normally, he avoided having any association with the wretched man. Their last meeting five years ago had ended with them at each other's throat, and Arioch only knew how each of them had walked away with all their limbs still attached.

Had the stakes of the game he now played not been so high, he never would have *considered* asking Mordant for his help, but he grudgingly admitted that the mage, however unpleasant he was to deal with, had considerably more mage powers in some aspects than he possessed. With a legendary mage factored into his plans of conquest, Roderick desperately needed every ounce of those extra powers if he was to have any hope in triumphing in the end.

Thus, he tolerated Mordant's complaints in silence, promising himself that when he ruled the world, the first thing he would do was order Mordant's head removed and mounted—alive by Arioch's power—on his wall.

Roderick calmly picked up a slice of mutton and popped it into his mouth, taking great pains in chewing it and swallowing before he answered his "guest." "Although we most certainly have had our differences in the past, I assure you that I'll make it worth your while if you agree to assist me in a little matter concerning Lamia."

Mordant laughed nastily and said, "You're still harboring that fool idea of conquering Lamia after all these years? Have you no pride? You know as well as I that nothing short of the end of time will ever cause that Shield to go down."

Now it was Roderick's turn to smile. "What if I told you that I have found a way to penetrate the Shield? Would that heighten your interests?"

Roderick wished that he had some method of preserving the dumbfounded look Mordant now sported on his face. He would have enjoyed taunting the Silver Mage with it in the future.

"How?" Mordant demanded after a moment of shocked silence.

"Not so fast, my friend," Roderick said slyly. "First I'll have your answer."

"And if I agree," Mordant asked slowly, suspiciously, "what do I get out of this?"

And now for the bait— "I'm prepared to offer you the throne of Bar'taiver," Roderick replied, knowing instantly that Mordant was as good as his when he noted the look of sheer glee that Mordant struggled to suppress.

However, to his annoyance, Mordant feigned uncertainty and demanded that Roderick give him a few days to think it over. The man was putting a real strain on his patience.

"I'll have your answer now or not at all," Roderick said firmly. "I don't have the time for any nonsense."

Mordant glowered at him, but all the same, nodded his agreement as Roderick knew he would.

Roderick sat back in his chair, satisfied, and said,

"Good. Now we can get down to business. First and foremost, know you of the Lamian Prophecy of the Golden Mage?"

"Of course," Mordant growled. "Do you take me for a fool?"

That and more, Roderick thought dryly and said aloud, "As it is, those old Seers in the Calamon Mountains spoke the truth of this legendary figure, and—"

"What, she's *appeared*?" Mordant interrupted in disbelief.

Roderick glared at him irritably. Nothing pissed him off more than being interrupted, and what made matters worse was that he knew Mordant knew this and insisted on doing it anyway.

"Yes," he replied curtly, "and if all goes as I plan, it'll be *she* who destroys that damned Shield and *she* who will ultimately place me on the throne of Lamia."

"And if she's within that Shield, pray enlighten me on how you propose to bring her out from it and under your power?" Mordant said dryly.

"That, my friend, is where you come in," Roderick said with a grin, "and how the sole spy I have planted in Lamia has finally proven its usefulness."

CHAPTER NINE

The steady, hypnotic thump of hoof beats was the only sound all around her. The infinite *clip clop, clip clop* of the hoofs beating on the worn path they traveled was enough to almost drive Allison mad. For the third time that night, Allison found herself slumping over onto her saddle in exhaustion. The moment she felt the smoothness of the pommel brush against her cheek, she instantly jerked awake and irritably forced herself to sit up again.

As the depths and sand-marks ticked by, Allison was finding it more and more difficult to force herself to stay awake. She feared to even allow herself to drowse for even a moment lest she suddenly awakened to find herself on the ground with a broken neck.

Sighing, she glanced around at what she had come to think of as her four jailers riding within a few feet all around her, the living bars to her moving prison. All mages, she had instantly known the moment they had taken up their positions around her. Just as Aidric had explained to her, Allison could easily feel the tingle of residual Mage-field energy all around their forms that was present around all mages who had channeled energy at least once in their lives.

Even in the darkness, they all seemed as alert and fresh as if they had been in the saddle a mere five depths and not half the night. For the life of her, she didn't know how they managed to endure it when she, herself, was ready to collapse at whatever cost—even a broken neck.

She had thought that once they reached the Lamian border and were into Kal that Eban would call for them to halt for the night, yet after they were allowed to pass through by the border guards, Eban seemed even more determined to ride out the night.

Domnae Eban had opened a portal just outside Ell to the border—why he had waited until they had ridden several marks before he did it, he had not felt obliged to enlighten her. Allison had hoped that once outside the Shield he would transport them all to Kal, but as the sand-marks crawled by and still they rode, it became apparent that Eban was bent on making them all suffer through a grueling night and day of riding. The long sand-marks of riding only served to allow her hatred for the Domnae to grow.

Passing through the Lamian border, itself, had been an interesting experience. Allison had felt her skin begin to tingle from what she knew was the result of being so near the infamous Shield around Lamia a full thirty depths before they actually reached the border. To plain eyes, the Shield was invisible, but when she had used inner-sight, Allison clearly saw the matrix of energy that composed the Shield.

The guards had passed them through without much delay. They clearly knew Eban well, greeting him by his name. Her, they merely stared at with widened eyes, in fascination or horror, she wasn't sure, though she suspected the latter.

Allison didn't truly understand what exactly they did to open the Shield, but she knew that it had been a mage who did it. He did a lot of gesturing and muttering in a language that must have been Ti'ar, but he channeled no energy, nor did any energy leave his hands. A hole big enough for them to pass through if they rode single file had appeared in the Shield once the mage dropped his hands and fell silent. She had promised herself that she would ask Aidric about it when she returned to the palace. He surely would know how it was done.

Allison glanced ahead at the barely visible figure of Eban riding at the point of their group, cursing him silently and willing her exhaustion to him, wishing for the thousandth time that night that Aidric had gotten around to teaching her the use of her Empathy so she could have truly sent her weariness to him. This time she didn't bother to hide her tired sigh when it became apparent that Eban didn't plan to stop for the night anytime soon, if at all.

Glowering in silence, she turned her attention to the young, black-haired man to her right with the same forest-green eyes as her own who looked to be around her age and wished he would at least talk to her. Conversation would at least help to keep her awake. However, she knew that any attempt at conversation with him was useless.

She had tried several times earlier to engage him in conversation by asking him questions about Kal and this Temple of Seni that they were taking her to, but her efforts only brought on the glares of the three other men around her and the young man's apologetic shake of his head, reminding her that they were not allowed to speak.

Allison even contemplated thought-speaking Aidric, but she figured that the range was too far for her wearied mind to make. At the moment, her mind was so fatigued that she was surprised that she could even remember her own name. Furthermore, Aidric was likely asleep, and she would not have disturbed his rest even if Roderick, himself, suddenly appeared in the night.

When the young man noticed that she was looking at him, Allison quickly lowered her eyes, feeling somewhat foolish. *I must look like a little lost puppy longing for attention*, she thought with a grimace.

She started and nearly lost her grip on the reins when an unfamiliar voice suddenly whispered in her mind, *"If milady wishes to rest, it's all right to do so. I'll keep close watch on you if you fear that you'll fall from your saddle should you nod off."*

Allison glanced over at the young man with a questioning look in her eyes, not sure if it had been he who had spoken in her mind. His gaze caught her eyes, and he smiled slightly in acknowledgment.

She returned his smile gratefully and sent back, *"Thank you...?"* She let the rest of that thought trail off into an unspoken question as she once again slumped over in her saddle and tried to arrange herself as comfortably as was possible in a saddle. She didn't think that he would answer her, but as sleep began to creep into her mind, Allison heard his voice, as if whispered from a far off place, say a name in answer to her unspoken question.

"Soren."

***

The dream was different this time, the landscape changed to what appeared to be the ruins of an ancient palace, though the same storm raged beyond the stone walls, water seeping in through its many fissures. Roderick found himself standing in the very heart of the place, water beginning to pool at his feet. He knew he should have been drenched and freezing, but his clothing was as dry as the deserts of Sonon. He also felt pleasantly warm.

Almost immediately, he sensed a presence in the room with him, a familiar presence. Roderick half turned, expecting to see a figure of a man hiding in the shadows behind him, but the room was quite empty.

"Yes, Mihran king, it is I," Roderick heard the same voice from his battlefield dreams declare distinctly within his mind. *"Time is eluding you, so listen well. An opportunity has arisen, riding into the coming twilight. Only silver will give you the chance to find the gold you seek when darkness reigns again. Yet, beware the one enclosed within walls of light."*

"But—what—" Roderick managed to ask before another, familiar voice filled his mind and the palace's ruined walls began to fade into darkness.

In the next breath, Roderick jerked awake, and to his chagrin, discovered that he had fallen asleep sitting at his desk. However, his initial anger instantly dissolved when he realized that another Foresight dream had come to him.

"*An opportunity has arisen. Beware the one enclosed within walls of light.*"

What did it mean?

Only when Roderick realized that it had been his Lamian spy's mind-voice that had abruptly awakened him, did he understand.

CHAPTER TEN

Allison jerked awake to the sound of men shouting and to the sudden stomach-lurching feeling of her horse beginning to rear. With a strangled cry, she instinctively snatched up her reins and held on for dear life as Destiny continued to rear and dance around wildly. Hands reached from out of nowhere and grabbed for her reins. Beneath her growing panic, Allison was distantly aware that they belonged to Soren, and that he was struggling to get Destiny under control again.

Her eyes darted wildly around into the infinite blackness and met utter chaos. Shadows and shapes grappled together all around her, the clang of metal and the shouts and curses of men alive in what had once been a peaceful night. Horses pressed all around her, and she saw that it was her jailers, facing away from her in a tight circle of protection.

"What's happening?" Allison shrieked.

"Ambush!" Domnae Soren shouted above the noise of the battle around them. "And well planned. We never saw them coming until it was too late. Stay close to me!"

Ambush— she thought frantically. *Dear God, it's probably Roderick! He's come for me just as Aidric feared!*

Before she realized what she was doing, Allison had already begun to gather the life-energy within her body and started shaping it into several powerful shields around her. She had barely completed weaving the shields when a flash of light suddenly slashed through the air mere inches in front of her and struck one of her jailers. For a few seconds, his body glowed with a brilliant, white light as his shields harmlessly absorbed the bolt of lightning that had struck him. The boom that followed sounded like the world, itself, was cracking open, leaving her ears ringing painfully. The smell of ozone instantly invaded her nostrils.

Before Allison could open her mouth to scream, four more bolts of lightning shot out of the darkness, each striking the men who desperately guarded her and blinding her with the resulting backlash of power. The world around her seemed to turn upside down and to explode at the same time. Men shouted. Horses reared all around her, including Destiny.

Blinded and gasping with terror, Allison fought desperately to stay in the saddle, but before she knew what was happening, a bolt of lightning struck at Destiny's forelegs, sending her flying. Destiny released a scream that sounded far too human for her peace of mind as they both tumbled to the ground. Allison landed hard on her side, her breath painfully wrenched from her lungs.

Gasping for breath, Allison blindly tried to scramble to shelter as dozens of lightning bolts struck the ground all around her, some hitting mere inches from her body. She couldn't escape them. Everywhere she turned, a flash would assault her eyes. The lightning had her trapped, lost within a world of brilliant chaos.

Frantically, she sought out the familiar shapes of the men that had been accompanying her. At that point, even the sight of Domnae Eban would have been welcome.

Then through vision blurred by tears and light, Allison saw a glowing figure dressed in shimmering silver robes easing his way towards her out of the darkness, leisurely, as though he had all the time in the world and the nightmare around them didn't exist. His hands glowed with an angry red power he had yet to cast forth.

He's coming for me—

"Crap!" Allison cried in English as she struggled

to rise to her feet, only to be knocked flat on her back with a blow of sheer power that shattered all of her hastily-built shields as if they were cracked egg shells and left her stunned and gasping for the breath she had only recently found.

A crimson light immediately enveloped and penetrated her body, a light that seemed to drain the very life from her body like some kind of magical leech. The pain of it was like something out of her worst nightmare, feeling as if thousands of tiny needles were being driven deep into her flesh and her blood drawn out. Allison struggled against the draining she didn't understand with every last inch of willpower she had left in her, but she knew that it was a losing battle. Distantly, she could hear herself screaming.

So it ends here, she thought despairingly as darkness began to invade her mind. *I longed for death—God help me, but not like this—not before I could tell Aidric how I really feel—*

Then abruptly, the glow all around her winked out and the draining stopped. Allison weakly lifted her head and saw through blurry eyes Domnae Soren standing before her, his back turned to her, golden power swirling in his hands. A few feet before him stood the mage in silver, fury clearly twisting his features despite the gloom. His eyes seemed to glow a red as angry as the power in his hands.

"She's mine, fool!" the mage in silver growled. "Do you think your pathetic powers of light are a match for mine?"

"We shall see," Soren spat back, and before Allison could blink, Soren had spun the power in his hands into a large, luminescent-green fireball and flung it at the mage.

There was a tremendous explosion as the fireball hit the mage's shields and was immediately reflected back into a thousand sparks that sped towards Soren. Wind instantly came alive around Soren and met the multitude of sparks dead on, dissipating them on contact.

The silver-robed mage then began to batter Soren with lightning bolt after bolt, pounding away at his shields until Soren was forced to stagger back a step. Allison could see that Soren was faltering, and it would not be too long before his shields gave away and the mage would defeat him.

I have to do something! she thought with determination.

Yet what, she had no idea. Allison knew that she was too weak to attempt to draw power from the Mage-field and expect to control it, much less to actually shape it into something she could use against the mage. She was too new to magic. She hardly thought that a ball of light in her palms would be much help to

Soren!

She cursed Eban bitterly for taking her away from the palace before she was able to learn any offensive spells from Aidric. She was supposedly the most powerful mage in all of Seni's World, and she was utterly helpless.

Damn it all, there has to be something *I can do! I'm supposed to be a damn legendary mage, after all!*

Then the sight of Soren's shields shattering caused a memory to surface of Aidric telling her that she had somehow shattered all of his shields with merely the power of a mind-scream the day he had found her. She sucked in a sharp, excited breath. Maybe there was some way she could do it again using her thought-speaking ability.

Clearing her mind of all thoughts and doing her best to ignore both the ache in her body and growing weakness, Allison concentrated on forming a high-pitched scream in her mind and sending it as forcefully as she could to the enemy mage just as Aidric had taught her to send emotions mind-to-mind. She only prayed that it worked the same for a scream.

The lightning attack on Soren abruptly ceased, and the silver-clad mage suddenly shrieked and threw his hands over his ears. Encouraged by his response, Allison closed her eyes and concentrated even harder on sending that high-pitched scream as strongly as she could to the mage's mind. She felt his shields shatter a moment later, and with them, his screams grew more horrible. Then, in the next heartbeat, his screams abruptly fell silent.

A wave of fatigue washed over her as Allison stopped her sending and slowly opened her eyes. The mage had vanished.

"Where is he?" she whispered hoarsely.

"He has fled," Soren replied, turning around to look down at her with puzzled eyes. "You did—*something* to him, didn't you?"

Allison nodded slowly and wearily shut her eyes. "I had—to help—you," she managed to croak out before the fatigue overwhelmed her and her mind knew no more.

CHAPTER ELEVEN

S prawled out on one of the two large couches in the room, a novel opened in his hands, Selwyn frowned as he watched the figure pacing anxiously in front of the windows in his sitting room out of the corner of his eye. With his white hair hanging in untidy wisps that half concealed his eyes and a scowl that seemed to have become a permanent feature on his face within the last sand-mark, Aidric looked uncannily like one of the many statues of the mage heroes of the past that lined the walls of the Temple of the Horae. Their hair was sculpted in such a way that it cast off the illusion that the wind whipped through their hair, mouths fixed in eternal snarls of hatred for the enemy.

"You know, you're beginning to give me a headache," Selwyn said dryly.

He might as well have been talking to himself for all Aidric heard him. More so, Aidric's pacing only seemed to increase in vigor and his iron scowl deepening, a feat he hadn't thought possible.

He tried a different approach. "Raya just walked into here naked."

Aidric's eyes didn't even blink.

"Hey, isn't that Allison with Patrym out there?"

"What!" Aidric boomed, turning his head so sharply to peer out the window that Selwyn could almost imagine hearing Aidric's neck crack.

"Well, now that I've *finally* captured your attention," Selwyn began with a wry grin, "need I even ask what or should I say *who* is behind this sudden urge to pace? There are much better methods of wearing grooves in my floor, you know."

Aidric glanced a second time out the window as if he didn't truly believe that what Sel had said about Allison and Patrym was a joke before the scowl returned to his face, and he strode somewhat stiffly to one of Selwyn's overstuffed chairs.

He plopped himself heavily into the enveloping cushions and said, "Spare me the lectures, okay. I'm neither in the mood nor have the patience for it today."

"So I gathered," Selwyn muttered, eyeing his friend's sullen figure worriedly.

It was clear that Aidric hadn't slept at all the previous night by the deep circles under his eyes and the unruliness of his appearance in whole—untidy hair and clothes that were slightly wrinkled—when usually Aidric didn't dare to show his face in public if even a speck of lint showed anywhere on his clothing.

In an attempt to relieve some of the choking tension that had been growing in the room since Aidric had come barging in a little over a sand-mark ago and set to pacing, Selwyn said lightly, "I haven't seen you this anxious since the time you thought Diryan had learned of your late night streak across the palace lawn with only your drunkenness to cloth you!"

"Aidius, you would mention *that* incident now," Aidric groaned, but with a shadow of a smile on his lips. "Will you never let me alone about it?"

"As long as I'm still young and not so senile to have forgotten it, no."

Aidric grimaced as if he had suddenly eaten something sour and then chuckled softly. "Damn you, Sel. I was brooding so beautifully before you had to go and ruin it—as always."

"I swear you worry more than a house full of grandmothers before a war," Sel chided good-naturedly. "I'm sure she's fine. By now she's probably resting comfortably in the Temple charming the breeches off those stone-faced Domni and Senini with that shy smile of hers."

When Aidric's smile suddenly melted into a frown, Selwyn could have kicked himself twice for mentioning the Domni. He was well aware of Aidric's black hatred for one Domnae in particular, a hatred that stemmed from an unrevealed secret that weighed heavily on his soul. What that secret was, Selwyn doubted anyone would ever know.

"I should be damned to the worst of the six hells for allowing that demon to even go near her!" Aidric suddenly spat out bitterly. "Sel, something has happened to them during the journey—I don't know what, but I've sensed it."

"It could merely be your nerves, Aidric—" Selwyn started to say before Aidric snarled in anger.

"It's *not* my nerves, damn it!"

Then as quickly as his fury rose up, it instantly abated. "I'm sorry," Aidric said with a frustrated sigh. "I know snapping at you does no good. You asked why I'm so anxious today. It's because I've tried on numerous occasions ever since I began to have these feelings of unease to thought-speak her and she is simply—not there."

"Perhaps she's too far away for you to reach her," Selwyn suggested tentatively, not wanting to set off

Aidric's temper again.

"Perhaps," Aidric muttered though he didn't sound convinced, "but if I don't hear from her soon, I fear that I'll go mad!"

"Well, brooding and scowling all day long isn't going to help you any," Selwyn said firmly. "Raya and I were planning on riding into Biros today to visit my sister for a couple of days as soon as her duties are done for the day. Why not come with us? It would do you well to get away from all of this. I know Jana and the kids would love to see you."

"As much as I would like to, my friend, I cannot," Aidric replied with a wistful sigh. "I have a meeting with Diryan, his councilors, the Lord Commander, and General Caith in a sand-mark."

Selwyn nodded sympathetically. It seemed all their time lately had been spent sitting on their rumps and debating in the Council Room over the growing tension between Mihr and Lamia. Since Raya was not a member of the Circle, they had not had much opportunity to spend time together whenever she was at the palace and not on duty at the Kemosian-Mihran border. Today was one of those rare days that they both didn't have any duties to attend to.

Only, do I have any right to complain? Selwyn thought. *If I seldom have time to devote to my personal life, Aidric has even less so, and it's really he, not I, who desperately needs it.*

"Life was so much easier back when we were only apprentices, wasn't it?" Selwyn said. "After we suffered the torment of lessons for the day, we were as free as the birds for whatever it was we had mind to do. Whether it was chasing a fair maiden or enjoying an afternoon of hunting, we never had to concern ourselves with the likes of politics and war as we do now."

Aidric smiled and then shook his head amusedly. "And to think how we use to grumble at least a hundred times a day about how we wished that we were no longer novices but a *true* mage and empath with *important* and *exciting* duties to attend to." He chuckled softly. "Sometimes I wish I could go back to those times past and kick myself for having such foolish notions. Only, if I did, then I likely wouldn't want to return to the present!"

Selwyn laughed and said, "As that old adage says, 'Take care in what you yearn for, for you will obtain it just as you deserve.'"

"As troublesome and mischief-makers as we were, I would say we are doing our fair share of penance for those yearnings now."

"You more than I, I'm afraid," Selwyn said with a wry grin, "but there is always tomorrow."

"Yes tomorrow—" Aidric said distantly, more to himself than Selwyn. "One more day too many that Allison must spend among strangers and the man I loathe perhaps even more than I loathe Roderick."

"So we are back to Allison again," Selwyn said, "I was beginning to wonder whether or not I would have to bring her up again."

Aidric looked at him sideways. "Something tells me that there's going to be a lecture in this somewhere."

Selwyn glared at him. "You make me sound as if I'm a nagging old bag. I was merely going to ask why you haven't told Allison that what you feel for her is more than friendship? Are you still afraid that what happened with Alina could—"

"Allison is *not her*," Aidric cut in sharply, then fell silent for a moment, turning his eyes to stare out the window. When he finally spoke again, Selwyn detected a note of uncertainty in his voice. "Now isn't the time. Ever since her lessons began, the atmosphere between us has been something less than friendly. I drive her mercilessly as you understand I must, and she is none too pleased with me at the moment."

"But, if you let her know that there's affection underneath all that sternness," Selwyn insisted, "then perhaps it would make her lessons that much more bearable."

"You make all too much sense for your own good, do you know that?" Aidric grumbled, though he was grinning.

Selwyn grinned back and replied, "I think I'll take that as a compliment. Then it's settled?"

Aidric hesitated for a moment before saying, "Yes, nosy, I'll do it when she returns from the Temple. Are you satisfied?"

Selwyn sat back into the couch with the air of a poor man who had just been informed that all his debts were to be dismissed. "That's all I wanted to hear," he said smugly.

CHAPTER TWELVE

When Allison jerked awake from disturbing dreams of spells and battles, the first thing she saw was Domnae Soren standing guard over her from the opening of the tent.

Tent? What—who—

Now completely awake, her eyes darted all around her and saw that she was in a small, makeshift tent, the type Lamian soldiers often used during their tours of duty. Aidric owned one similar to it. She was lying on a thin bedroll that did nothing to soften up the hardness of the ground, a slightly damp cloth folded across her forehead.

Vaguely, she could hear the sounds of people walking outside the tent as well as the sound of men moaning in the distance. Pulling the cloth from her forehead, Allison tried to sit up and discovered that her limbs felt as if they bore lead weights.

Soren immediately turned his head towards her when he heard her stir and knelt down beside her. "Here, allow me to help you sit up. Despite your rest, you still should feel as if you've been ill for over a moon."

That was by far the most she had ever heard him speak aloud. Silently, Allison accepted his help in propping herself up into a more appropriate position and then gladly took the mug he pressed into her unsteady hands when she realized that her mouth was as dry as the Sahara. She sipped at the liquid slowly at first until she discovered that it was watered down wine—an underlying bitterness signifying that it had probably been doctored with medicines. Nevertheless, she eagerly downed the rest of it in only a couple of gulps.

"Easy now, milady," Soren chided gently. "It will make you ill if you drink too much. Are you hungry? I can bring you some food if you don't mind travelers' rations."

Ignoring his offers of food for the moment, Allison asked instead, "Where are we?"

"A little over half a day from the Temple," Soren replied. "Although Domnae Eban had not initially planned to pause for more than a sand-mark to rest the horses and to break our fast, last night's unexpected battle of course changed everything. Many of the guard were seriously wounded, and we feared to move you as drained as you were. Thus, we made a somewhat crude camp here and sent for some healers from the Temple."

He looked at her askance and added, "I had thought *you* were in need of one, though they said otherwise after they examined you. I'm surprised that you've awakened at all. That blasphemer dark-mage drained you of your life's energy almost to the point of death. It's a wonder that you have regained it so quickly. I hadn't thought you had the strength to channel the power to replenish yourself—or the knowledge."

"I didn't channel," Allison replied uneasily, frowning at what he had implied. "At least I don't remember doing any such thing. I've channeled before in my sleep, so I suppose that it's not entirely impossible." She shuddered at the thought. "Please—can we not talk about this any longer? I don't like thinking about the things I can do."

"Of course," he said quickly. Apparently, he didn't like thinking about the things she could do, either. "I should leave you to your rest, and I must go report your condition to Domnae Eban. You should be well enough to ride soon, and the beds of the Temple are certainly more comfortable than the ground."

He started to rise, but she caught his arm. He looked down at her hand in surprise, and Allison couldn't help thinking that his expression made him appear younger than he was.

"Wait, Sor—I mean Domnae Soren," she said hastily. "I just wanted to thank you for saving me from that mage, for being so kind to me and not treating me as if I was a prisoner like all the others do."

To Allison's surprise, he actually blushed at her compliment and seemed to be at a loss for words.

"It was no large feat, milady," Soren said modestly after a moment's hesitation. "I did only as I should have—as my brothers have also done. You remind me much of my twin sister, and wouldn't I do everything that could be done to protect her?"

Then he nodded his head politely at her, rose, and quickly strode out of the tent. Allison gazed after him with a small smile on her lips, the first since that hellish night had begun. However, it was gone in a flash when she realized that Eban would more than likely come to see her himself. Something about the man made her skin crawl even though she reminded herself that he was a member of a holy order.

Yes, but Kiryl is a holy man, and I don't think he was

being totally honest with me, her mind stubbornly reminded her. *Plus, there's also what Aidric told me. He certainly hates Eban enough. I wonder what it was Eban did to him to create such bad blood between them?*

Against her better judgment, Allison climbed unsteadily to her feet. She would be damned before she faced Eban sitting down where he would tower over her again as he did back in King Diryan's study. That incident had shaken her more than she cared to admit to herself. She certainly didn't want a repeat of it if it could at all be helped.

Just as she finally got her bearings and the room had stopped spinning so insistently, Eban stepped into the tent, followed by Domnae Soren, two of her jailers, and a man she didn't recognize. Allison was relieved to see that her jailers had survived the ambush despite her dislike of them. She had enough to worry about without adding their deaths to her conscience. Eban frowned when he saw her standing quite steadily instead of sprawled out on the ground, weak as a kitten, as he had likely expected to find her.

"You do not look ill at all," Eban barked accusingly, his eyes moving over every inch of her body in such a way that it caused the hair on the back of her neck to begin to rise.

With an effort, Allison forced herself to look directly into his eyes as she answered, "I assure you,

Domnae Eban, that I still feel very weak, but I didn't think it was proper for me to see you while sitting or lying down."

He blinked in surprise, his expression clearly showing that he had expected her to be cowed in his presence as she had been back in Diryan's study. She thought she saw Soren's mouth twitching as though he was struggling not to smile. However, Eban's expression quickly melted into a scowl when he realized that he had allowed them to see his surprise.

"We shall leave immediately for the Temple, then," he said firmly and turned to leave.

"But Domnae Eban," Soren spoke up suddenly, causing Eban to stop abruptly and fix him with a glare so cold that it could have easily frozen the fires of hell, "should she not eat first? It's a long journey, yet, to the Temple. She is still—"

Eban cut him off coldly. "When I have need of your opinion, *Domnae* Soren, I shall ask for it. Perhaps you would do well to be demoted back to a novice until you learn the proper respect for your superiors. If she wants to eat, she can eat in the saddle. We have wasted enough time here as it is."

Allison could clearly see the anger flash in Soren's eyes before he dropped them and bowed, though somewhat stiffly, to Eban. She didn't think Eban had seen his anger, or else the man surely would have raged till nightfall.

Allison followed Eban on unsteady legs as he retreated from her tent, afraid that her legs would crumble beneath her before she reached the herd of horses that was a few feet away. Then Soren was at her side, taking her arm gently and urging her to lean up against him. She smiled at him gratefully and all but collapsed against him. She could hardly believe her luck in finding an unexpected friend amongst this sea of hostile faces.

Eban glared daggers at both of them but said nothing. Soren met that glare serenely, and it was Eban who first looked away. Soren's smile was smug. It seemed as if Aidric was not the only one who disliked the man.

When they reached the horses, Allison started when she realized that Destiny was among them. Her eyes anxiously scanned the filly's body and front legs, but she didn't see so much as a scratch on her. From the terrible way Destiny had screamed, Allison was surprised that she had even survived that lightning bolt.

Soren graciously helped her mount before seeking out his own mount.

The rest of the journey to the Temple was uneventful compared to the chaos of the previous night. Allison once again found herself nodding off on countless occasions, not only from the weakness she still suffered but also from boredom. Kal seemed to be composed of nothing more than flatlands and dust. In the last sand-mark she had seen only a handful of trees, and even those were small and sickly.

The second sun had been just barely visible over the horizon when they had resumed their journey. Now it shined down on them brightly without remorse next to its mate, which baked them with equal cruelty. The back of her dress was already damp with sweat, and streams of it were falling steadily down the sides of her face and dripping from her chin no matter how many times she wiped at her brow.

You'd think this place would be a desert with all this damn heat! Allison thought irritably. She took a quick glance around at the yellowed grass and the treeless landscape and amended, *Although, it's not far from becoming one. Just take away the dead grass and add some sand instead of this dirt—*

A drop of sweat dripped into her eye, causing her to break out of her thoughts to rub her eye in annoyance. She glanced up at Eban to see how he was faring against the heat, and bit back a curse when she saw that his face was quite dry and his hair rippled a little even though there was no breeze.

Damn him! Allison thought as it suddenly dawned on her. *The bastard is using magic to keep cool!* A quick glance around at her escort showed that they were all sweating as profusely as she. *The bastard probably doesn't allow anyone to do the same*, she thought angrily. *Mage or no mage, he's still a priest of some sort, and I thought priests were supposed to endure all hardships readily. I guess he didn't get the memo. I think I'm starting to despise the man as much as Aidric.*

"How much longer 'til we reach the Temple?" she sent to Soren, trying not to let her irritation show in her mind-voice. She felt as if they had been riding forever.

"Perhaps another sand-mark, milady," he replied. His mind-voice sounded weary, though outwardly he appeared as alert as ever.

Thank God, she thought and then sent, *"I hope that the Temple isn't as hot as it is out here. I feel like I'm about to faint if I don't cool down soon."*

"Oh, the Temple is quite cool," Soren assured her. *"We have set wards against the heat and cast dozens of cooling spells throughout the Temple's many chambers."*

"I'm happy to hear that," she replied, relieved.

As they pressed on, Allison found her thoughts inadvertently wandering towards the previous night's attack, a memory she had been trying unsuccessfully to bury. Had that mage in the silver robes been Roderick? She had heard his name mentioned often enough in the palace, but no one had ever offered her a description of the man. She shuddered to think of how close she had come to being captured by the Mihran king, especially now that she knew that he had not intended to kill her.

Earlier as they rode, Allison had hesitantly asked Soren about the mage and what he thought about the attack, and Soren had brushed off her question, which was unusual for him.

"By attacking a Temple procession," Soren had explained, *"the question of the mage's actions became Temple business. Thus milady, I cannot disclose anything I know of the matter to you. I'm sorry."*

And just like that, Allison had been forced to accept his words without further question. More and more, the Temple and their secrecy were beginning to remind her of the CIA. Domnae Soren had practically told her that the previous night's attack had just been deemed "classified" by the Temple, even if he had not used that exact word. Strange, how two worlds completely alien from one another, virtually ignorant of the existence of the other, could turn out to be not so dissimilar.

Now, she knew that she would have to wait until she could thought-speak Aidric to know if the mage had been Roderick or not. She almost dreaded telling Aidric about the attack. To say that Aidric would not be pleased with her news would be the understatement of the millennium. Why in the hell did the Temple have to drag her away from the only safety she knew in this world?

Soon, Allison saw the faint shapes of what looked to be farmhouses in the distance. She blinked in surprise when she first realized what they were, wondering how anyone could want to attempt to grow anything, much less actually produce anything, in this wasteland. They had not passed any rivers or lakes along the way, and she wondered where their water source came from. When they passed the second farm, she had her answer.

The fields behind the stone farmhouse were vast and green, looking out of place in the barrenness of the land around it, but that wasn't what had Allison gaping in shock and not quite sure that the heat had not affected her brain. Above the fields, shaped identically to the rectangular layout of the rows upon rows of crops, thick, dark clouds released torrents of rain to nourish the crops, while the skies surrounding the fields remained cloudless and scorchingly dry.

A lone figure dressed in robes of pale blue stood in the center of the fields, arms raised to the heavens, untouched by the rain that fell all around him. His robes flickered in a wind that did not reach beyond the ends of the plowed fields.

"How is that possible?" Allison asked Soren aloud, forgetting Eban's order of silence in her awe.

She felt Eban's eyes fix on her, but for once, she was able to ignore them.

Soren appeared to ignore her question on the outside. He never shifted his gaze from staring straight ahead.

When Eban turned his attention before him again, Soren sent, *"Have you not heard of weather-mages?"*

Of course...

"Aidric mentioned them to me a few times, but I had no idea that they could do—that!" She glanced over at the fields again and shook her head in amazement. *"I thought that they merely predicted the weather or tampered with it, not created it out of nothingness!"*

His chuckles rippled across her mind. *"Well, not exactly nothingness. I see your mentor has much yet to teach you. If all goes well in the Temple, then I see no reason why you cannot return to your lessons in less than a quarter-moon."*

That was certainly reassuring. She had learned that they judged their time by the cycles of the moon, and that a "quarter-moon" roughly equaled an Earth week, give or take a day or two. If Domnae Soren was correct, then she would only have to spend a few days at the Temple. If.

Allison glanced up at the Eban's back and was suddenly not sure. If he had any say about it, then it was entirely possible that she would be there for a long time, if for nothing more than just to spite Aidric. She quickly dismissed such a troubling thought from her mind.

After a while, the scattered farmhouses gave way to shops and inns, and the dusty road they traveled upon to paved roads of cobblestones. Swarms of people milled around before them, haggling prices at shops or standing around gossiping and laughing. Children dashed around getting underfoot, to the annoyance of their mothers.

Compared to the Lamians, the people of the Temple City wore rather drab clothing, simple tunics and dresses of white or light earthen tones. They *would* dress so circumspectly, Allison mused, since they forever had the eye of the Temple upon them.

However, being under the shadow of the Brothers in Divinity did nothing to thwart their tongues, it seemed. Even from a distance, she could clearly hear an angry customer accusing a fruit merchant of selling vermin infested wares, calling him a few choice names that were anything but circumspect. Allison doubted that even a decree by Seni, Himself, would squelch a person's angry tongue. Nevertheless, it was a scene that matched the one she had seen when Aidric and she had visited Ell.

As their entourage headed towards the central part of the town, everyone, even the children, immediately stopped what they were doing and fell down onto their knees, bowing down to the ground until their chins touched the cobblestones in worship. Allison found the act disconcerting, but reminded herself that this world was alien to her, and their customs wouldn't always agree with her sense of righteousness.

As they made their way through the mass of kneeling bodies, it was then that she finally got her first glimpse of the Temple. Located on a slope in the center of the town, it was a monstrous building that seemed to loom ominously over the surrounding village. It looked more a fortress than a temple, constructed out of a rather dull-gray shade of granite. Five wide towers rose at least a dozen stories to the heavens, ending with pointed domes of what she suspected was solid gold that made her think of giant spears. Only a few windows dotted the structure. It did indeed appear as if she was being led to a prison. Allison shivered at the thought.

By no means did the structure look anything like a holy temple where priests resided and people gathered to worship their god. A vision of the breathtaking majesty of St. Paul's Cathedral floated at the surface of her mind. Where the Providencen priests' abode had seemed gloomy and desolate, it was nothing compared to the foreboding atmosphere surrounding the Temple. Allison almost wished that she was back at the

Providencen abode facing down Master Kiryl's knowing, taunting eyes instead of being forced to enter the
Temple.

"What happens to me now?" she thought-spoke
Soren anxiously, eyeing the Temple with a new sense
of fear.

Some of her fear must have leaked over into her
mind-voice because Soren turned to her and flashed
her a sympathetic smile before he answered, *"Don't fret,
milady. You won't be taken before the High Priest for questioning and oath-swearing today. You'll be taken to the novice wing,
given fresh clothes, food, and drink. There, you'll be visited by a
Seninae who will advise you spiritually before you pledge your
oaths."*

Allison was about to ask him what a Seninae was,
then thought better of it. She had heard Aidric mention the word on a few occasions, but he had never
elaborated on it. Everyone at the palace, even the
Providencen priests had tolerated her ignorance of
Seni, but would Soren or anyone at the Temple do the
same? From the stories concerning them that Aidric
had spoken of, she didn't think it was very likely. They
might very well decipher her ignorance as heresy for
all she knew of them.

If they were ruthless enough to execute a queen
just because she gave birth to a child who was destined
to be a mage, she didn't think that they would have

any qualms about doing the same to her, Golden Mage or no Golden Mage. The majority of Lamians most certainly wouldn't object to ridding themselves of her and all she symbolized.

What a fantastic thought, Allison, she thought sardonically.

They rapidly rode up a steep incline to the Temple grounds where they were immediately surrounded by a group of white-robed men. They bowed and began to rattle off to Eban in a strange tongue.

"What are they saying?" she asked Soren.

"Just a ritual greeting. These Senini will be your escort from henceforth."

Allison glanced over at each of the newly arrived men, noting the lack of expression on their faces and shuddered. *"Will I ever see you again?"*

"Perhaps," Soren replied hesitantly. *"Domni are not usually allowed to have any contact with those we bring to the Temple for oathswearing, but since you are an apprentice-mage, a Domnae will be assigned to you along with the Seninae. Perhaps it is I who'll be assigned the position, but perhaps not."*

"I hope it's you," she said sincerely. *"You're the only one that's been willing to talk to me out of this bunch, and those white-robed men over there don't look too promising, either. If I had you to talk to, then my stay here wouldn't be so bad."*

"I can't make any promises," he warned, *"but I'll see what I can do."*

She was about to thank him, but a hand suddenly fell on her arm, and Allison shook herself out of her thoughts and looked down to see one of the white-robed men standing next to her horse, urging her to dismount. Quickly, she obeyed, wincing when she noticed how stiff her legs felt from being in the saddle so long. When her feet hit the ground, she was immediately surrounded by the rest of the white-robed men as if they feared that she might bolt given the chance.

"The Senini welcome you to the Temple, daughter," the man who had urged her to dismount said in Lamian with the barest hint of a smile. He had a peculiar, thick accent that made his words almost indecipherable. It was similar to Soren's, though Soren's was not near so prominent. "Here you will find the true path to salvation in accepting the Lord Seni as your true and righteous master. Come."

CHAPTER THIRTEEN

Mutely, Allison followed the Senini through a pair of iron gates, up a short flight of marble steps, and through a couple of massive, silver-plated doors. Beyond the doors was a huge, high-ceilinged chamber that finally showed the magnificence she had expected of the outside of a holy temple.

The room was lined from end to end with golden statues of men, women, and animals, some of the creatures familiar and others alien, standing regally alone or intertwined in various scenes of action. The eyes of the statues were precious jewels—emeralds, sapphires, amber, and diamonds—that glittered in such a manner as to give the impression that they gazed about the room.

The walls were entirely gold plated, emitting a luster so bright that it was almost painful to look at them. Allison squinted at the golden walls and noted that carved into every inch of them were intricate and breathtaking murals that she suspected were of various religious scenes, but knowing next to nothing of their religion, she was not entirely sure.

Supernatural battles of beings who could not be mortal against creatures that Allison couldn't even began to put a name to made up a single mural that appropriated an entire wall. Other murals were of various figures, some kneeling before great alters, others before a giant throne seat that was illuminated with golden light, projecting lightning bolts from behind.

Another mural portrayed various scenes of a great gate in which a featureless being that stood three times as tall as the kneeling people around it looked to be either waving people through or pointing a large finger away as if denying them entrance. That mural, she was certain could only be of Aidius, the once mortal man Aidric had spoken of briefly that was supposedly the first man to die because of a man's treachery.

Aidric had told her that Seni had felt a special sympathy for Aidius and granted him the eternal position at the gates to the thrones so he might judge every soul who wished to pass beyond the gates, denying or granting entrance as he chose. Aidric had said that those souls denied entrance were either sent back to live another mortal existence until they lived one worthy of Aidius's judgment, or if the soul was purely evil, banished to one of the six hells of Ter-ob. Only then had Allison understood the devotion everyone had to both Seni and Aidius.

The domed-ceiling rose several stories above them. In the center was a large multifaceted skylight that allowed the rays of the suns to shine down into the room at many different angles. Everything, from the ceiling to the marble floor, glittered brightly with precious stones that reflected the light that shone down on them. The whole effect of the room was uncanny, and as she gazed, wide-eyed, around at the magnificence of it, Allison suddenly had the urge to run screaming from the room, escort or no escort.

With a great effort, she managed to force her legs to move through the chamber towards an opened door on the far side, their footsteps echoing loudly all around them, sounding like boulders crashing down a mountainside to Allison's ears. Her escorts ushered her through the door into a much smaller and vastly plainer room in which several corridors branched off into an intricate maze. They led her through what seemed an endless amount of corridors and passed dozens of identical closed doors before they stopped before one of the doors.

One of the Senini opened the door and gestured for her to enter. Warily, she stepped through the threshold into an unimpressive, not surprisingly, windowless room that held only a small bed and a wash station consisting of a small basin, pitcher, and half a dozen linen washcloths folded into a neat stack. Over to the right was a narrow door that probably led to a bathing room. Lying in a neat pile on the center of the bed was a drab, beige garment of an indeterminable type and equally drab slippers to match.

"This will be your cell for the duration of your stay," the Seninae said as if Allison didn't know already. "Over on the bed you will find suitable garments for wear while you are inside the Temple. A servant will come shortly to bring you food and drink and to take away your civilian garments for laundering. Seninae Seweryn will come to advise you in a few sand-marks when you have been amply rested."

They stared at her from the doorway as if they expected her to say or do something. "Uh—thank you—milords Senini," she stammered awkwardly, bowing her head humbly and bending her knees into a curtsey.

Allison breathed a sigh of relief when they seemed satisfied with her response and firmly shut the door. She didn't move until she could no longer hear their footsteps echoing down the corridor.

Rather stiffly, she walked over to the bed to inspect the clothes she was expected to wear. She wrinkled her nose in distaste when the beige garment proved to be a simply cut dress of coarse wool that she knew would feel itchy against her skin. The slippers were constructed of the same itchy material.

With a resigned sigh, Allison gathered up the dress and shoes and headed over to the narrow door. Sure enough, it proved to be a bathroom in the simplest sense, a privy and small tub that was already filled with lukewarm water. As dusty and sweaty as she felt, she would not have cared if the water had a thin layer of ice coating its surface. It probably would have felt a thousand times better than the warm water.

A few depths later when she emerged from the bathing room dressed in the irritating dress and slippers, nevertheless feeling clean and refreshed, a tray of food awaited her on her bed. The insistent grumbling of her stomach when she eyed the food reminded her just how long ago it had been since she had choked down a few slices of dried meat and a couple of bites of rock-hard journey bread. She was delighted to discover that the same assortment of foods she had grown accustomed to eating in the palace had been brought to her, although she had been given some sort of bitter tasting tea instead of wine.

Allison was in the process of devouring down her

meal when there came a sudden knock at the door that nearly caused her to spill her tea down the front of her dress. She jumped to her feet, hastily wiping her mouth with the sleeve of her horrid dress before she called out for her unexpected visitor to enter.

I thought that the Seninae said this Seninae Seweryn wasn't supposed to come for another few sand-marks, she thought anxiously as the door swung open.

She breathed a sigh of both relief and delight when she saw that her visitor was Domnae Soren. He had changed out of his riding clothes into a gray tunic and breeches. He sported the same large sword and lightning bolt emblem on the breast of his tunic as Domnae Eban had.

"You seem nervous," he observed as he closed the door behind him.

Allison curtsied respectfully and said, "I thought you were the Seninae that was supposed to visit me. I'm glad it was you instead, although I'm surprised to see you so soon."

"I've been officially assigned to you," he said, smiling warmly as she cleared the tray from her bed and gestured for him to have a seat. He hesitated a moment before accepting her offer. "I spoke with the Ans-domnae and luckily a Domnae was yet to be assigned to you. He agreed that since I've already accompanied you for some time and have witnessed some of your abilities that I would be the logical choice."

"What exactly are you assigned to do here?" Allison asked curiously.

"I'm to guard you from using your powers without authorization or from harming yourself or others."

"And to prevent me from trying to escape, right?" she added with a wry grin.

He chuckled. "Yes, milady, that as well, but I don't think I'll have to worry about that in this case."

"I couldn't escape even if I wanted to," Allison insisted. "With all these identical corridors and doors, I'd never be able to find my way out!"

"With enough determination, I believe you could find your way eventually."

"Yes, but to what punishment if I'm caught?"

"Have you rested and eaten well?" he asked, choosing to purposely ignore her question because the truth was more than likely something that was too horrible to contemplate. She decided that it was best to let it slide for the moment.

"Yes, but I do admit that I'm a little scared about talking with the Seninae I'm supposed to talk to and then going before the High Priest."

"Why should it frighten you?" Soren asked with a puzzled frown. "Oathtaking is as common as breathing. Scores of children take oaths here every day. As a matter of fact, there are about one hundred children rooming in this very hall along with you and will swear their oaths before the High Priest along with you."

"You don't understand," Allison said, shaking her head in agitation. "For them it's something that's simply a part of their lives. They grew up with this religion, but I'm not from this world. I don't know much about Seni or anything else associated with your religion. I don't even know what a Seninae is!"

Soren drew in a sharp breath and stared at her with shocked eyes. "How can you not know of Seni?" he managed to ask after a few moments of dead silence. "Did your mentor not teach you of our divine master? It should have been the first lesson to come from his lips!"

Allison winced at the outrage that tinged his words and she hastily explained, "It's not his fault! He *did* explain some of it to me, but I never thought to ask for more instruction than he gave. I just didn't think it was as important as I'm coming to learn it is."

"'Not that important'?" Soren all but sputtered. "If Domnae Eban or even the Seninae who is to come see you heard such words from your lips, they most certainly would order you to be hanged immediately for the blasphemy!"

Her hands flew up to her neck instinctively and she felt all the blood drain out of her face. "Hanged?" she whispered. "But—but—how can they expect *me* to suddenly be as devoted to Seni as everyone else is when I was born and lived in a different world?" She felt tears start to swell up in her eyes. "How can I possibly expect to swear an oath truthfully to a god and religion I know next to nothing about?" she cried desperately. "Aidric told me they would know if I was lying, and I will be if I'm forced to swear an oath now!"

Soren's hand was suddenly across her mouth, and he gazed around uneasily as if he feared somebody was hiding in the room. "Never, *ever*, speak those words in this temple again," he hissed. "There are those in the Temple that would condemn you to a fate worse than death if they got wind of even a third of what you just revealed to me! *Never* reveal to another soul what you have just confessed!"

"But what am I going to do?" Allison cried when he had removed his hand from her mouth. "They'll know I'm lying! Aidric said they would. They'll—" She couldn't bring herself to finish the thought. Just thinking about never seeing Aidric again made her feel like collapsing in total despair.

His eyes reflecting conflicting emotions, Domnae Soren slowly raised a hand and placed it on her shoulder in comfort. He stared at her with troubled eyes for a long while, his expression shifting from anger to understanding to anger again.

Finally he sighed, his eyes softening, and said, "I

know of a way to get around the lie-detection spell. I shouldn't know this, but there's a group of people who live beyond the Phaedrian Sea who do not worship Seni but a being named Ingmar. A half dozen of them appeared in Kal a few years ago—some sort of exploration expedition. They were extremely vague on their explanations, it seems. My father is also a Domnae, and he learned that these people planned to settle in our kingdom. Of course, he immediately set out to bring them to the Temple to swear oaths to Seni, yet they refused. They said they would not serve a divine master other than Ingmar.

"My father believed, as I do, that Ingmar was just another name for Seni, so he warned them of the consequences they would suffer if they refused to swear. This didn't seem to faze them in the least. They explained that their people had come across 'the likes of us' in the past and knew a way to fool even the most powerful of the lie-detection spells we could cast. I now hold the secret to such means. I'll share the knowledge with you, but it will be successful only if you worship a divine master in your own world."

"I do," she said with a sniff, wiping her eyes.

He nodded and continued, "When the oaths are recited to you before the High Priest, imagine that they are oaths to your deity, but you must focus intently on your beliefs or else the ruse will fail. When the time comes for you to swear your oaths, your mind must totally believe that you are swearing oaths to your divine master and not to Seni. Only the slightest disbelief is needed for this method to fail."

He paused a moment, drew in a breath and then said, "I'll allow you to do this against my better judgment, but only on the condition that should you be successful and leave the Temple, then you must learn all you are able from your mentor about Seni. Then I want you to journey to the Temple again and swear your oaths to Seni to me only, but this time swearing them truthfully."

Allison looked at him intensely. "I promise," she said firmly. "Even if it takes me the rest of my life, I promise I'll swear them to you before my death."

He nodded and said, "You seem a good and honest person, Allison. I believe Seni did well to choose you as his messenger."

Allison perked up immediately at his first mentioning of the legend she was. Maybe Soren knew more about the Prophecy of the Golden Mage than anyone else had been willing to reveal to her. He was, after all, a member of a holy order as the Providencen priests and the Horae were. Surely he had been taught everything that had anything to do with Seni and his plans for mankind. She might at last have a chance to get some straight answers about who she was, provided he was allowed to even talk about such things.

"Domnae Soren," she began carefully, "you've never really mentioned the legendary mage I supposedly am until now. Ever since I arrived here in this world, no one has really given me a straight answer as to who I am. All I've heard is talk of prophecies and truths I'm supposed to discover, but nothing more. Recently, Aidric and I visited the Providencen priests, and I know that Master Kiryl didn't reveal everything he knew about me and my destiny. Is it possible that you know what he's been hiding from me, maybe something that was taught to you here in the Temple?"

He looked puzzled for a moment, frowning as he mulled over her question. Then he shook his head and replied, "As novices here, we are, of course, taught all the legends and prophecies of all of Seni's World, so I know well the Prophecy of the Golden Mage. However, I don't know anything more than what your mentor could have revealed to you about what is destined for you to decide. I'm not a Seer, thus not entitled to their knowledge as they are not entitled to the knowledge of a Domnae. If what you believe is true about Seer Kiryl, then no soul will know what it is he conceals until Seni, Himself, orders him to speak. Those of The Order of the Providence do nothing that is not the will of Seni. I fear I cannot help you any more than your mentor or Seer Kiryl has."

Allison sighed, disappointed, but resolved not to let it depress her. Instead, she steered the conversation to something else that troubled her, which she hoped Soren could shed some light on.

"Well, maybe you can clear up another mystery for me."

"You certainly are full of questions, milady," Soren said, his tone teasing, "but if I'm at all able to answer them, I would be more than happy to. I seldom am able to talk with anyone these days. Your curiosity is a refreshing change from some of the stiff-necked old goats around here."

Her eyebrows rose. That was certainly a curious attitude for someone who was essentially a monk to express. For the moment, Allison put the thought aside. She would question him about it if she got the opportunity later. For now, she had more pressing questions.

"This question may not be as refreshing as you think," Allison warned. "It seems there's a lot of hatred between my mentor, Aidric, and Domnae Eban. In fact, 'hatred' is an understatement. The confrontation Aidric had with him over my being brought here under Domnae Eban's escort troubled him immensely. Had they have had swords, I don't think either one would've hesitated to run the other through.

Do you know why there's so much animosity between them?"

"Perhaps," Soren said, his tone suddenly hesitant. "I've heard several rumors whispered among the Domni and even some of the novices that Domnae Eban was to be promoted to Ans-domnae if he succeeded in convincing Lord Aidric to take vows as a Domnae. It was said that Domnae Eban flew into a rage when Aidric announced to the High Priest that his decision was to swear oaths to the Horae as a mage duty-bound to the defense of Lamia. According to some of the Domni, something unpleasant transpired between the two during the last quarter-moon Lamia's Mage-general was here—what, only the men in question know. Although I did hear—"

His voice cut off suddenly, and he looked uncomfortable.

"Yes?" Allison prompted when it became clear that he wasn't going to continue.

"No," Soren said maddeningly, vigorously shaking his head. "I cannot repeat such a whispered tale. I'm afraid that I've spoken far too freely as it is. My father always said my tongue knew no bounds." He looked almost rueful. "If you wish to know more of the quarrel between Domnae Eban and Lamia's Mage-general, then I think it is best that you ask the Mage-general, himself."

Strike two. She nodded, hoping that her disappointment didn't show.

"I'm sorry, Domnae Soren. I shouldn't have asked."

Allison quickly directed the conversation to safer grounds, asking about Soren's family, about Kal, and about the meaning of the symbol on his breast. He explained in more detail than she would have liked that the symbol was the emblem for the Domni and how it came to represent their order.

He was in the middle of an explanation of a festival that took place in Kal every year after the main harvest when there came a soft knock at the door. Soren started and quickly scrambled off the bed and promptly stationed himself in the farthest right-hand corner. The door was swinging open before Allison could even open her mouth to invite her visitor in.

For all they know, I could've been buck naked and in the process of dressing, she thought irritably.

An unfamiliar man with hair as white as Aidric's stood at the threshold, dressed in immaculately white robes lined with thick, golden braids of *sholkie* thread. A symbol, different from the one on Soren's tunic, conspicuously stood out from each of his sleeves— the symbol of the Senini, no doubt. To Allison, it looked like the Greek letter "gamma" encircled by an oval.

Soren nodded politely at the man, and she belatedly remembered to curtsy. Thankfully, the Seninae didn't seem to notice her blunder.

"I am Seninae Seweryn," he announced in a high tenor in flawless Lamian that told her he was probably a native, fixing her with hard eyes that seemed to warn against keeping anything from him, "and I shall be your spiritual advisor for the duration of your stay with us."

And from the looks of him, my stay'll probably feel like an eternity, Allison thought dryly as the door slammed behind him with an ominous bang.

***

"You are certain, Eban?" High Priest Casimir asked with a frown as he peered down at the kneeling figure before him from his seat behind the High Alter. "This girl, this Allison McNeal you say she is named, you believe she will fail to swear oaths to our divine lord?"

"Quite certain, Your Grace," Eban assured him firmly, all the while seething inside for having to lower himself to groveling before another man, especially when the "man" in question was much younger than him.

He still couldn't for the life of him understand why of all the people Seni could have chosen to bear the mark of the High Priest on his brow—namely himself—when the last fool had finally lost his battle with Death, he had chosen this—*child* to gain the most powerful seat in the world. Casimir, in fact, had been a novice under *his* instruction when he was chosen as successor at the ripe old age of seventeen. Casimir had once called him Master, and now Eban had to endure the daily humiliation of acknowledging the brat as *his* master.

But not for long, Eban thought darkly as he gazed up at that cursed silver symbol of Seni preternaturally branded on the boy's brow with eyes that revered while his heart secretly swelled with the blackest hatred. *Soon she will be mine, and where she is, Aidric is bound to follow eventually if his actions in that fool king's study are any indication of how he truly feels for his pretty* ward. *Soon, they both will be mine and with their aid, so will the high altar. All the world will bow down under my hand!*

"It's difficult to believe that one chosen by Seni to be one of His messengers should not swear allegiance to serve His will!" the high priest boomed angrily. "It's an abomination!"

"It is heresy!" Eban spat out with false passion. "She will be dealt with accordingly, Your Grace. I—"

"She cannot be hanged, Eban," Casimir interrupted, to his annoyance. Eban slowly counted to ten—then to fifteen. "She was sent here to fulfill a prophecy, and it would be Seni's wrath if we interfere."

"That is precisely why I sought your presence, Your Grace," Eban said as coolly as he could manage. Casimir already had his temper hanging by only half a thread as it was. He hoped that the brat would decipher the slight edge in his voice as anger towards the Golden Mage, else it would be *his* head swinging in a noose in the morning not hers.

"I have come to humbly ask, as unworthy as I might be, (he almost choked on his tongue saying that) to have her sentenced over to my instruction when her heresy becomes known before the congregation tomorrow. I shall instruct her to properly humble herself before Seni. By keeping her here among us, perhaps we shall even prevent the tragedy of Lamia's downfall the prophecy speaks of."

Casimir stared at him for a moment, considering. *If you dare deny me, I swear I shall hang you with your own mother's entrails while she is still alive and screaming!*

"I grant you permission, Eban. I know only too well your stern hand, and I feel that is precisely what the maiden needs to steer her away from the darkness that now holds her in its grip. Now leave me."

Gritting his teeth so firmly that his jaws began to ache, Eban forced himself to bend his face to the marble floor and plant the ceremonial departing kiss at the base of the altar before rising and walking stiffly from the chamber, vowing that it was one of the last times he would do that.

CHAPTER FOURTEEN

With a sigh of relief, Allison made her final curtsy to Seninae Seweryn as he *finally* prepared to leave. She had begun to think that the decrepit old man would never leave. For what seemed like days even though she knew it had been about four sand-marks, he had questioned her endlessly about every aspect of her life, no matter how personal it was.

When he had asked her if she was a virgin, she nearly laughed in his face, thinking that surely he wasn't serious, but when she had tried to brush the question off by telling him it was none of his business, he had clenched his fists and looked as if he was about to have a heart attack from shock.

"How dare you speak such words to me," the Seninae had said through clenched teeth, and for one alarming moment, she had thought that he was going to strike her—or burst a blood vessel in his head. "Insolent child!"

In the end, Allison had finally told him that yes, she was still a virgin and then after all that fuss, the old coot hadn't even believed her! She had been forced to listen to a half-sand-mark tirade about how she would be condemned to Ter-ob for lying to one of Seni's priests. For a moment, she had been afraid that he would send her to the Domni to test her word, but he had finally relented when it became clear that she wasn't going to change her answer despite his dire threats.

All the while, Soren stood silently in his corner, his face expressionless, but every so often, she got the feeling that behind those passive eyes, he found the whole scene amusing. Several times she had to bite back a retort at him. Had she said something spiteful to him, Domnae Seweryn most assuredly would have had her lashed for the insult.

"I hope you enjoyed yourself," Allison said irritably to Soren the moment she could no longer hear Seninae Seweryn's retreating footsteps.

"I cannot lie. It was indeed most entertaining," Soren replied with a wry grin that suddenly made her feel the urge to slap him. "Although I do sympathize with you for being assigned Seninae Seweryn. Out of all the stiff-necked old goats in the Temple, Seninae

Seweryn could give lessons to a diamond column."

"Hmm—and how is it that you're nothing like any other man I've met in your order?"

"Oh, give me a few years and a few headstrong novices to instruct, and I'll catch up to the others fairly quickly," he replied, his eyes twinkling with mischief. "I've yet to lose my sense of humor, so as long as I still possess it, I might as well make as much use of it while I'm still able."

"When you talk this way, you remind me so much of Aidric," Allison said wistfully.

God, less than a day away from him and she already missed him a ton. The thought of her being that needy made something deep within her squirm unhappily.

Soren tilted his head to the side. "Indeed? Do I hear a note of longing in your voice? Am I correct to assume that he is more than just your mentor?"

It was a fairly innocent comment, but to her chagrin, she felt the blood rising to her cheeks. "Yes, he's more than my mentor—but not in the way you think," she said quickly. "He's just a dear friend. I didn't lie to Seninae Seweryn."

Soren's smile said that he didn't believe a word of it, but to her immense relief, he didn't press the issue.

"Well, milady, it's been a most entertaining day, but I should probably leave you to your rest, now," he said. "Remember all I've instructed you to do, and I'll come for you in the morning to bring you before the High Priest. May your dreams be pleasant, and may Seni guide and protect you."

"The same to you," Allison said, her eyes following him as he left the room.

After all the hell she had endured under Seweryn's interrogation, she felt battered and drained and desperately in need of a long soak in warm water. Her stomach also growled insistently for dinner, and she had no idea when a meal would be brought to her.

With a sigh, she plopped herself onto a bed that was somehow more uncomfortable than she imagined sleeping on a bed of rocks would feel, hoping that someone would come along soon with food. Although she had been in this world for the equivalent of a few Earth months now, her body still hadn't adapted to the longer time of their days. She still found herself sleepy in the middle of the day, and her stomach grumbled for meals at the oddest hours.

I wonder if Aidric's busy right now? Should I risk thought-speaking him? I'd hate to interrupt him if he's in one of those Circle meetings.

Her anxiousness to hear his voice quickly won out over any other misgivings, and she settled herself as comfortably as she could and began the process of clearing her mind. Once her mind was sufficiently blank, Allison concentrated on conjuring up a picture in her mind of Aidric as he had taught her to do for a long distance sending. Then she cracked open one of her shields in her mind and with a little effort, channeled a small trickle of Mage-field energy to aid in sending her thoughts and receiving his from such a great distance. It was the first time she had attempted to do it, and she half expected it to fail.

When all was prepared to the best of her ability, she sent, *"Aidric?"*

"Allison?" came his deep voice, dripping with what sounded like a mixture of relief and anxiety. *"Where in Seni's name have you been? I've been so worried!"*

"What do you mean 'where have I been?'" she asked, puzzled. *"I'm here at the Temple of course."* Then the probable reason for his anxiety suddenly dawned on her. *"You've already heard about the attack?"*

"Attack?" he all but shouted in alarm.

Apparently not.

"We were ambushed just on the other side of the border," she explained, shivering at the memory. *"Aidric, I was so scared! There was a mage who attacked us with lightning bolts and a small army, and he did—something to me. I felt like I was bleeding to death even though I didn't have so much as a scratch!"*

"Are you all right?" he asked anxiously.

"I'm fine," she quickly assured him. *"I think I was*

attended by a healer. Aidric, that mage—I think he was Roderick."

"Describe him," Aidric prompted.

"He had silver hair that fell way below his shoulders and was dressed in silver robes. That's all I was able to see of him before he blasted me with his power."

"Mordant," Allison heard faintly, so faintly that she thought she was losing control of the power she channeled.

"Aidric?"

"Sorry, I was just thinking. That mage wasn't Roderick. Roderick wears nothing but his kingdom's colors of black and gold, which, not coincidentally, are the same colors of his hair and eyes. That was the dark-mage, Mordant, but in all probability, he was there under Roderick's orders. Aidius condemn the bastard! Lately, he's managed to be one step ahead of us, which could only mean that somehow he has planted spies in Lamia. We've suspected this for some time now. This latest incident merely confirms our suspicions. How else could he have known that you would be beyond our borders?

"Only two groups knew of your departure, the Temple and those present in Diryan's study. Roderick couldn't have planted a spy within the Temple. The Domni would sniff him out instantly, for all allied or bound magically to Roderick carry a taint of the Dark Powers about them that cannot be concealed. Only Eban I would suspect of those within the Temple, but I cannot believe that even Eban is a cohort of Roderick's, mainly

because Eban wouldn't tolerate taking orders from another. The only reason Eban bends knee to the High Priest is because it's an absolute. Not even he would dare to contest the High Priest's authority—which leaves the Lamian palace."

"But who could it be?" Allison asked worriedly. She had always thought she was absolutely safe from Roderick as long as she remained within the Lamian border. The thought of spies in the palace made her stomach knot up painfully. She didn't think that she would ever be able to walk through the palace again without looking over her shoulder and jumping at every shadow.

"That's the problem," Aidric replied solemnly. *"Anyone in the palace could be a spy. Roderick could gain a great deal of damaging information by placing spies both among the servants and in a high palace position. Servants are all but invisible since no one pays them the slightest mind, and if Roderick somehow managed to get a spy into the Circle—well, need I say more? Until the spy is weeded out, everyone will be under suspicion. As far as Diryan is concerned, it could very well be the Seneschal, one of his councilors, or even me."*

"That's not funny, Aidric," she retorted sharply. *"I have enough to worry about as it is without having to wonder if one of my friends is really working for Roderick."*

"As much as I don't wish to add to your worries, I would be remiss in my duties as your mentor not to warn you of the possibility. It really irks me that I had no choice but to allow

Eban to carry you off at such a dangerous time. If he's harmed you in any way——"

"*His unkindness was just words,*" Allison interrupted hastily. *"I don't want to wake up tomorrow morning to find you in chains because you tried to take me from this awful place. Besides, I haven't even seen Eban since I was brought to this room."*

"I just hate the idea that you are there alone with no one to stand up for you against that bastard or any other of those stiffed-necked old goats there."

"That isn't entirely true. There has been someone watching over me."

"*Oh?*" His mind-voice suddenly sounded tense.

"One of the Domni who stood guard over me on the way up here has been looking out for me. His name is Soren. Do you know him?"

"*Now there is a man I haven't seen in a while,*" Aidric replied, the tension in his mind-voice lessening. *"I didn't realize he was part of Eban's little entourage. He was a novice during the time when I was at the Temple. Poor man was forced by his father to become a Domnae."*

"That explains it," Allison sent absently.

"Explains what?"

"He's nothing like anyone here. I swear, all these priests make me feel like I'm in a military camp. He says I remind him of his sister, so he feels an obligation to watch over me. Aidric, he saved me from that mage. He stood between us and faced him.

He bought me enough time to do what I could before I passed out. Strange, how you can find friends in the most unexpected places."

"Indeed. I'm grateful that your paths crossed. From what I remember of him, he has a good heart and will make sure you are treated fairly. It's a load off my heart to know that you have at least one protector there, but I still don't cherish the idea that Eban is so near at hand."

The opening she had been waiting for, at last. *"Aidric—maybe I shouldn't ask this, but it's been bothering me ever since I left the palace. What did that awful man do to you to make you hate him so much? Can you tell me?"*

Aidric didn't answer for a long while. Allison was suddenly afraid that she had made him mad, that she had meddled into something that was too personal. She had just begun to form an apology in her mind when she heard his mental sigh ripple across her mind, sounding like the wind brushing against a lonely valley.

"That, Allison, even to you, I can never reveal," he said slowly, almost apologetically. *"It's something I wish to keep buried in the past where it can do no more—damage to me. Please understand."*

"I shouldn't have asked," she said immediately. A sudden rush of guilt washed through her. How could she have been so insensitive? She felt like the world's biggest idiot. *I'm sorry. I shouldn't have brought it up at all. Sometimes I'm too nosy for my own good."*

"I should be flattered that you care enough to ask me about

it."

"Of course I care! We're still friends, aren't we?"

"We are," he said firmly. *"Whatever happens in the future, little cat, never forget that."*

CHAPTER FIFTEEN

"So that's about the sum of it," Aidric said gravely, sitting back into his chair and gazing critically at Diryan's face for his reaction. Just as he expected, Diryan's face showed no flicker of surprise, only a grimness that matched his own.

"The man is bold—and no fool, I'll give him that," Diryan said, running a hand irritably through his hair. "He bloody well knows that we cannot prove that he was behind that ambush, even though we all know damned well it was him. He knows if we send troops to lay siege to his palace, the Brothers in Divinity will bowl us over like so much sagebrush, and I would be hung for heresy. Perhaps that is exactly what the bastard is hoping for! All the easier to get his foul hands on Allison and the Mage-field."

"And the spy?" Aidric prompted, knowing Diryan

was avoiding touching on the subject.

He nearly jumped out of his skin when the king suddenly slammed his fist onto his desk and growled, "Who can it be? Ion? Liam? Ambrus? Perhaps one of my servants? One of yours? Damn it all, I do *not* need this!"

"I can't believe it of Ion," Aidric said. "He's too much your man and infinitely suspicious. Half the time, I think the insufferable man is suspicious of *me*! Besides, he has never set foot outside the Lamian border, so Roderick couldn't have gotten a hold of him that way. As for the rest of your councilors or even the representatives in the Circle, all are likely suspects."

"The way I see it, the whole blasted kingdom can be a suspect," Diryan grumbled. "We cannot very well cast a lie-detection spell on every citizen. That could take several moons, moons in which Roderick will have ample opportunity to plan and make his final move. Yet, something must be done about this spy, and soon."

"If one of your councilors or any member of the Circle is the spy, then I'll find them," Aidric said confidently. "Surely they won't object to undergoing such a test under the current circumstances, and if any should suspect me, Lady Kiara can subject me to the test."

"Do it," Diryan said. "The situation is too serious

for me to worry about bruised egos. I'll call a meeting of the Circle for ten sand-marks past the midday mark and explain the matter. You may conduct your testing then."

Aidric nodded and watched with concern as Diryan wearily laid his head down onto his desk regardless of the ever-present piles of documents strewn about the surface. For the first time, Aidric really *saw* Diryan and noticed the dark circles under his eyes that had not been there last quarter-moon. There were also deep lines around his eyes and mouth, and his auburn hair sported more strands of silver at his temples. It also looked as though he had lost some weight. His clothes hung loosely on him.

Aidric touched the king's shoulder and said, "Diryan, you've been working yourself much too hard lately. Fool that I am, I didn't realize it until now. The meeting won't be for many sand-marks yet. Go rest awhile. The kingdom and your duties will be here when you return."

"I cannot," Diryan replied with a heavy sigh. "I have a Council meeting in a sand-mark. As weary as these old bones are, they know that Roderick has little consideration for the lives of others, and any time I don't give to our defense is that much more time Roderick has to gain the upper hand in this silent war."

"Even a king has need for sleep," Aidric said quietly. "Bright Thrones above, Diryan, you aren't made of marble! You must rest *sometime*. This is advice from a man who learned that the hard way—remember, when I collapsed that time a few years ago, I was bedridden for a half-moon building up my strength. Seni knows you can't afford to be bedridden for such a long time now. Postpone the meeting a sand-mark or two, and catch a short nap. Surely a sand-mark will not make any difference."

Diryan smiled thinly at him. "Perhaps you're right. I admit that I feel as if I'm ready to rub noses with the floor. I *am* the king, after all, and entitled to a few breaks when I need them, right?"

"Good," Aidric said firmly as he rose from his seat. "I'll let you be, then. I'll see you at the meeting."

As Aidric walked out of Diryan's study, a flash of brown disappearing behind a group of potted plants caught his eye. Only servants wore brown uniforms in the palace. Aidric stalked over to the plants, and sure enough, it was Diryan's scribe, Voytek, who cowered behind the massive leaves, staring up at him with the terror-stricken eyes of a rabbit that was cornered by a wolf.

The spy—

His eyes blazing, Aidric grabbed the scribe from the front of his tunic and demanded, "What are you doing here, boy?"

Voytek let out a strangled cry and tried to twist out of Aidric's grasp. "Please, M-Milord Mage-general—I was—I was only waiting for you to c-come out."

"Why?" Aidric all but growled.

To his surprise, Voytek stopped trying to struggle out of his grip and flushed a deep scarlet. "Forgive me, milord. I was just resting my eyes for a few depths! I swear!"

Aidric laughed and gripped the boy more tightly. "So you just happened to be shirking your duty outside the king's study. Do you honestly expect me to accept such a ridiculous excuse as that? What do you take me for, boy? A fool? You are the *spy*! Roderick sent you, didn't he?"

The boy squeaked and looked absolutely horrified at the accusation, which, in Aidric's eyes, only proved his guilt. Voytek's face was so red that Aidric feared that he would soon burst a blood vessel.

"*No!* No, milord!" Voytek protested desperately. "I serve only King Diryan! I'm not a traitor! I'm *not*!"

To Aidric's annoyance, the boy began to cry.

"We shall see," Aidric retorted angrily, flinging him to the floor and immediately casting a paralysis spell over him.

Aidric then pulled energy from the Mage-field and

channeled it through his body until it came to rest in each of his hands. He muttered a few words into the air, and with a sweep of his hands, he flung the power around Voytek until the boy was encased inside a golden globe of energy. Aidric cut off the flow of power and then lowered his hands to his side.

He lifted the paralysis from Voytek's throat and said in a surprisingly calm voice, "I shall ask you again, Voytek. Are you a spy sent here by Roderick? You would do well to answer quickly, for I shall not release you from this spell until you do. Whether you answer falsely or truthfully, the spell will tell me. Answer!"

If Voytek spoke the truth, then the boy's words would penetrate the magical barrier and be heard. If a lie was voiced, then the globe would absorb the sound and nothing would be heard beyond the barrier. As far as Aidric knew, no one had learned to trick the spell.

Voytek stared up at him with eyes that almost bulged out of their sockets in fear, but at Aidric's command, he couldn't get the words out fast enough. Aidric nearly jumped out of his skin when he heard the meek denial that was unmistakably Voytek's voice emerge from the energy globe. He had been so certain that Voytek was the spy that the disappointment of being proven wrong hit him like a dagger to the chest.

Damn it all to the lowest of the six hells, he thought as he dismissed both spells around the cowering boy. *I was so certain—so bloody certain, but the spell can't be wrong. What a relief it would have been if he had been the spy, but now, all I have accomplished is frightening a boy.*

He reached a hand down to Voytek, who accepted it warily, and hoisted him up onto his feet again. "I'm sorry, lad," Aidric said sincerely. "Your behavior—dashing out of sight and hiding behind these plants—only roused my suspicions. From henceforth, I suggest that you do nothing more of the sort unless you want a repeat of what happened here."

"I p-promise I'll never do it again, m-milord!" Voytek replied instantly, his voice still a little shaky from the ordeal.

Aidric waved him away and stared at his back as he scurried away towards the servant's quarters. "I was so certain," Aidric muttered under his breath as he turned to leave the king's rooms. "I was so certain."

CHAPTER SIXTEEN

The narrow, dim corridors of the Temple made Allison feel a bit claustrophobic as she was led through an endless maze of them by Domnae Soren and unfortunately, Seninae Seweryn. Her stomach was painfully tied up in knots, and she longed to just go and be done with it. She wasn't sure if she could pull off her attempt to fool the lie-detection spell, and the resulting consequences if she did fail terrified her.

How do I get myself into these messes? she thought miserably. *Isn't it enough that I was plopped down into a strange world and given these terrifying powers? How much more must I suffer before I'm left alone, if ever I am?*

By the time they reached the High Priest's audience chamber, Allison was feeling sick to her stomach and ready to bolt despite the consequences. Only the firm grip of Soren's hand on her arm prevented her from attempting it.

The audience chamber was just as magnificent as the chamber she had seen when she had first entered the Temple. The domed ceiling was a match for even that chamber, rising some hundreds of feet above them. The dome was faceted in a blue-stained glass that seemed to make the chamber more foreboding than anything. Blue light bathed everything, making the whole room seem to be a surreal scene from a dream.

Four marble columns rose from floor to ceiling against the four corners of the chamber, each containing symbols carved into them in a pattern that suggested that they were letters and words from a foreign alphabet, possibly even the Kalite alphabet. She was not surprised to see four more columns, carved out of diamonds just like the ones outside the door to the Lamian Throne Room, surrounding a dais that rose at least a hundred feet.

Allison blinked stupidly up at the figure who sat on a throne-like chair high up on the dais. *That can't be the High Priest*, she thought incredulously.

The man she saw seated so serenely and regally high above couldn't have been more than sixteen, if not younger. He looked as if he wasn't even old enough to shave much less hold such a powerful position. The fear Allison had felt suddenly left her as she strained her neck up at the High Priest. She had been afraid all along of a boy!

She was led over to an empty pew behind a group of children who were already anxiously waiting their turn before the High Priest. She had been so wrapped up in her nervousness that she didn't even see them when she had first entered the chamber. Somehow, their presence there was comforting.

Silently, Allison watched the first child, a girl of about seven years, being summoned before the High Priest. The girl knelt at the foot of the steps leading up to the high seat and very humbly bent her small face to the marble floor to plant a kiss there just as Seninae Seweryn had schooled her to do. She remained kneeling, head bowed, as a man stepped out of the shadows.

Allison started when she looked at his face. The man could have been Soren at fifty. Allison vaguely remembered Soren mentioning that his father was also a Domnae.

"Domnae Soren, is that your father?" she thought-spoke him as she stared at the newest arrival.

"Yes," Soren replied somewhat stiffly.

"Is he the Domnae who will cast the lie-detection spell?" she asked curiously.

"He is the Ans-domnae, thus it is his duty."

The tone in his mind-voice said that he didn't want to talk about his father, so she left it at that and turned her attention once again to the ceremony. The Ans-domnae stood directly before the little girl and immediately began to cast the spell.

Allison felt a slight tingling on her skin, and the hairs on her arm began to rise as they always did when channeling was being done near her. She saw Soren's father sweep his arms around the girl in a deliberate pattern, but nothing visibly emerged from his hands. The girl flinched a little, and a split-second later, the Ans-domnae dropped his arms in completion and stepped back into the shadows of the tall dais.

The High Priest's voice, surprisingly powerful and commanding from one so young, began to speak the ritual words of the Oathtaking. The girl swore her allegiance to Seni quite diligently, and Allison strained to see how the spell worked, but nothing around the girl gave any indication that a spell had even been cast over her in the first place.

When the ceremony was completed, the Ans-domnae appeared once again and laid his hand onto the girl's brow. As before, Allison felt the tingling along her skin that signaled that someone was channeling, and for just an instant, a blinding white light flashed from his hand onto the little girl's forehead. Allison instantly knew that the girl had been given some sort of magical mark just as Aidric had done to her when she had obtained citizenship in Lamia.

Good. At least you'll only have to do this once since nobody can mistake that mark.

She sat quietly in her pew for what seemed like a dozen sand-marks before the last child completed his oaths and took his seat. Allison wondered if they had purposely made her last just to unnerve her. She had caught the High Priest frowning down at her more than once with mistrustful eyes that seemed to have already judged and found her guilty of heresy. She had a sudden suspicion that a certain Domnae had been whispering tales in his ear recently.

Allison stiffened when the Ans-domnae at last called her name to stand before the dais. On wobbly legs, she rose and slowly made her way over to the foot of the dais. She knelt onto the cool, marble floor and bent to kiss the floor as was required, though she felt a slight wave of humiliation wash through her when she thought of all those eyes watching her do such a degrading thing.

Eyes—

Oh no—not this time, she scolded herself before the panic could begin to take form. *The only thing you'll accomplish by panicking now is to make yourself look like an idiot in front of all these strangers.*

Allison drew a couple of deep breaths before she raised her head from the floor—to stare up into the eyes of Domnae Eban. She bit her tongue against the cry that had almost involuntarily escaped her lips and stared up at him with widened eyes. *What the hell is* he *doing here?* The Ans-domnae was nowhere to be seen.

Eban returned her stare, but more coldly, wearing a most peculiar half-smile that plainly said he was up to something. From what little Aidric had been willing to speak of concerning the man, she knew that whatever the reason he had suddenly appeared in the chamber now, it meant nothing but trouble for her.

Determined to let him know that his presence there didn't bother her in the least, Allison stared up at him almost defiantly and didn't even flinch when it became apparent that it was he, not the Ans-domnae, who would cast the spell over her. She felt him begin to channel, suspiciously more power than she had felt the Ans-domnae channel for the other children. That made her nervous. What if he made the spell too powerful for her to trick?

Before she could even blink, Eban had woven the spell all around her, and to her surprise, it was quite visible to her eyes, a globe of golden light that surrounded her kneeling form. As to what purpose the globe of power would serve to weed out any lies she might speak, Allison hadn't the faintest clue, and that really terrified her.

What if all this power strikes out at me like a Taser or something if my lie is caught? Could it possibly even kill me?

Allison distantly heard the voice of the High Priest drift inside the globe, and she immediately focused her attention on the ritual words, spoken in Lamian to her immense relief. She didn't understand a word of Kalite.

"—born through the might of Seni as one of His servants," the High Priest was saying. "Your duty is to give thanks for the gifts He has bestowed upon you and use them to the best of your ability to serve only His will."

As he spoke, Allison concentrated on convincing herself that the god the High Priest was speaking of was her god. After a while, as she listened to his voice, she began to believe that she heard him referring to her god and not Seni, that in fact they were one and the same. When the time came for her to swear her oaths, she wasn't anxious in the least.

Seninae Seweryn had instructed her in the wording of the oaths she was to swear. He had drilled her over and over until she thought she could recite them backwards. Now, they rolled easily from her tongue as though she said them every day.

In a steady, clear voice she recited, "I, Allison McNeal, citizen of Lamia, swear that I am a child of my lord, Seni. I swear that I hold allegiance to no other false divine master, and I swear that until the end of my days, I shall serve my lord, Seni, to the best of my ability with the gifts He has bestowed upon me."

Each time she had mentioned Seni's name, in her mind, she was talking about the Christian god and believed with all her heart that she pledged her allegiance to Him and not to Seni. When she finished her oaths, there was only silence.

Eban looked down at her through a mask of passivity, but his eyes betrayed his true feelings. He stared down at her with the eyes of a viper ready to strike and devour its prey. Her suspicions had been well-founded. He *had* been hoping that she would fail, but to hurt Aidric through her or for his own purposes, she had no idea.

Allison glanced up past Eban's shoulder to see the High Priest's reaction. However, he was not as good as Eban in hiding his true feelings. He wore a very open expression of astonishment as if he had truly expected her to fail in her Oathtaking. If the situation hadn't been so serious, she would have laughed.

I don't know what you were up to you slimy bastard, but now there's nothing holding me here, Allison thought smugly. *I damn sure will leave this awful place the second I'm able!*

With an air of reluctance, Eban dismissed the spell. When his hand touched her forehead, a wave of revulsion instantly washed through her. It was all she could do not to flinch away as he magically gave her

Seni's symbol of fealty. The first thing she would do once she was back in her room would definitely be to wash his touch off her skin.

After bending her lips to the floor for the parting kiss, she slowly rose and made her way back to her pew, all the while feeling two pairs of eyes boring holes into her back. For the first time in her life, Allison didn't in the least bit care.

***

"Aidius, I never want to go through another meeting like this one," Aidric groaned, his arm slung around Selwyn's shoulder, as his friend helped him down the Mage Hall. It was all he could do to stay on his feet.

"Seni help us all if we do," Sel agreed in a voice just as exhausted as his friend's.

The Circle meeting had gone just as Aidric had expected—badly. Everyone, especially the dukes and their envoys, were outraged when they were told that they were to be questioned under the lie-detection spell. Diryan's councilors and the Seneschal were none too ecstatic about the prospect, either, but at least they took the news more calmly.

He was not in the least bit surprised when Lady Gaelle had dramatically risen and loudly demanded that he be the first tested. *Insufferable woman*, Aidric thought resentfully, *always ready to point the finger at me first whenever a problem arises. I must have wronged her in a previous life and caused Aidius to deny her entrance to the Thrones for her to despise me so much!*

Not wanting to upset her or anyone else further, Aidric had readily agreed—but not without scowling at Gaelle in annoyance—and allowed Lady Kiara to cast the spell over him while Diryan conducted the actual questioning. He suspected that Gaelle was disappointed that he passed the test. She resented all mages, especially him who held the highest position, since it was whispered that she had longed to be a mage herself. It seemed she blamed everyone but fate that she was born with only mind-mage abilities.

He had hated having to subject Selwyn to the test. He had warned Selwyn before the meeting that he would have to undergo the test with the rest of them. Sel had just shrugged and said that "what has to be, has to be done," but Aidric couldn't quite shake the feeling that it really bothered him. So far, Sel had said nothing about it, and more than likely, he never would. That was just Sel.

In the end, they had trampled over the Circle's pride for nothing. All had passed the test easily, so the question of the identity of the spy still remained unanswered. Perhaps when they questioned the servants tomorrow, their search would end. He was still feeling disappointment from his mistake with Voytek, not to mention guilty for frightening the lad so much. If they didn't find the spy among the servants, then Aidric had no idea what to do next. Diryan was right. He couldn't very well test every single Lamian citizen!

If we don't find this spy soon, I fear I'll go mad!

Since Raya was away on a tour of duty along the southern Kemosian border, Aidric asked his friend to stay awhile. Although he had lived alone most of his life, he was suddenly feeling that loneliness more keenly ever since Allison had left for the Temple. He had grown so accustomed to her presence in the few short quarter-moons she had been living with him that he felt as though a part of him was missing.

—of which one of those quarter-moons she was shooting daggers at me with her eyes. He chuckled softly as he all but collapsed into his sofa.

"What's so funny?" Selwyn asked as he plopped down into the cushions next to him.

"I was just thinking about Allison," Aidric replied.

"As always," Sel said, rolling his eyes. "I hope you haven't changed your mind about telling her how you really feel about her."

"I haven't, nosy," Aidric said good-naturedly. "For better or for worse, I intend to settle this once and for all, but that doesn't mean that I'm not anxious about it."

"You shouldn't be," he said. "I've seen the way she looks at you, how her eyes soften. She does care about you."

"Yes, I've seen that too, but does she care for me as friends do, or more?" Aidric worried.

"You are such a pessimist, Aidric," Sel scolded. "You need to start thinking more positively. I believe that all will be well when she returns—as you should."

Aidric's face clouded over instantly when he once again thought of her at that place under Eban's eye. "*If* she returns," he muttered under his breath, thinking that it was too soft for Sel to overhear.

He heard.

"Why wouldn't she?" Selwyn asked, eyeing him suspiciously. "They have no right to keep her there once she swears her oaths. Besides, the prophecy—"

"—says nothing about her having to stay in Lamia," Aidric interrupted. "You forget the hate between myself and Domnae Eban. By my actions in Diryan's study, he knows how deeply I care for Allison, and I wouldn't put it past him to try to keep her there with some pathetic excuse or another just to spite me. He knows my rank here holds no precedence over his."

"But why, Aidric?" Selwyn asked in exasperation. "What happened between you two that was so terrible that you won't even confide it to your best friend?"

"You know I cannot speak of it, Sel," Aidric said wearily. "I cannot."

Selwyn rubbed his temples in frustration. "You have lived with this secret for so long now. I can tell that it's eating away at your wellbeing. How much longer can you hold it within your soul?"

"Until the last shovel of soil is cast upon my grave, if needs be. I've told you a million times, and I'll tell you a million more. I don't wish for sympathy—only to forget."

Selwyn sighed heavily, but nodded his reluctant understanding. It had been nearly a year since they had last had this conversation. Did Sel actually believe his answer would be any different this time? Perhaps his friend had hoped, but Aidric knew he could never give in to the temptation of revealing the darkest secret of his soul no matter how much of a relief it would be.

Never.

They sat in a tense silence for a few moments before Selwyn rose and excused himself with the excuse of wanting Aidric to rest. He did, after all, still have to cast more lie-detection spells on the servants in the morning and needed to build up his strength. Aidric nodded and silently watched his friend leave. The banging of the door after him made ripples of loneliness start to wash through him once again. Seni help him, but he missed Allison.

And I need her, Aidric admitted as he began to rise from the couch, intending to drag his weary bones to his bed for a short nap.

However, the sound of Allison's voice calling his name in his mind nearly sent him bowling over head-first onto the marble floor. With an effort, he regained his bearings and awkwardly settled himself back down onto the couch.

"Allison?" he inquired.

"You sound tired," Allison remarked. *"I didn't wake you did I?"*

"Of course not," he assured her, his mood instantly improving several notches. *"I just returned from a Circle meeting, and it was very draining. It was very disappointing, actually."*

"Well, at least I can give you some good news," she said almost giddily. *"I'm off for Lamia in the morning!"*

If he would have had the strength, Aidric would have sprang up and danced for joy. *"Words cannot describe how glad I am to hear that! I feared that Eban would try to keep you there indefinitely."*

"Oh, I think he tried." Her mind-voice was colored with tinges of anger. *"I think he was counting on me failing to give my oaths to Seni judging from his expression when his spell didn't detect a single lie from me. I think he even told the High Priest that I would fail. He isn't as apt at hiding his emotions as Eban is."*

"That's hardly surprising since the High Priest is still young enough to get a switching from his parents."

Ripples of laughter echoed throughout his mind, sounding like a chorus of souls rejoicing at the foot of Seni's holy throne. How he longed for her to be in his arms, his hands running through that glorious golden mane and his lips caressing her full lips—

"Aidric, are you still there?" her voice cut through his reverie.

Blushing scarlet even though there was no possibility of her having heard his thoughts, he hastily replied, *"Yes—I'm sorry. I guess I'm—wearier than I thought."*

"Then I should let you rest," she said. Her voice dripped with concern, which only made him feel worse for fibbing to her.

"Don't sound so concerned, little cat," Aidric sent firmly. *"It's nothing that a sand-mark of sleep won't remedy. If anything, it's you who should be resting. You have a long journey in the morning—and plenty of mage lessons waiting for you when you return."*

"I can hardly wait," Allison said dryly, but there was a touch of amusement layered within her mind-voice. *"May your dreams be pleasant, and may Seni guide and protect you."*

Aidric nearly choked when he heard her speak those phrases. *She learns quickly*, he mused before he sent his own good-byes. *I do believe that she's starting to accept her destiny for what it is.*

He rose from the couch, still feeling a little weak and lightheaded, but for once, he retired to his bed with also a light heart.

***

"You try my patience, Mordant," Roderick growled, not bothering to hide his annoyance for the man who paced in front of the huge window in his study.

The silver-haired man immediately ceased his pacing and shot Roderick a glare that would have cowed any other man, but Roderick was more or less used to Mordant's frequent rages. Mordant's hands were tightly fisted, which signaled that the mage was trying very hard to keep his temper in check, the wisest thing the fool had done in the past few days.

"Do I now?" Mordant replied coolly. "You are a far too impatient man, my dear Roderick. You don't seem to realize that for the game you insist on playing, the only way you can win the upper hand is with time." Mordant flashed him that patient smile that Roderick despised, the smile of a man who knew he was talking to a fool.

"Oh, and I suppose you have figured it all out, haven't you?" Roderick all but sneered at him. *Damned if he will be smiling so broadly when I rip his lips off and hang them on my wall!* he thought darkly.

To his chagrin, Mordant's smile only broadened as he replied, "Of course. Unlike you, I am a man of strategy. Don't you realize that the reason why all of your attempts at conquering Lamia have failed is because you rush too quickly into them? What you need is time—time to strengthen your armies, both magical and non, and to devise a plan that has no room for failure."

"I see," Roderick said. He took a couple of steps towards the mage. "If I'm not mistaken, Mordant, you are naming me a fool, aren't you?"

"You said it, not I."

Mordant was suddenly flying into the opposite wall with all the strength of Roderick's fury. The Silver Mage hit the paneled wall with a sickening crunch and landed in a crumbled heap at Roderick's feet.

"Now who is the fool?" Roderick asked pleasantly, though his eyes still blazed with the flames of Ter-ob. Mordant could only grunt painfully. "Only a fool would face another mage, ally or no, unshielded, or perhaps it's because you are too overconfident. That golden-haired wench certainly proved that. You may be more powerful than I in some aspects, but you would do well to remember that it is *I* who possesses the uniquely combined powers of the Domni and Lord Arioch. Cross me again, and you will be nothing but a pile of living ash before you can even *think* to channel."

Mordant muttered angrily under his breath as he stiffly picked himself off the floor, but otherwise, he remained silent. Roderick nodded his approval

"You believe I don't have a plan, do you?" Roderick said. "These little diversions I have sent you on were merely the honey on a sweetcake. I admit that I had hoped that you would have been successful in acquiring the Golden Mage in Kal, but I didn't really expect success. What I plan is to take the Mage-general and not the wench. My spy in the palace has informed me that there's much talk of the pair being lovers. That's her weakness, a woman's weakness. If Aidric is captured, then the Golden Mage is sure to follow, and when she does, we'll be ready for her."

"And if she doesn't?" the Silver Mage asked.

"She *will*," Roderick insisted darkly as he turned and stalked to his desk.

It was perhaps fortunate for Mordant that Roderick didn't see the look of scorn that flashed momentarily on the dark mage's face. Mordant's lips would not have been the only part of his anatomy that would have been gracing Roderick's walls.

CHAPTER SEVENTEEN

For one sleep-blurred moment, Allison wasn't sure what had awakened her. Her mind felt disoriented and exhausted, as if she had been channeling energy from the Mage-field for a long period of time. Her temples throbbed dully, similar to the one she had experienced after setting her shields for the first time.

Absently, she began to rub her left temple as she attempted to clear her foggy mind.

Something's wrong.

Suddenly more alert, Allison quickly scanned the darkness around her with both her regular eyes and mage senses, but she didn't detect anything other than the normal shadows cast along the walls of the tiny room from the dim light that bled through the thin cracks along the doorframe. Over the few quarter-moons that she had been in Lamia, her senses had easily doubled, and now, there wasn't a soul that could walk within a hundred feet of her without her sensing their presence. Thus, she was pretty sure that no one had been in her room, but if not that, then what *had* awakened her? A sound?

As she eased out from beneath the coarse blankets and slowly sat up, she instantly had her answer. The skin on her entire body abruptly began to tingle insistently, almost to the point of pain. Someone had just started to perform high-level magic nearby—within her wing.

It had taken Allison quite a while to become semi-comfortable enough to fall asleep, and now, despite her mild headache, her body felt rested enough to have been asleep for at least a handful of sand-marks. It was probably still the middle of the night, though she couldn't confirm this since her room had neither a sand clock nor a window. Everyone except the night guards were supposed to still be sleeping if what Soren had told her about rigidity of schedules in the Temple could be believed.

He had claimed that *nobody* was ever late for prayers or duties unless they wished to find themselves permanently expelled from the Temple. Allison couldn't help thinking that the Brothers in Divinity were appallingly harsh about their policies and laws.

Nobody was perfect after all. Did they think themselves gods among men?

Besides, even if it wasn't as late as she thought, this was the novice wing. Didn't Soren tell her that the use of magic among novices and prospective Oath-takers was forbidden without proper authorization and supervision? Wasn't that why a Domnae was assigned to watch over her in the first place?

Allison knew that the sensible thing was to stay under her blankets and forget that she had even noticed the spellcasting, but curiosity had her slipping quietly out of bed anyway. She carefully glided across the room on cat feet to the door, and put her ear against it, listening for a few moments for any movement. It was so quiet that her breathing and heartbeat were extraordinarily loud.

Tentatively, Allison sent out a Probe of Inquiry down the length of the corridor and around three corners. It detected no one. Outwardly, it appeared as though everyone in the novice wing was deep in slumber, but she didn't believe it for a second.

It was *too* quiet. That's what was wrong, what had probably made her wake up, and considering what had happened to get her to this point in her life, she had definitely learned the hard way to trust her intuition and be wary of extreme silence. She wasn't about to ignore that painful lesson now.

Allison could scarcely believe it when she found herself carefully edging the door open and soundlessly slipping out of her room into the suspiciously dark corridor. Not one mage-flame burned within the lamps suspended above. With no windows, the corridors of the Temple gave new meaning to the words "absolute darkness."

At that point, Allison's alarm exploded nearly tenfold. How would she ever find her way back to her room if she continued on? She hardly thought that she could find her way back when the corridors were illuminated much less now when she couldn't even see the *outline* of the corridor.

Her hand still firmly gripping the handle of the door, Allison started to step back into her room when she was nearly bowled over by a wave of what could only be Mage-field energy as it violently washed through her faster than she could blink.

There had been no sound, no manifestation of golden light, no warning, period. The wave had simply appeared so quickly that her senses had not had time to detect it.

Allison slipped to her knees, stunned and infinitely grateful that she had been tightly gripping the door handle when the power had struck her. She shuttered to think what might have happened if she hadn't also been heavily shielded. Never mind broken bones, she doubted if there would have been enough of her left against the far wall of her room to even identify her as human.

What in God's name had happened? That power—she had not felt magic so powerful since she had been faced with the untamed power of the Mage-field when Aidric had forced her to construct the shields in her channels. Who was the mage? And more importantly, what had he or she done?

Her mind still reeling, at first Allison didn't hear the pounding footsteps until the first lantern far down the corridor roared to life with mage-flames. Startled, she could only sit there on her haunches helplessly and stare at the scene unfolding before. The whole thing felt surreal, almost as though she was watching herself and the figures emerging into the green glow as an ob-server within a dream.

A score of both white and grays robes alike—Domni and Senini—flooded into the hall, uncannily resembling ghosts as they moved through the eerie, green gloom. They immediately headed to the second door to the right of her own, and without preamble, one of the Domni sent a strong wave of faintly blue energy forth from his hands towards it that had her mage senses tingling madly again and shattered what had clearly been a magical shield.

The door was kicked open, and a half dozen

Domni rushed inside. Scant moments later, they emerged, carrying between them a frightened boy of about fifteen. He was dressed only in breeches, his hair wild as if they had dragged him from his bed. He was babbling in what was probably Kalite and sobbing both, words that Allison couldn't even begin to understand. He was too old to be one of the Oathtakers, thus he could only be a novice.

Suddenly, hands grabbed her shoulders from behind and yanked her to her feet. Allison cried out in reaction before she could stop herself. The gray robes of a Domnae flashed into view as the lantern above their heads sprang into life. The sudden bright assault to her eyes instantly made them tear up, momentarily blurring her vision.

After rubbing at her eyes vigorously, she found herself staring into the face of a rather hard-looking Domnae.

"What are you doing here, girl?" he demanded harshly, his eyes layered with suspicion.

"This is my r-room," Allison stammered, gesturing awkwardly towards her opened door. A knot of fear lodged itself within her throat as three more Domni and a Seninae moved to encircle her. "I felt— I came to see—"

"I see," the Domnae holding her said coldly. She

knew without reading his emotions that he did not believe her. He turned to the young Domnae to his left and commanded, "Rouse Domnae Soren A'ban and bid him come to his charge's cell at once."

Allison did not in the least bit like the gleam in the Domnae's eyes. What exactly did he suspect? No—what did they plan to *do* to her? Would they even listen to her? Surely Soren wouldn't let them to hurt her—would he?

"What did I do?" she cried as they urged her back across the threshold into her room.

At the same moment, the Domni holding the frightened novice passed by, dragging the boy between them as though he was a ragdoll, and for a moment, the novice's eyes fastened on hers. The overwhelming fear she saw within his dark eyes caused Allison to forget her own fear for the moment. What had he done? Those were the eyes of a condemned man.

Then he was gone and her door was being closed. However, before it could click shut, the novice's hysterical voice echoed throughout the corridor, "Eban—*ne*—Ans-domnae—*vartunor*! *Vartunor*!"

Although she didn't understand a word he had shouted, it was clear by the others' pinched expressions that whatever he had said cut deeply, especially the word *"vartunor."* A couple of the Domni muttered the word to themselves and then began to rattle quietly at each other in the same language of the boy, casting several cursory glances at her during their discourse.

The atmosphere in the room quickly became heavy with feelings of uneasiness and suspicion. She knew that they were talking about her, that they likely thought her and the novice somehow connected. Allison found herself resenting the fact that Master Zenas had not given her more than the Lamian language.

"Sit there," the Domnae who held her abruptly ordered, pointing down to her bed.

Silently, she did as she was told. She didn't dare speak again. Allison had a feeling that her questions would either go unanswered or punished. They hadn't hit her once, but that didn't mean they wouldn't do it later if they thought the situation warranted it. Her status as the ward of the Mage-general of Lamia offered her no protection within these walls. How did she always manage to get herself in these fixes?

I knew I should've stayed in bed, she thought bitterly. *But oh no, I had to be nosy. I swear, Allison, are you ever going to learn?*

It seemed to take an eternity doubled for Soren to arrive. By then, Allison's nerves were wound so tightly that when someone abruptly knocked on the door, a little cry escaped her lips.

Soren's face was unreadable as he entered the room, though she felt the sharpness of his eyes as keenly as the edge of a razor. She desperately wished to thought-speak him, but she had enough sense left to not even make the attempt. In a room full of Domni, it would be suicide.

After Soren performed the perforate greetings to his comrades, he asked in Lamian—purposely for her, she was sure, "Was she involved, Domnae Janus?"

Domnae Janus hesitated, glancing at first her then his brothers before replying in Lamian as well, "We are not certain, Domnae Soren. All in the novice wing but she had succumbed to a sleep spell. She was kneeling outside her door when the novice, Ren, was taken. We wish to put her to the question."

Soren nodded curtly, as if he expected as much. His eyes fell on Allison once again, clearly questioning. Instantly, she understood.

He doesn't know what to believe, she thought, suddenly feeling exhausted. *Maybe he even thinks that I've been playing him.*

Domnae Janus stepped closer and began his spell. Instantly she found herself entrapped within the golden globe of the lie-detection spell.

"I don't need to explain to you what will occur should you answer falsely," Domnae Janus said sternly. "Why were you out of your cell?"

Taking a deep breath, Allison proceeded to explain how she had been awakened by a feeling of wrongness, how along with a mild headache, she had felt a surge of magic and thinking it odd, had intended to find its source. She even described the sensations she had experienced when the wave of Mage-field energy had struck her.

Her eyes never left Soren's face, his familiar features giving her some comfort despite his stoniness. She was surprised that her voice remained steady throughout her discourse.

Allison had thought that her explanation would be enough, but when she fell silent, Domnae Janus made no move to dismiss the spell.

Instead, he asked, "Are you acquainted with the novice, Ren?"

"I never knew he existed until today," she answered.

"That answer does not suffice. A simple yes or no, child."

"No," Allison said a little indignantly, and instantly regretted the edge in her voice when most of the Domni looked offended.

Soren merely shook his head in warning. Crap. She was probably dangerously close to crossing over the line. Maybe she even already had a foot on the other side.

Allison bit her lip and lowered her eyes meekly. "No," she repeated more softly.

When she raised her eyes, Domnae Janus was regarding her peculiarly. The silence that followed seemed to stretch into eternity.

"Do you know what happened in Ren's room tonight?" Domnae Janus finally asked.

Allison started to shake her head, realized that type of answer wasn't going to cut it, and spoke, "The corridor was too dark. I was afraid that I would lose my way. I never got beyond a *foot* of my door."

"'*Foot*'?" Domnae Janus repeated in confusion, glancing questionably at Soren who shrugged and shook his head.

Feeling the blood rising to her cheeks, Allison hastily amended, "I'm sorry. I used a word from my native language. What I meant to say was 'handspan.'"

Unfortunately, her slip of the tongue caused the Domni to only grow more uneasy. She could see it in the stiffness of their stance and how a couple of the Domni kept glancing at the door. It was as if she had announced at the top of her lungs "I am the Golden Mage! I am fated to destroy a kingdom!"

Soren cleared his throat, and all eyes instantly fell on him. "The spell has proven that she speaks the truth, but even if we hadn't used the spell, her explanation rings true. She said she had awakened with a slight headache. The strain of breaking a sleep spell is enough to cause a headache. Her abilities are said to be extraordinary, more powerful than any man has seen since the Natian Six. I, myself, have seen her exercise these abilities when we were attacked on the way to the Temple. It doesn't surprise me that one little sleep spell couldn't contain her.

"Although—" He looked sharply at Allison, causing her to involuntarily shrink back. "I do not condone her leaving her room without permission. However, I believe the fright she received tonight is punishment enough. I shall remain here with her for the remainder of her stay to ensure that no such future mishaps will occur."

"I agree," Domnae Janus seconded. "Her mentor has yet to curb her curiosity and her disobedience. Perhaps it should be *he* who is given reprimand."

To everyone's surprise, Soren chuckled. "Have you all forgotten that her mentor is the Mage-general of Lamia? Reprimanding Aidric Stanisnik for not teaching his ward to lessen her natural curiosity is like reprimanding you for not teaching the worst of your headstrong novices to be more sedate. Neither the Mage-general, nor you, Domnae Janus, can help being who Seni deemed you to be. Let us leave it at that, shall we?"

The look on Domnae Janus's face said that he couldn't decide whether or not he had just been insulted. Luckily for Soren, the older Domnae didn't press the matter. He did, to Allison's relief, dismiss the spell about her.

"Very well," Domnae Janus said. "I shall report this interrogation to the Ans-domnae."

"Already done," Soren said with a smile. "I have relayed all through thought-speech, but he does request the presence of everyone as soon as possible." His smile melted into a frown. "Tonight's incident is far from resolved, I'm afraid."

The direness of his words hung in the air even after the Domni and Seninae left her room. For a moment, neither one of them spoke, Allison still feeling chastised. Heavily shielded, she couldn't even begin to feel or guess what the young Domnae was thinking.

"You're furious with me, aren't you?" she asked quietly, no longer able to stand the silence.

"No," Soren said evenly, walking over to the bed and seating himself beside her. "You just stumbled into a bad situation. That's all."

Allison sighed. "It's a gift of mine, it seems. If you want trouble, then just hang around me for a while."

"I want to apologize…"

"Shouldn't it be me saying that?" she interjected, tilting her head in confusion.

Soren shook his head. "When I was summoned, I didn't know what to believe. Here I had trusted you with a secret that only one other knows, and now it had appeared as though you were conspiring with the young novice doing Seni-knows-what. It made me nervous. I didn't even give you the benefit of the doubt, and I'm sorry."

"You barely know me. How could you have been sure?"

"Because you trusted me with a secret that should have never been told," he explained, looking away. "The least I could have done was extend you the same courtesy. I like you Allison, more than perhaps I should, especially as a Domnae whose emotions are supposed to be disassociated from the people who seek spiritual guidance."

At a loss for words, Allison merely nodded.

Seemingly embarrassed, Soren rose from the bed and took up his previous place in the corner of her room. He regarded her for a long moment before he spoke, his eyes betraying none of the emotions she now knew he struggled against.

"You should rest," he said softly. "We have a long journey ahead of us in the morning."

"Can I ask you something first?" Allison inquired hesitantly. When he nodded, she continued, "What does *vau*—" She stumbled over the word. "—*vartunor* mean? The novice the Domni took was screaming it as they dragged him down the hall. I assume it's Kalite?"

Soren's expression changed instantly into something indecipherable, and for a moment, Allison didn't think he would answer.

"Sacrilege," he finally said dully. "It means sacrilege."

She stilled. "But—what did he—"

"Please," Soren hastily interrupted, "ask me no more."

The peculiar look in his eyes as he stared intently into her own was disturbing, so much that it was many sand-marks after they fell silent before Allison finally, out of sheer exhaustion, succumbed to sleep.

They never spoke of the incident again.

CHAPTER EIGHTEEN

T he vast lawns of the palace stretched for miles in all directions around her as Allison rode towards the dark line and white dot in the distance that was Lamia's wall and palace. The lush grass waved lazily in the cool breeze that was a relief after the harsh climate of Kal, and the sky was dotted with thick, dark clouds that promised rain later on. Allison didn't realize how much she had missed the palace until she caught her first glimpse of it after riding nonstop for more sandmarks than she cared to think about and suddenly felt like shedding tears of joy.

She sensed Soren ride up next to her, but he didn't immediately speak. For most of the journey home, her young Domnae friend had kept up a cheerful conversation about his home life before he had pledged his life to the Temple. It had made the ride more pleasant than it had been when she had first set out for the Temple.

The rest of their entourage were as stone-faced as the men had been in the first, and if not for Soren's company, Allison thought that she would have gone mad after a sand-mark of their sullenness. Now, as she looked at him, Soren seemed almost sad as he scanned their surroundings with eyes that held a deep longing.

"I can almost envy you your home," he said distantly, his eyes never turning away from the landscape he gazed at so longingly. "Such beautiful lands and such a sense of freedom—the wind blowing so coolly through my hair and the smell of rain thick in the air. Quite the opposite from Kal. Other than coming here to retrieve you, it had been years since I had last set foot in these lands, and I was too young at the time to fully appreciate its beauty. If I had not gone into the Temple, perhaps I would have come to lead my life here."

"Can't you still do that if that's what you really want?" Allison asked carefully, not sure if she should let him know that she knew his father had forced him into the Temple.

His laugh sounded bitter. "Once a Domnae, always a Domnae. There is no renouncing of oaths—at least honorably. My life belongs to the Temple and to Seni—but not to me."

Allison didn't know how to respond. She shifted uneasily in her saddle and focused her attention on smoothing her skirts around her—her apprentice uniform and not the horrid, itchy dress from the Temple. The *sholkie* material felt cool and soft against her skin, a relief after two days of scratching her skin raw. She hadn't been in the least bit sorry to leave those godawful garments behind.

She chanced a glance over at Soren and saw that his attention was once again turned to the land around them. She pressed her lips together with worry. He had sounded as if his life was already over, and in a sense, from what he just told her, it was. She couldn't imagine such a way of life.

At least she had been able to escape her stepfather's hand after her mother had left him. From the little she had experienced of life in the Temple—and little of that time had been pleasant—Allison could well imagine how much a man of Soren's friendly personality longed to be free from those confining, secretive walls.

The previous night's incident was still fresh in her mind, the young novice, Ren's, words echoing ominously through her memory as they had through the shadowed corridors as he was being led to—what? The Temple dungeons? His death? Allison knew that she would likely never know his fate. So much secrecy, even danger within those mazes of corridors.

How did Soren bear it? How much longer before he became as cold and stone-faced as the rest of the Domni? The thought depressed her.

Yet, when she thought about it, was she really as free as Soren thought her to be? She couldn't ever leave Lamia on her own without the King's permission—not that he would probably ever feel inclined to give it—nor even something as simple as the palace grounds because of who she was. She was forced to fester within the Lamian borders because of the threat Roderick posed to her and to the kingdom.

My walls are just as confining as his even though they're walls of air, Allison mused.

She stared harder at Soren's face. Although his expression was as stoic as ever, there was just something so—forlorn about his entire demeanor. Suddenly she felt guilty for that last thought.

I'm being incredibly shortsighted. Even though I'm not as free as I would like to be, I at least can wander the palace grounds out in the sunshine and fresh air. Even if I can't go alone, I can still visit villages or go riding. Can he say the same? Those old bastards in that Temple probably don't even leave those walls unless they have to bring children or someone like me before the High Priest. If that's the case, it's no wonder that Soren jumped at the chance to escort me back to Lamia.

"I'm sorry," Allison said contritely into the heavy

silence that had fallen between them. "I have a bad tendency to accidently poke people's sore spots."

Soren's eyes softened as he turned them to her again. "You didn't," was all he said before flashing her a smile that didn't quite reach his eyes.

He was silent for the rest of the ride to the palace, and Allison was content to have it so. She suspected that he was trying to savor this little freedom as much as possible before he had to resume the stifling life he was forced to live.

To her delight, Allison immediately spotted the familiar face of her friend when they neared the stables. Raya was casually leaning up against the gate to the large pen where several horses were stretching their legs before the rains came. Allison's eyes darted around for Aidric and was more disappointed than she wanted to admit to herself when she didn't see him anywhere.

Telling herself that she was being stupid for expecting Aidric to be there when he had so many other pressing duties to attend to daily, Allison quickly dismounted and ran to hug the younger girl, paying no heed to the Domni and soldiers that rode up behind her.

"God, I've missed you all so much!" she exclaimed as she squeezed Raya tightly.

"Aidius, you sound as if you've been gone for a

couple of moons and not a few days!" Raya teased, smiling broadly. "I, myself, have just returned from a tour of duty, and believe me, I feel the same way. A couple of days without Sel's jests and pranks becomes rather dull fairly quickly."

"So why are you still standing here?" Allison demanded. "If I were you, I would've already sought him out."

Raya chuckled. "I believe it. Aidric and you are similar creatures—no patience! Master Ahern said that he was expecting you any depth now, so I decided to wait. I thought after being among strangers for so long that a familiar face would be a welcomed sight."

"You thought correctly." Allison turned her attention to Soren and said, "Raya, I'd like you to meet a friend of mine from the Temple, Domnae Soren. Domnae Soren, this is Raya Phelannike."

"A pleasure, milady," Soren said with a warm smile and a slight nod of his head.

Raya smiled up at him and replied, "The pleasure is all mine, Domnae Soren. I do believe that the Mage-general has spoken of you a time or two."

"All good, I hope," he said with a grin, all traces of his earlier sadness gone from his eyes.

Raya laughed and said, "If he hadn't, I would've said he 'snarled' of you, not 'spoke'!"

Soren chuckled. "I see he's still his same charming

self. I once had the opportunity—or shall I say misfortune—of witnessing one of his bouts of temper back when I was but a novice. The very walls shook so that I feared the ceiling would come crashing down on us all! I could feel nothing but pity for the poor fool who ever found himself on the receiving end of that temper. He roars like a snowcat with a toothache!"

"More like a dozen snowcats," Raya amended, her eyes sparkling.

More than one throat cleared behind them, and Soren glanced over his shoulder at them with an expression that was suddenly unreadable. *The goats are becoming restless, I'm afraid,"* he sent to her, and from the choked sound that came from Raya's direction, he had also sent the thought to her.

"Come," he said aloud. "My brothers and I have yet a long journey ahead of us, and I must deliver you safely into the hands of the king before we may depart."

Soren gracefully dismounted, handed his reins to the nearest Domnae, and urged them before him with a wave of his hand. Stifling giggles, Allison and Raya obliged.

When they were once again out of earshot, Allison asked Raya, "Do you know if Aidric is in his rooms, or is he in another one of those Circle meetings? I've tried to thought-speak him several times to-day, but my mind keeps coming up against a brick wall."

"You don't waste any time, do you?" she teased.

Allison felt her cheeks grow hot, and the knowing look in Soren's eyes only made her blush more furiously. She really hated herself sometimes.

"You know I've missed him a lot," Allison replied, keeping her tone light, "and it wasn't because I'm eager to return to my mage lessons! If it weren't for Domnae Soren's company, I think I would have gone mad in that temple."

"It's nice to feel needed," Soren said dryly, but from the mischievous gleam in his eyes, she knew he was teasing.

"Oh, you know I'm going to miss your company," Allison said sincerely. "I just wish there was some way I could visit you from time to time. Does the Temple allow you to have any visitors?"

He sighed and replied solemnly, "Only family, I'm afraid, but who knows? Perhaps if you come in the company of the Mage-general, then the Ans-domnae will allow it."

However, the look on his face was doubtful.

"We can only try," Allison insisted gently.

Their trio earned them a few sideways glances from the handful of people they passed on their way to the palace's main entrance. Servants and guards both nervously avoided making eye contact with her, yet they still all bowed or curtseyed respectfully. Allison supposed they made a very disconcerting trio—a barbarian mage, the Golden Mage, and a Domnae. Not your everyday combination, and had she been in their shoes, she likely would have behaved similarly.

A few inquiries of the guards directed them to King Diryan's chambers where they were told the king was resting. Allison hated the idea of interrupting him, but Soren did need to return to the Temple. That lot outside was restless enough as it was. She did not envy him his journey home.

Raya left them by the steps to the lone corridor leading to the king's rooms, saying that Selwyn was waiting for her in the Mage Hall. Allison understood only too well her friend's desire to see her husband. She, herself, was itching to see Aidric. Although Raya had informed her that Selwyn didn't know where Aidric was at the moment, she promised to tell Aidric that Allison had arrived on the way to her quarters if he was in his suite.

At the doors to King Diryan's quarters, Allison was relieved to see that the guards at the door were not the same two who had treated her as though she was a criminal, although they wore no less hardened expressions and eyed her with the same suspicion. At least this time there wasn't a chance she would be manhandled by them with Soren at her side.

As it turned out, the king was not resting but working quite feverishly in his study. When they were admitted, Allison was surprised to see the queen working alongside him, frowning down at a couple of maps spread before her. Ileanna had been quite fervent when she had told Allison that she tried to leave all matters of warfare and council to her husband while she handled the people, themselves. Something serious must have been stirring in the wind for the queen to have become involved.

Allison curtsied, but Soren merely nodded his head in respectful acknowledgment of the royal couple. *It must be strange for a king to have to answer to a power above him.*

Soren cleared his throat and then stated in a formal voice, "King Diryan of Lamia, I, Domnae Soren, return to you the Lady Allison McNeal as the charges of heresy have been dismissed due to the oaths she has sworn before the High Priest to serve our lord, Seni. The Brothers in Divinity thank you and your kingdom for your cooperation in the matter, and know that the light of the Thrones above continues to shine down upon Lamia in approval."

"Lamia is always happy to oblige the will of the High Priest," Diryan replied just as formally. "I thank the Temple for returning the Golden Mage to us safely. May Seni guide and protect you and all who ride alongside you on your return journey to the Temple."

Soren nodded again to first, the king, and then the queen. Then he reached over, took Allison's hand, and delivered the parting kiss.

"It has been a pleasure, milady," he said softly.

"A pleasure," Allison agreed, feeling a heavy sadness.

Would she ever see him again?

With one last nod at the royal couple, Soren swiftly left the room, leaving her standing before the king and queen without a clue as to what she was to do or say now. However, Ileanna saved her from her awkwardness by walking over to her for a completely unexpected embrace.

"We are glad to have you back," Ileanna said sincerely, "and if Diryan won't apologize to you, then *I* shall for abruptly herding you off to the Temple with little explanation."

Allison blushed in embarrassment and protested hastily, "No, no, I'm the one who should apologize, Queen Ileanna." She turned her eyes to King Diryan, who watched them soberly. "Your Majesty, I want to apologize for causing such a big scene when I was last before you when it obviously could have been avoided. I acted foolishly, and I disobeyed Domnae

Eban."

Blinking at her in surprise, King Diryan replied, "Yes, milady, your actions were in the wrong, but what is done is done. I believe you have done penance enough within the Temple walls, so I shall forget the matter. You have my leave to return to Aidric and your lessons. I trust you are anxious to see your mentor?"

He wore a most peculiar wry grin that instantly had her blushing furiously again. *My God, he knows*, she thought with horror. *Has he told Aidric?* When she looked at the queen, Ileanna bore a knowing look as well. They both seemed to find the whole situation amusing, a development she had never in a million years expected, much less how to react to.

Allison somehow managed to stop blushing and stiffly nodded her head to the king's question, not trusting her voice. She curtseyed then gratefully escaped from the study with a promise to Ileanna to come see her and her ladies soon.

"We have much to discuss," the queen had said, all but winking and making her want to just sink into the floor.

Despite her embarrassment, Allison's heart raced with anticipation as she strode down the gloomy corridors of the Mage Hall to Aidric's rooms. Her hand shook as she reached for the door handle.

You're being stupid! she scolded herself. *You're not*

some fourteen-year-old on her first date!

Taking a deep breath to calm the pounding in her chest, Allison swung open the door and walked across the threshold.

CHAPTER NINETEEN

H e had sensed her presence when she had first set
foot inside the palace, so he had not been surprised when Raya had come to report the news of Allison's arrival. He had envisioned the moment of her
arrival a thousand times, how he would draw her into
his arms, tenderly gaze into her eyes, and say he wished
to speak about their relationship. He imagined himself
laying his soul bare to her for good or ill and her smiling that incredible smile of hers that always sent his
heart racing and confessing that she felt the same.
Then he would embrace her again and their lips would
finally meet. After that, the Thrones were the limit.

Aidric refused to even think about rejection. If he
focused too much on that, he knew he would lose his
nerve. That was why he had blocked his mind from
receiving all thought-speech. He was nervous enough

as it was, and hearing Allison's voice unexpectedly would have likely pushed his nerves over the edge.

Despite the weakness and dizziness he felt as the aftereffects of that morning's spellcasting, he had forced himself to crawl out of bed and to dress in his best *sholkie* shirt and breeches. Aidric cursed as his fingers shook when he fumbled with the laces of his shirt. He couldn't remember the last time he was so nervous.

He could almost hear Raya teasing him in the back of his mind about how fussy he was about his appearance. Praise Seni that she was occupied with Selwyn at the moment, or else she would no doubt have still been there poking fun at him until Allison arrived.

Aidric was just walking out of his bedroom when he heard his front door open and close softly. He forced himself to walk slowly and calmly down the hall and into the sitting room. Like a statue enveloped in gold, Allison stood in the center of the room, her hair hanging in untidy, windblown waves and her uniform dusty from travel. He thought he had never seen her look more beautiful.

"Well, are you just going to stand there, or are you going to give your mentor a hug?" he demanded, knowing that he was grinning like a fool and hating himself for it.

She flashed him a smile, though he noted that it

was a bit strained. *She's probably just weary from the trip*, he mused as she stepped into his outstretched arms. At least he hoped that was the cause. He was still half-afraid that she still begrudged him his sternness during her lessons.

However, his mind quickly drifted away from those unpleasant thoughts as he savored the feel of her in his arms.

Now is the time.

He opened his mouth to speak, but to his chagrin, he found that he couldn't make the words he had rehearsed so meticulously emerge. It was as if someone had suddenly cast the paralysis spell upon his throat, the words stuck like a cold lump in his throat. It was then that Aidric knew his plans of confession were doomed from the start—and why.

Although his mind insisted that he had put that whole mess with Alina behind him, his heart and soul knew better. The fear of giving himself so completely to another again was still alive and strong within his spirit. It was the fear of rejection, the fear of betrayal.

Coward, a little voice inside his head taunted him, a voice that could easily have been Selwyn's.

"It's good to be back," he heard Allison say as though from a great distance as she pulled out of the embrace.

And just like that, the moment was gone.

She grinned wryly. "After being in that awful temple for a couple of days, even the thought of coming back here to my mage lessons was something to celebrate, but I did miss the company."

After her lessons are complete. I'll reveal everything to her when her lessons are complete. Aidric promised himself suddenly, though deep down he knew he was only stalling the inevitable, making excuses. Aidius, he really was pathetic.

Aloud, Aidric said warmly, "Indeed, I also missed the company, so much that I'll even postpone your lessons until tomorrow in order for us to talk awhile."

"You're too kind," Allison said a little too sweetly as she brushed a lock of her hair out of her eyes in such a way that suddenly sent his pulse racing again.

After her lessons, his mind repeated stubbornly. *Lamia comes first, even above your own feelings.*

Maybe if he said it enough, he would start to believe it...

"Come, sit," Aidric said, forcing himself to sound cheerful. "You must be exhausted from your long journey."

"Exhausted yes, but not so much that I'm in a hurry to sit down again," Allison replied dryly, but nevertheless, she carefully seated herself onto the couch. "If I ever have to see another saddle again, it'll be too soon. We won't even discuss how many saddle sores I have."

Aidric laughed as he followed her example, careful not to sit too close. However, before he could even ask her all about her experience in the Temple, she was already asking him her own questions.

"So, have you found Roderick's spy yet?" she asked steadily, though her eyes betrayed her anxiety.

Rage surged within him as he was reminded of how close he had come to losing her because of that spy.

"Only here for no more than a few depths and you are already worrying over political matters," he teased as he tried to get his emotions back under control. The last thing she needed was to see just how worried and frustrated he was about the whole thing. "Didn't I tell you that you should be a member of the Circle?"

Allison's eyes widened in something like alarm. Aidric was well aware of her dislike of politics. She had stressed her dislike vocally enough on several occasions, nearly biting his head off the last time he had brought up the subject. *Of course, she had already been cross with me over the way I had pushed her mercilessly through her lessons that day.*

Aidric shook his head in amusement and said, "Don't worry. I'll not force the seat on you if you are so against it. I can only hope to change your mind."

"Not happening," she said dryly, "but you've ignored my question." She raised an eyebrow. "Purposely?"

"Of course not," he assured her. He had been trying to do just that. "I have tested everyone in the palace under the lie-detection spell, from Lord Ion to the youngest servant, and all passed easily. Even *I* underwent the test! I'm at my wits end over the matter. Whoever the spy is, Roderick has concealed him or her well."

An image of Alina inadvertently formed in his mind, and he viciously banished it in almost the same instant. No—he would not think of *her* now.

"At least you know that it's no one at the palace," Allison said, trying to sound optimistic, but the tension in her voice betrayed her worry.

Aidric paused, disturbed by the brief burst of fear that suddenly leaked beyond her shields. "Perhaps that only makes matters worse," he continued reluctantly.

Although he would do anything to erase the fear that bastard, Mordant, had etched into her heart, it was more dangerous to leave her out of the loop. As long as the spy or spies were still uncovered, he needed her eyes open and sharp.

"The spy could be any of the peasants or even petitioners from the out-kingdoms who attend court daily. I couldn't possibly test every single person. I simply don't have the time, and even if I did, channeling so much power from the Mage-field on a daily basis would burn me out until I was a useless husk. We have enough to worry about with our problems with Roderick to solve one of the bastard's largest problems by ridding him of me ourselves."

"Then we'll just have to be more careful," she said firmly.

His lips quirked up. "Oh, I plan to. Roderick may think we are fools, but sooner or later he'll wake up one morning, gaze into his mirror, and realize that he was staring at the face of the biggest fool all along.

"Now, enough about Roderick. You must tell me more about your stay at the Temple. I find it very hard to believe that Eban did not—Allison?"

Allison's eyes had suddenly focused inward as if she was thought-speaking with someone. However, he didn't sense any of the strands of energy about her that signaled thought-speech.

Aidric touched her arm lightly. "Allison?"

She shook her head a little as if waking up from a daydream and fixed him with eyes that were now blatant with worry. "You said that you tested everyone using a lie-detection spell?" she asked with an edge of seriousness he had never heard in her tone before.

A sense of foreboding washed over him. "Yes—why?"

His answer made the worry in her eyes strengthen. "Did you use the same spell that the Ans-domnae uses to test the sincerity of those who pledge their oaths to Seni before the High Priest?"

"There is only one lie-detection spell," he answered, puzzled.

Allison grimaced as though she had suddenly bitten into something bitter. "Did you know that there is a way to fool that test?"

Aidric nearly fell out of his seat.

"*No*," he replied quietly, refusing to lose his calm. He stared intently into her green eyes. "You are certain of this, Allison?" *Seni help me, she* must *be mistaken!*

Allison nodded her head slowly, and Aidric felt as though he had suddenly swallowed a boulder.

"Yeah, I'm sure," she said, "because I've fooled it myself."

Her cheeks colored in what could only be embarrassment as she quickly lowered her eyes, but not before he could see the flash of shame in them.

That was when he understood what she had done.

"Your oaths to Seni—they were not sincere," he said slowly, knowing that he should be angry that she had committed such a blasphemous act but unable to summon up any such feelings.

She nodded unhappily, refusing to meet his eyes. "It had to be done, Aidric," she mumbled so that he had to strain his ears forward to make out her words. "I feel no loyalty to your god—at least not yet—and I just couldn't accept the thought of being hung because of something that really isn't my fault. I wasn't born here, so how could they expect me to be loyal to a god I hadn't even known existed until a few short quarter-moons ago?"

"Tell me how it was done," he said calmly, though inside his stomach was beginning to painfully knot up. It was all he could do to prevent himself from tearing out his hair in frustration. Only the thought of looking like a fool in front of Allison prevented him from doing so.

"I remembered how you said that they would know I was lying in the Temple," she began, "and I instantly knew that I was in a bind because there was no way I could truthfully swear oaths to Seni, a god I know next to nothing about. The only person I had to turn to in the Temple was Domnae Soren."

Aidric wanted to ask her why she hadn't consulted *him* on the matter, but he held is tongue, not wanting to possibly agitate her further. *If I didn't know that Domni are sworn to chastity, then I might have been jealous.* He ignored the little voice in the back of his head that snorted derisively.

"I was incredibly lucky that he *could* help me, or more accurately, that he decided that I *should* be helped," Allison said. "He said that he and his father had encountered a group of people—I can't remember if he told me their name or not but they came from beyond the Phaedrian Sea, wherever that is—that worshipped some deity named Ingmar. They were to swear oaths before the High Priest, and they revealed a method of getting around your lie-detection spell. Apparently, they had done it on several occasions. Both Soren and his father believed that Ingmar was just another name for Seni, so they kept their secret, allowing them to swear falsely."

"Did they use a form of mind magic?" he asked.

She shook her head. "As far as I can tell, it's simply a matter of self-conviction. I made myself believe that I was swearing oaths to my own deity, even when I said Seni's name, so in a sense, I *was* speaking the truth. I'm not sure how that lie-detection spell works, but I did succeed in fooling it or else I would probably be in a hangman's noose right now."

Aidric was silent for a moment, curses in every language he knew flashing through his mind with the speed of his growing rage. *All that testing,* he thought darkly, *it all may have been for naught. If these people came across the Brothers in Divinity, then it is very likely that Roderick learned of them as well—learned and was taught their secret. Shall I ever be able to place my trust in that spell again?*

"They wouldn't have dared to hang you," he muttered absently, his mind still half on his dark thoughts. "You are here because of Seni's will, and executing you would most certainly be considered blasphemy unless Seni, Himself, deems otherwise. You don't need to worry about that, but I stray from the real issue here. If what Domnae Soren has taught you is known by even a few outside those who have come from beyond the Phaedrian Sea, then perhaps now I know the reason why I've failed to locate the spy."

He ran his hands agitatedly through his hair and then fixed his eyes thoughtfully on her. "Could you demonstrate this technique for me?"

"I suppose," Allison replied, "but I don't think I can do it at the spur of the moment. I need some time to brainwash myself first. Maybe five minutes— sorry—*depths* will be enough. I also have to know what it is I'll be lying about."

Aidric nodded and couldn't help feeling a slight sense of relief that at least there were limits to the ability. ...*or are there?* his mind countered stubbornly. With an effort, he pushed that thought away. The forever pessimist.

"How about saying that your hair is black?" he suggested.

"All right. I'll nod when I think I can do it."

Allison sat back more comfortably into the cushions and turned away from him. Aidric waited as patiently as he could, but it seemed as if an eternity and a day crawled by before she turned her head back and gave him a slight nod. He immediately began to channel energy from the Mage-field and cast the spell around her.

A sharp sting similar to rubbing a hand across a freshly-skinned knee assaulted his mind, and he barely stopped himself from physically wincing. It seemed his channels were more chaffed from all the overload than he had initially thought. Seeing him being affected adversely while channeling what was for him a negligible amount of energy would definitely make her worry, and the last thing he wanted to do was to add to her seemingly infinite string of worries if he could at all help it.

When the spell was complete, Aidric asked, "What color is your hair?"

"Black," came the immediate answer, as clearly and confidently as if the golden globe was not there.

Aidric grunted, knowing that he could no longer deny it. *Well, now that I know it can be done, I might as well test its limits.*

"I would like to try a few things, if you don't mind," he said hesitantly. He hated subjecting her to it, but he knew it had to be done.

"Not at all," Allison assured him, though it did little to ease his conscience.

He asked her to repeat her oaths to Seni. At first, he only saw her lips move, but no sound penetrated the globe. He still didn't feel even an inkling of anger at the undeniable lie, a fact that he was probably better off not scrutinizing too closely.

About halfway through the oaths, Aidric began to hear her voice, faintly at first, and then more clearly towards the end. He then asked her to lie to every question he asked her. Even though she was prepared to lie, Allison still failed in her next ten attempts to fool his spell. Finally, after ten more attempts, each ending with a failure, Aidric dismissed the spell, not missing Allison's little sigh of relief when the last of the energies had been dissipated.

"I didn't mean to exhaust you," he said unhappily.

Allison shook her head and offered him a sheepish smile. "You didn't. I'm just glad that the spell is gone. All that energy was starting to make my skin crawl unbearably. Did you find all the answers you were looking for?"

"Yes and no."

Her eyes narrowed in puzzlement.

"No question is ever entirely answered, unfortunately," he added before she could open her mouth to speak. "My questions are answered, yes, but how can

I be certain that there aren't others that should have been asked?"

She stared at him blankly for a long moment before she made a face and said, "You sound like one of those Providencen priests."

"Seni forbid," Aidric said dryly, but he couldn't resist grinning at her disgruntled look. "Lord Othos used to always say that, and I've found it a priceless bit of advice. If you remember nothing else I say, then at least remember that."

"Hey, I thought you said that you were postponing my lessons until tomorrow morning," Allison teased.

"Right. Sorry," he said with false solemnity. "Old habits are hard to break. Perhaps it's this room. What say we take a stroll through the courtyard if you aren't too weary? Keldan said that the bards would be entertaining there today."

Allison's eyes instantly lit up. "I'd love to. I haven't had the chance to hear any of the court bards or minstrels since that awful night Roderick attacked Idona." Her grimace was an echo of his own distaste for that nightmarish night.

"Then it's settled," Aidric said cheerfully, refusing to let that memory spoil his mood. He rose to his feet. "Of course you'll probably want to change out of that dust-covered uniform into something more casual. I would ask if Selwyn and Raya would like to join us, but I definitely don't want to disturb—" He cut off in mid-sentence when he suddenly felt Allison's hand fall onto his upper arm.

Her unexpected touch caused his heart to begin to beat so loudly that he was sure she could hear it, and it was all he could do to keep the sudden surge of strong emotions from his expression. *Stop it you fool!* he chided irritably. *Remember—she cannot know your feelings until after her training. After! Only when you have come to terms with them yourself.*

Aidric managed to pull himself together and look down at her questionably, not trusting himself to speak.

"Aidric," Allison said quietly, her eyes gazing intently up at his face, "before I change, there's something I really need to tell you."

He stared at her mutely, his mouth suddenly feeling as dry as the air of Kal. Could she possibly—he scarcely dared to hope. Luckily, she took his silence as a signal for her to go on. He didn't think he could've said a word even if Aidius, himself, declared that it was the only way he could gain admittance to the Thrones.

"Earlier, although your facial expression didn't change," she continued in that same, quiet voice, "I could see it in your eyes that my swearing falsely to Seni really—upset you."

Aidric released the breath he didn't realize he was holding as waves of disappointment and self-beratement began to thunder through him. Of course it wouldn't be that easy...

"You have every right to be angry with me," she said quickly, casting her eyes down with that same look of shame he had seen earlier.

Aidric instantly felt like a total heel. Apparently some of the anger he felt for himself had managed to creep unknowingly into his expression, and she had thought it was directed at her. He started to reassure her that he wasn't in the least bit angry with her, but she put a delicate finger to his lips that instantly silenced him.

Damned if she will drive me mad if she touches me again! he thought miserably.

"Please don't say anything," Allison entreated. "Just let me finish. For what it's worth, I made a promise to Soren to return to the Temple one day and swear those same oaths truthfully to him."

So, it's just "Soren" now, is it... Aidric suddenly felt an invisible hand start to painfully squeeze his heart, though thankfully Allison didn't seem to notice his distress.

Her hand squeezed his arm tightly, her eyes wide and vulnerable. "I also want to make that promise to you, Aidric. I want to make this right."

"I'm not angry with you, little cat," he assured her gently, "but with myself. It was *my* duty as your mentor to teach you more of Seni and Aidius when you first arrived in this kingdom, but I foolishly allowed it to slip my mind. What's past is past and cannot be done differently. What say we forget this whole business of Oathswearing until at least tomorrow? For now, I want you to go change your clothing into something more suitable. I'll not have my ward looking disheveled!"

"As you wish, *milord*," Allison retorted with mock meekness as she rose from the couch and bent her knees in an elaborate curtsey that would have done every highborn lady proud and hurried to her bedroom.

To Aidric, it seemed as though only yesterday that he had stifled a chuckle when she had awkwardly curtseyed before Diryan for the first time. Now she did it with hardly a moment's thought.

She's finally adapting to this new life, and how much of you is afraid that now she'll no longer depend upon your company? Perhaps Selwyn is right. You're worse than a fool for not confessing your love, but deep down I know I'll just clam up again should I attempt to share my feelings with her. Now isn't the time, but I pray that when the time does come, I'll not be too late.

Aidric frowned, not liking that last thought at all.

CHAPTER TWENTY

Allison felt those eyes on her again, like an itch that refused to go away. Without turning her head, she looked out of the corner of her eye and saw that same dark-haired young man next to Aren staring intently at her as his fingers plucked skillfully at the strings of his lute.

It was the fourth time she had turned her eyes to him and caught him staring at her ever since Aidric and she had entered the courtyard for the performance. Unconsciously, she inched nearer to Aidric before she realized what she was doing, and blushing, she stilled her movement.

She didn't at all like what those eyes were suggesting no matter how handsome he was. He made her feel as if she was a side of beef and he, a hunger-maddened wolf. A name tugged at the edges of her memory, but no matter how hard she tried, she couldn't remember it, nor really remember seeing him elsewhere.

Determined to ignore him, Allison focused her attention back onto the fantastic music that the five men and three women were creating. Never had she heard music so hauntingly beautiful in all her life. The tune they were playing was a popular lament Aidric had said was called "Yesternight." She could almost hear the woman who had lost her husband and daughter during a raid wailing her pain in the minor chords the bards and minstrels played.

More than once, she had caught herself shivering with the chills the music was causing her to feel, as well as nearly bringing her to tears. It was a little disconcerting. Music had never made her feel like this!

It was no wonder that a large crowd had gathered in the courtyard to enjoy the concert. Allison noted that about three-fourths of the crowd were female, no doubt there to swoon over the twins, although a good many of them were making moon eyes at the handsome lute player with his hungry stare.

Quite a few people had also eyed Aidric and her askance a few times, more so when they had first arrived and had settled themselves onto the lawn. Allison had to bite her lip against a snort when some of the groups and couples seated around them had started to nervously inch away from them. She was finding it surprisingly easier and easier to accept the Lamians' reactions to her.

Aidric, on the other hand, was not amused in the least. He frowned openly at them, his eyes reflecting his annoyance. Everyone carefully avoided eye contact after that.

After a while, when it became apparent that she wasn't going to go mad and sear everyone away to Seni's Thrones, everyone began to pay her no more attention than they would a stranger sitting next to them in a crowd. Allison had even chatted with several of the women around her about the performance, they having lost their fear more quickly than their husbands or boyfriends, while Aidric looked on in approval.

In fact, she had been really enjoying herself for the first time in weeks until that black-haired man had taken to staring at her. After feeling him practically lick her with his eyeballs for over a sand-mark, now all she wanted to do was leave—not that she planned on saying anything to Aidric about it. She knew that he wanted to talk to the twins after the performance, so even though the thought of being under *their* eyes would be just as uncomfortable, Allison held her tongue and concentrated in keeping her rising tension from both her body and expression. She didn't need to give Aidric yet another reason to stress over her.

Thinking about the bardic twins sent a new wave of anxiety through her. She had been doing her best to avoid them since their first meeting, afraid that they would tell her that she needed to begin her training with her bardic-mage abilities. So far, Aidric hadn't mentioned the lessons, and she would've rather eaten her slippers than bring up the subject herself. She didn't know why, but she dreaded those lessons more than her lessons with Aidric, unsure if it was because of the twins, themselves, or even worse, a touch of her Foresight abilities giving her a nudge.

"Aidric, who is that man?" Allison whispered into his ear, discreetly pointing at the black-haired man.

She was taken aback when Aidric's face immediately darkened with a mixture of hate and disgust when his eyes fixed on the bard. His lips twisted as though he had just tasted something vile.

"Patrym," Aidric all but spat out, scowling. "He's someone I advise you stay far away from."

"Ah, the infamous Patrym I keep hearing everyone mention," Allison said.

It was no wonder he was known as a womanizer. He most certainly had to looks to pull it off. Add to that a great talent for music, and that made him this world's version of a rock star.

She grimaced. "You *really* don't have to worry about me steering clear of someone with a reputation as—*infamous* as his. His type always have 'trouble' written all over them, and I've had enough trouble to last me a lifetime, thanks."

"Good," Aidric said with a satisfied nod, "because mark my words, from the way he was staring at you just now, I believe he has just targeted you as his next conquest to add to his surprisingly ever-growing collection. He may be handsome and a marvelous bard, but as far as I know, those are his only two virtues— if being handsome can be called a virtue."

"Is that why you're glaring daggers at him?" she asked boldly, thrilled that he was being so protective. "To protect my virtue?"

He looked at her sideways and answered, "Mostly. I *am* your mentor and friend after all, but that isn't the whole of it. Our paths crossed badly a while back, and there's still a mountain of ill feelings between us. I tolerate him only when I must, and I admit, I hate to think of him being anywhere near you."

Allison shook her head. "If I'd known just how much the thought of him would upset you, I never would've pointed him out to you. I only asked because he seems to have developed a staring problem that I find annoying, but enough about him. Can you tell me the name of this song? It has a nice melody."

For the next hour they sat in a comfortable silence

as they listened to the music, broken only when Allison leaned over to ask Aidric about a particular song or those around them engaged them in conversation. In truth, Allison enjoyed being near Aidric more than the performance, itself. Even when Keldan and Aren sang a love duet for the ladies in the crowd, their tenor voices blending together in a harmony so perfect and beautiful that it was almost unearthly, she was still very much aware of Aidric's nearness. Not even the strong power of the bardic-mages singing in concert could entirely hold her in rapture as it seemed to be doing to everyone else, including Aidric.

However, despite the distraction of both Aidric's nearness and the beautiful music, a particular phrase in the twins' song stirred the memory of her incident at the Temple. Once it surfaced, Allison annoyingly couldn't seem to get what had happened at the Temple out of her mind. She had stumbled into something strange and frightening last night.

Again, she found herself wondering for the thousandth time what the novice, Ren, had been doing. Surely casting spells without permission would not have necessitated such a brutal response from the Domni and Senini. Why had he shouted "sacrilege"? Why had he mentioned Domnae Eban and the Ansdomnae? What had he been trying to convey?

Allison was still torn about whether or not to even

mention the incident to Aidric. She knew that Lamia would declare her queen before the Brothers in Divinity acknowledged it to anyone other than their own order. Before she had departed the Temple, the Ansdomnae, himself, had ordered her to never speak of the incident again.

Was it really that important? Would she dare defy the Ans-domnae's command? Was she making too much out of nothing? Besides, what if the incident turned out to be more than the Temple's rather harsh methods of disciplining its members?

She glanced over at Aidric's relaxed demeanor and frowned. Aidric had enough to worry about without her adding more to his ever-growing pile of problems than she already had. Maybe it was best to forget that last night had ever happened and just enjoy the performance. After all, she seldom saw Aidric as relaxed as he was now. She hated the thought of ruining it for him now. In the end, she decided to keep her thoughts and fears to herself.

After the performance came to an end and the bards and minstrels took their final bows before the cheering and clapping crowd, Aidric and she approached the twins, although the going wasn't easy. What seemed like hundreds of ladies—anywhere from girls who looked to be barely on the edge of puberty to women whose faces could no longer be called middle-aged—crowded around the twins, each trying to be the first to talk to the bards.

Neither Keldan nor Aren seemed in the least bit perturbed over the mass of women shoving and professing their undying love in shouts they hoped were louder than the girl next to them. They merely preened under the attention to the point where Allison could almost swear that she could see the arrogance radiating from them.

Aidric shot her an amused glance that said volumes, and she just rolled her eyes and shook her head. She couldn't for the life of her fathom how Aidric had ever become friends with those two characters.

However, in all fairness, she really didn't know them all that well. Her only interactions with them were those brief moments at the celebration on the Eve of the Birth of the World and a few times thereafter, so who's to say that underneath those layers of arrogance lay two of the kindest, noblest hearts in Lamia? There had to be a good reason why Aidric had chosen them as friends. She hoped.

Out of the corner of her eye as Keldan (or was it Aren?) caught sight of them, Allison noticed with some alarm that Patrym had been making his way towards them with a determined and self-assured expression on his face, no doubt to seek her out, no matter that she was in the company of Aidric. Given what Aidric had told her about their mutual animosity, she suspected that it was *especially* because she was with Aidric. However, Patrym stopped dead in his tracks when he saw where their destination lay, scowled, and then retraced his steps back into the crowd of waiting ladies who were more than happy to shower their attentions on him.

Allison couldn't help but grin. *Score one for us, thank goodness.*

When Aren spotted them, he all but fell over himself to reach her ahead of his brother. Before Allison could even think to shrink away, her right hand was already at his lips, and Keldan was raising her other hand to his.

"It's been far too long since you have graced us with your lovely presence, Milady Allison," Keldan said more civilly than she had thought was possible for the man. She had been almost afraid that the first thing out either of their mouths would be something that would make her blush.

Aren, however, didn't disappoint. "Aw, Aidric just wants her all to himself," he accused, doing his best to pout. "Although as stunning as she is, can we blame him?"

Allison surprised herself by managing to keep the

blood from rushing to her cheeks by sheer will alone. She'd be damned before she willingly gave them more ammunition to tease her with.

"And can you blame me for keeping her away since you insist upon speaking of her as if she's a piece of property?" Aidric said dryly, folding his arms across his chest.

Aren tilted his head to the side. "Have we really?"

Before Aidric could respond, Keldan quickly asked her, "So, did you enjoy the performance, milady?"

Allison smiled at him, deciding in that instant that she liked him much better than Aren. "Please, just call me Allison, and yes, I really enjoyed the music, especially that duet you two sang. It was beyond beautiful. If I didn't know any better, I'd have thought you were using magic during that song."

Keldan laughed and said with a hint of mischief, "We were. It's something that only Aren and I can do, and perhaps in time, you will as well. We use the lesser of our bardic magicks to strengthen the notes we sing in order for the audience to actually experience the music down to their very souls. It's somewhat tiring, so we don't do it often. Perhaps someday you'll join us in a song or two."

She shook her head regretfully. "I doubt it. Remember, I told you I couldn't sing, and I really meant it. I couldn't find a right pitch even if it grabbed me by the throat."

It was the twins' turn to laugh. "Nonsense," Aren chided. "I haven't once heard nor read of a bardic-mage not able to sing."

"There's always a first time for everything," Allison muttered, wishing they would drop it.

"Then, I'll make it my next task to prove you wrong!" Aren exclaimed somewhat smugly.

"I guess that leaves the actual teaching of bardic spells to me," Keldan said wryly, shooting a glare at his brother, while Allison groaned to herself at the thought of being cornered into the bardic-mage lessons she had tried so hard to avoid. "I knew you would leave the hardest part for me."

"What are little brothers for?" Aren said with a devilish grin.

Aren and Kat would make the perfect couple, Allison thought bemusedly, then in the next instant, started at the thought. *What the hell am I even thinking? All this talk of magic has finally driven me insane!*

"It's funny that they automatically assume that I want to even learn these bardic magicks," she thought-spoke Aidric. *"I wish someone would've at least asked me first before they started planning out a huge chunk of my day."*

He raised an eyebrow at her, but his smile was understanding. *"I could tell you why, Allison, but you would probably strike me if I did."*

"I know, I know," she sent irritably, her sigh purely mental. *"It's because Seni wills it, right?"* When he nodded, she smiled thinly and added, *"I'm glad you didn't say it because I probably* would *have hit you!"*

"Hello..." Aren said, abruptly stepping between them. Allison blinked owlishly at him. "Enough of that secret thought-speech," he scolded. "It makes me feel as though you two are talking about me."

Keldan swatted his younger brother on the arm and chided, "Stop being so paranoid." He then turned to Aidric and asked seriously, "Do you think she's ready to begin learning the lesser bardic magicks?"

Aidric frowned and shook his head. "If that bastard, Eban, had not dragged her off to the Temple, then perhaps she would have been. She's a fast and efficient learner." He smiled fondly at her. For some reason, she found that irritating. "However, since her lessoning *was* interrupted, she won't be ready for a while."

Keldan nodded, looking thoughtful. "She can, at the very least, begin her music lessoning." He glanced over at Aren. "Despite what my brother believes, we'll *both* take a hand in teaching her the fundamentals of music."

"I have no objection if she doesn't," Aidric replied, raising his eyebrow ever so slightly at her.

Allison really, *really* didn't want to add anything else to her day. Her mage lessons were exhausting enough in and of themselves. Furthermore, she already had to add her study of the Ti'ar language to her day.

Her shoulder slumped. Yet, she knew she couldn't say no. As Aidric and everyone else had their duties to perform, so did she.

Maybe it won't be so bad. Maybe some of the lessons will coincide with some of Aidric's Council meetings. At least then I won't have to be alone even if the company is less than charming.

"It's fine with me even though I still insist that I'm a musical half-wit," she warned.

Keldan and Aren looked at each other before saying in complete unison, "I like a good challenge."

Aidric grinned, but seeing the scowl she directed at the silver-haired men, he smartly did no more than grin.

Something tells me that these are going to be the longest months of my life, Allison thought with a sigh.

CHAPTER TWENTY-ONE

For the thousandth time that day, Allison wondered why she had ever agreed to these music lessons as she sat in Keldan's sitting room. His room was much smaller than Aidric's, perhaps half its size, but more elaborately decorated. Instead of wall-to-wall bookcases like Aidric's sitting room, Keldan's sported at least a dozen paintings by probably as many different artists as none were of the same style.

The largest of the paintings hung on the opposite wall facing the main door where no one could miss seeing it upon entering, a portrait of the bardic-mage, himself, holding his lyra. Allison admitted grudgingly to herself that he did make for a striking picture, although she would have rather undergone torture than to admit as much to him. His head was already crowding up the room as it was.

The rest of the paintings consisted of dazzling sunsets against the backdrop of the palace and other exotic places she couldn't name. Maybe they were of places Keldan had traveled to or only visions of a talented artist's imagination. Either way, they were simply exquisite beyond words.

For as many chairs and couches that lined the walls, Keldan had insisted on sitting on the floor instead. She didn't mind, already accustomed to it from her lessons with Aidric. Aidric had explained that most mages found sitting in a chair disruptive to their spell-casting, so it made sense that a bardic-mage felt the same way, even if what they were currently doing had nothing to do with spells.

Seated on a pile of cushions across from where she sat, Keldan gazed at her serenely, though his mouth twitched ever so slightly from the effort of not laughing. Allison, however, wasn't in the least bit fooled, and she had no qualms of openly glaring back at him. She had just completed singing the scales he had assigned her, and they had sounded every bit as bad as she had warned him they would.

"It's as I thought," Keldan informed her. "You are singing through your nose, thus the high, off-key nasal sound. I take it you have never had any musical training?"

"No, I haven't," Allison retorted sullenly, wondering what "singing through your nose" meant and wishing he would crack another smile so she could wipe it from his face.

At least he hadn't tried to come on to her. Yet.

He sighed. "You are every bit as unique as the prophecy says. You have the potential to become a very powerful bardic-mage, but the singing ability is not inborn in you. In any bard, that is simply unheard of. At the moment, even if you were apprenticed to a Master Bard, then all you would ever have hope to become is a street minstrel. It's almost as if Seni gifted you with your bardic-mage abilities as an afterthought."

"Then, is there any point in learning how to use my bardic-mage abilities?" she asked hopefully.

Keldan smirked and replied, "Nice try, but yes, there are many reasons why we should still pursue this. The most important reason being that left untrained, you could one day unconsciously hum a tune and suddenly find the person next to you lying sprawled out on the ground, dead from a heart attack at the worst or at the best, under a sleep spell only the caster could lift."

Allison shuddered at the thought. How she longed for the days when all her newfound abilities lay dormant and unimagined in her mind. Keldan watched her carefully, for her reaction to his words, she suspected. He almost seemed to be a different man now than the arrogant, womanizing man she had met. It left her feeling a bit unsettled.

"Fine," she said more forcefully than she had intended, "you've convinced me. I still have a lot to study before Aidric drags me to today's mage lessons, so we might as well get on with this."

"Your enthusiasm for music just overwhelms me, milady," he said sarcastically, but his smile took the bite out of his words. "Nevertheless, I pledge you that when your lessons are complete, you'll love singing as much as I do. Once the spirit of music begins to flow in your blood, nothing short of your death, if even then, will release it from your soul."

"If you say so," she replied skeptically.

The way her singing voice sounded at the moment, Allison thought Roderick would become a saint before she would ever love the sound of her own voice. Given the choice between listening to her singing or the screeching of fingernails on a chalkboard, most people would probably opt for the latter.

"I have often boasted that I could teach even a frog to sing beautiful laments," Keldan declared, "and I'll be damned to the six hells first before I allow you to make a liar out of me!"

Allison chuckled at the fervent expression on his

face. "I can only try my best," she promised. Then more mischievously, "However, I have a feeling that you had better stock up on ice and cold drinks if any of those six hells are anything like the one from my world."

Keldan glared at her, though his lips ruined the effect by curving up slightly in amusement. "I'll pretend that I didn't hear that. Now, the basics of singing are fairly simple. The first and most important element is breathing. If you don't breathe correctly, then the tones of your notes will emerge too breathy, weak, flat, or sharp. What we are aiming for is the purest tones you can possibly produce. Bardic magicks will not work properly, if not at all, if the tone isn't pure. Would a normal mage's spell work if the incantation or weavings of the energies were not done perfectly?"

She shook her head.

"When singing, you mustn't slouch your shoulders, else you cannot breath as deeply as you should. As you draw a breath, breathe deeply, smoothly, through both your mouth and nose to obtain the maximum amount of breath as possible. This is especially important if the phrase you are about to perform is a long one with many runs or trills. Now, let us practice breathing for a few depths."

Allison felt silly, but she did as Keldan asked without complaint. She practiced the exercise under his critical eyes for longer than she thought she'd have to before he felt she was ready to continue on to the next lesson. By then she was feeling lightheaded as though she had been hyperventilating or had just completed some kind of weird class on meditation.

And I thought Aidric was the only drill sergeant around here! she thought wryly.

"Now that you've mastered the breathing technique, next you must master focus," Keldan explained as she groaned miserably to herself. "What I mean by focus is the point to which you must direct your sound. As I said earlier, your focus is totally nasal, which will not do at all. When you sing the lower notes of the scale, concentrate on directing your flow of sound to your upper teeth. However, don't actually sing straight to your teeth. That would only cause you to close your mouth, thus closing off the sound. Allow the music to simply flow in that direction. The middle notes of the scale are to be directed in the same manner to your nose."

"But you said—" Allison interrupted in confusion.

"Yes, yes, don't sing *through* your nose," he finished patiently. "You won't be, Allison. The flow of music will only be focused in that direction. As for the high notes, they are to be directed to the roof of your head, but instead of allowing the sound to stop there, it should flow up and over in the pattern of an arc."

Keldan demonstrated with his hands to give her a picture of what he meant. The concept of it only puzzled her more.

"Do you understand all I have explained so far?"

"Not really," Allison admitted reluctantly, feeling incredible dense.

He smiled a little at her woebegone expression. "It's quite all right. I've had students in the past who have come to me with less knowledge of music then you have. At least you knew what a scale was when I asked you to sing one. One poor lad I had a few years ago gazed up at me as though I had just insisted that he eat my lyra when I asked him if he knew any scales and said, 'what do stairs have to do with music?'"

Allison giggled as she pictured that scene. In the Lamian language, the word used for both a particular type of spiral staircase used in the towers of temples and musical scales was the same.

Keldan laughed along with her. "I had thought the lad hopeless, but now he is well on his way to becoming one of the greatest Master Bards in Lamia. If I made a bard out of such a hopeless case as that, then surely I can make a passable bardic-mage out of you.

"Since you don't fully grasp the concepts I've explained, I'll demonstrate. Listen closely to the tones of the notes. I'll sing them first, correctly, then once incorrectly. You'll notice a great difference when I shift my focus."

Allison sat and listened in silence as he ran through several different scales, randomly shifting his focus on some of them. As he promised, she *did* hear the difference in the clarity of the tones. Some of the notes sounded flat and utterly lifeless. She could almost see him wince inwardly every time he sang an untrue note. It must have been like an artist being forced to paint over his carefully drawn lines.

"Do you see?" he asked after he completed the last scale.

"I think so," she replied thoughtfully. "Now I understand what you mean by your focus making a difference in the tones. I can plainly hear it, but I'm not altogether sure if I can duplicate it. How do I know on which notes to switch my focal point?"

"It's mostly instinctual," Keldan replied, frowning a little as he struggled to find the right words. "However, I suppose for the untrained, the ear and a little trial and error is all that's needed to detect when you should switch focuses. For instance, when switching from the lower to the middle register, as you near the middle notes, the tone will begin to sound slightly untrue. That's when you should switch focus. In time, you should be able to switch focus unconsciously. As with everything from swordplay to baking, it just takes practice. Now, do you wish to ask any more questions before we try the scales again?"

Allison started to shake her head no, but then one suddenly popped into her head. "Keldan, what happens if I don't ever learn how to sing properly?" she asked anxiously. "Will I not be able to perform any bardic spells at all? I mean, I find it hard to believe that to cast a spell it's either all or nothing. No one can be that perfect every time—can they?"

Keldan laughed. "Dear lady, of *course* one can't always be perfect. Bright Thrones above, not even *Seni* is perfect!" His grin became mischievous. "However, as far as music is concerned, Aren and I damn well come near to perfection. We are bardic-mages after all. But once in a single sun, I've sung a note that was untrue, and it indeed affected my spell, although it didn't cause it to fail entirely. Shall I demonstrate the effects?"

"If you don't mind—" Allison said diffidently.

"I'll create a mage-flame before your eyes. Watch the flame at all times, but at the same time, listen to the spell I'll be singing. If you watch and listen carefully, your question will be thoroughly answered."

Then before she could even blink, Keldan began to sing, a powerful, fast melody in a strange tongue that immediately had the hairs on her arms standing on end with the power it emitted. Every note was as pure as it could possibly be sung. Immediately, a green flame appeared a few feet before her, literally from thin air.

She watched it intently, fascinated to the point where she almost forgot to listen to the song. Then quite unexpectedly, the flame flickered and seemed on the verge of fading away as Keldan sang a note that sounded slightly off-key, even to her untrained ears. Only when Keldan continued to sing in pure tones again did the flame return to its previous majesty.

When he stuttered over a few of the words, the flame flickered violently and vanished for a while in a backdraft of immense heat that brought beads of sweat to her forehead and didn't return until Keldan sang flawlessly again. Despite herself, Allison was impressed with the demonstration.

"I see your point," she said after he banished the flames, "but your magic raises another question."

"Oh?" he said, raising an eyebrow.

"If I can create a mage-flame with the methods Aidric is teaching me," she continued carefully, "then is it really necessary that I learn how to use my bardic-mage abilities as well as you or Aren? No offense, but it just seems an unnecessary waste of both your time and mine to teach me more than just the basics I need to keep me from killing myself or the person next to me. You said it yourself; my bardic magic seems to have been only an afterthought to my regular mage abilities, if something like mage abilities can be called regular!"

"Aidric was correct," Keldan said. "You are indeed a hard maiden to convince." He fixed her with his blue eyes that always seemed to want to devour her, although she found it almost impossible to drop her gaze. "Many years ago, when I was but a lad of sixteen and only half-learned in my bardic magicks, I foolishly enlisted myself in a battalion heading to Oleria, the kingdom to the north, stowed away in a wagon of supplies with no one being the wiser.

"Now, during those days, I was a reckless youth with thoughts of war and personal glory swimming around in my head. I simply couldn't wait until I was fully trained to join Lamia's army. Of course, my brother thought I was missing a few marbles because pretty ladies and wine were not the things uppermost in my mind."

"Now that, I can believe," Allison said with a laugh.

Keldan grinned along with her. "Don't get me wrong, your mentor, Aidric, will be the first to tell you that I enjoy a kiss and a tumble as much as the next man, but my blood hungered for glory, and by Aidius, I was going to have it!" To her surprise, he actually looked a bit sheepish. "Little did I know that I had made the biggest and damn near my last mistake by leaving Lamia's borders before I was ready. A band of raiders had been plaguing a small border town in Oleria, and the king had sent the battalion to disband them. By some twist of fate, the brigands caught wind of us before we could even arrive and set an ambush."

Allison shivered, remembering all too well the ambush she had ridden into unknowingly. *Chaos all around me, horses screaming and the sounds of men dying in their attempt to protect me like I'd stumbled into the very pits of hell...*

Keldan nodded at her expression of horror. "Yes, my first ambush was likely as terrible as the one you recently endured. The brigands surprisingly had a couple of minor mages among them, and although they couldn't wield the greater magicks, the lightning they cast down on us was sufficient enough to cause considerable damage and chaos. I still lay hidden in the supply wagon and didn't know what was happening outside until a bolt of lightning struck the wagon and set it on fire.

"By the time I untangled myself from underneath several sacks of grain and stumbled out of the wagon gagging on smoke, most of our battalion lay in charred heaps all around me, and the rest had been taken prisoner. I was no exception, either. I was instantly bound and gagged and hauled off to a cave like so much baggage. Their plan was to ransom us off to King Diryan, and if the king didn't comply to their demands, then they had other uses for us for their entertainment which would *not*, to say the least, have been very entertaining for us.

"Had I been fully trained, perhaps I wouldn't have panicked back in the wagon and had been able to put out the flames and overpower the brigands with something as simple as a wall of music. I would have obtained the glory I had run off to seek and gone home a hero. Instead, I lay in the blackness of a cave, cold and frightened to the point of tears. However, the thought of being tortured to death knocked some sense into me, and I knew that I, alone, had the ability to rescue us from that unpleasant situation.

"Although gagged and obviously unable to sing a spell, I still had the means to hum even though a spell is considerably weaker than it would be if I had sung or played an instrument. I managed to put our jailers to sleep and free my fellow men and myself from our bonds. They were so relieved at being rescued that they didn't think to wonder why I was there until we reached the palace again. By then, not even my elders had been able to be too cross with me for running off. At least I found the glory I sought! However, my point is that had I been an adept-mage rather than a bardic-mage, I would've been limited to mind magic since my hands were bound and in all probability would have died horribly in that cave."

"So there really *was* a point in that story somewhere!" Allison teased and then laughed at his bewildered expression. "You could've just told me that I would need my bardic-mage abilities if one day I found myself bound and gagged and unable to use my hands for a spell, but instead you switched into story-telling mode. You Lamians are all the same. You guys have a love for telling stories. Aidric goes off on one at least once a sand-mark!"

For once, as long as she'd known him, the bardic-mage was at a loss for words. Keldan just stared at her with a befuddled expression for a long moment before he shook his head with a laugh.

"I stand rebuked," Keldan said and then added with a sheepish grin, "In fact, I've been forbidden to tell *that* particular tale unless the situation warrants it, so you know I couldn't resist!" Then he tilted his head to the side and remarked, "Aidric was correct on one other matter. There's more to you than just a beautiful face and unique hair."

"So I've been told," Allison said dryly.

"In fact," he continued as if he had not heard her, "you are one of the most fascinating women I've ever had the pleasure of knowing, and yet, you puzzle me, milady. My charms don't affect you as they do other maidens."

And the player returns...

"I puzzle you? Why? Because I don't blush and giggle like all the other ladies at court when you pay me a compliment? That's not my style. I'm more likely to think you're up to something no good."

He raised an eyebrow ever so slightly. "So I gathered, or perhaps I'm getting too old for this sort of thing."

"Old?" Allison echoed with genuine surprise. "You couldn't possibly be more than Aidric's age!"

Keldan snorted. "Aidric's age? I wish! Were that I was twenty-three again then perhaps my bones wouldn't ache so! Milady, I have lived for thirty-five summers and was bedding girls when Aidric and you were still in swaddling clothes! Although sometimes it seems like three times that—especially when I'm given some ruffian as a student who seems to exist only to make my life miserable! Truly Allison, I'm flattered that you think me so young. Although—"

He eyed her with eyes that were a touch wistful and full of regret and—she blinked and looked at him more closely—was he pouting? "Were your heart not given to another, I would most certainly take that flattery a step farther and try my hand at courting you."

That remark certainly caught her off guard. He

couldn't have surprised her more if he would've stripped naked and insisted that they dance the Tango.

"What do you know about my heart?" Allison asked cautiously, almost indifferently.

God, does everybody *in the whole damn kingdom know* except *Aidric?*

To her further agitation, her question only seemed to amuse him. "You can try to play innocent with me, milady, but I have enough experience with women that I know when they are trying to deny that a true situation exists. My father used to always say 'when looking for a whole treasure trove of secrets, always look behind a woman's indifference.' My dear lady, I'm well aware of your affection for Aidric, and unless I miss my guess, his affection for you."

His expression then became exasperated and he added dryly, "Although it seems you two are the only ones who are not. I understand Aidric's caution and uncertainty of the situation, but you—why don't you simply go to his bed?"

Well, nobody ever said that Keldan wasn't blunt, Allison thought uncomfortably, feeling the blood rushing to her cheeks, *but dammit! I wish he wouldn't be so blunt with me!*

"I-I don't make a habit of jumping into people's beds on just a whim!" she told him darkly, suddenly more irritated than embarrassed with the situation. To her chagrin, she also found that her irritation caused her tongue to flow freely. "Besides, Aidric hasn't once hinted to me that he's interested in starting that kind of relationship with me," she continued, her voice rising with every word. "He treats me like a student and friend, nothing more, and even if he did come on to me, I *still* wouldn't jump into his bed at the first crook of his finger!"

Keldan stared at her as though she had suddenly grown another head, and for the second time that day, was at a loss for words. She could've hit him over the head with a club, and still, she doubted that he would look as stunned as he did now. A deep, dragging silence suddenly filled the room, and that allowed her to cool down and begin to feel the first tinges of embarrassment for her little outburst.

"Keldan," Allison ventured hesitantly, "I—I'm sorry—I—oh hell! I didn't mean to start ranting like a madwoman. I guess—I guess I'm just a little touchy on the subject, especially these past few days ever since Raya told me that rumors have been circulating around the court that Aidric and I are already sleeping together. Everyone here seems to find the idea of mentors and their students sleeping together normal, but I don't."

He nodded, his face relaxing visibly from distress. "No Allison, *I* am sorry. My only excuse is that I easily forget that you weren't born into this world, and what seems normal and acceptable to us may not be so to you. We'll forget I even mentioned it, yes?"

Allison nodded vigorously, only too happy to change the subject. "Maybe we should quit yapping and get back to my music lessons. God only knows how we got off the subject in the first place, especially to a subject like *that*. Besides," she said, glancing at the small sandclock on the mantle, "even if you have nothing else to do today, *I* have mage lessons in a sandmark."

He grinned mischievously. "That you do, and we both know how much you're looking forward to those lessons no matter how much you say you detest them." When she glared at him, he merely widened his eyes and said innocently, "Shall we begin with the minor scale?"

CHAPTER TWENTY-TWO

*S*omething's *wrong*, Soren thought anxiously as he knelt with his fellow Domni before the high alter in morning prayer. He had been experiencing overwhelming feelings of uneasiness ever since he had awakened that morning, and since he had neither Foresight nor Empathy, at first he had ignored it, thinking that it was just nerves since today his father was sending a group of Domni on an important mission to the mountain palace of Sarim. King Calais's teenage son had enlisted the help of several mages to overthrow his father. Apparently, he had grown impatient and had decided that his father had ruled long enough.

Normally, the Temple didn't entangle itself with political matters unless any divine laws were broken, but since the Domnae ambassador was murdered in

Prince Derwyn's first attempt to usurp the throne, blasphemy had been committed directly against Seni. The prince now faced the full wrath and judgment of the Temple.

Nevertheless, his feelings of unease continued to grow throughout the morning, and now it wasn't so much a feeling of unease but a feeling of *wrongness*. Soren raised his head ever so slightly, careful not to draw any attention to himself, and scanned the many bowed heads all around him. The Domni appeared as passive as ever, and even those whom he knew had either Empathy or Foresight seemed at peace, distress the farthest things from their minds.

Frowning, Soren attempted to return to his prayers, but he just couldn't seem to concentrate on much of anything except the feeling of wrongness that was like an itch in the middle of his back that he couldn't quite reach. Finally, with a completely mental sigh of exasperation, he decided that he couldn't ignore his unease any longer. He needed to go try to find the source of it, even if it took him all day and his father learned that he had skipped out of prayers without permission. Seni would understand. His prayers could wait.

Soren carefully drew energy from the Temple's Mage-field, shielding it tightly in order to prevent the others from sensing it, a feat in which only three other

Domni could match. Then, so softly that his neighbors could not possibly make out the words if they even heard them at all, Soren whispered the incantation that shaped the spell of invisibility. Next, with a slow, careful sweep of his arms, he cast the finished spell over himself, praying that everyone around him would be so fervently lost in their prayers to notice any movement from him.

Unfortunately, luck was not with him that day. Several men glanced curiously over in his direction. Biting his tongue against a curse, Soren quickly seized their minds before he could stop to think about the seriousness of what he was doing, an action that could see him swinging from a hangman's noose on the morrow if discovered.

"You saw nothing," Soren quickly whispered into their minds. *"You heard a sound, but when you turned your head, all was as it should be."*

When he released their minds, the Domni resumed their prayers as if nothing was amiss. Relief flowed through him that his planted suggestion had been successful. He said a silent prayer of thanks to Seni that today he was positioned on the outer right-hand corner of the last row of Domni as he carefully rose from his knees without so much as a whisper of sound, wincing at the stiffness of his legs.

He exited the chamber without further incident,

and breathing a sigh of relief, Soren hurried down the endless spans of corridors towards the Ans-domnae's chambers, unsure of his final destination, but somehow sensing that he was heading in the right direction. His feelings of wrongness strengthened to the point where they were almost painful as he neared his father's chambers.

Something's wrong with Father, he thought with rising alarm as he quickened his pace. *I'm certain of it! No wonder only I sensed that something was amiss! It's as they say. Blood calls to blood, and my blood is telling me that Father is in danger!*

In his haste to reach his father, Soren didn't hear the echo of approaching footsteps as he raced blindly around a corner—and right smack into a Seninae. The Seninae, a young man whom Soren didn't know, was too surprised to do more than grunt from the impact. Soren had still been cloaked behind the spell of invisibility, so he could very well imagine the man's shock at turning the corner and suddenly being bowled over by what seemed to be the very air, only to have a Domnae appear before his eyes.

"What—" was the only thing the Seninae managed to choke out before Soren seized his mind in a panic before he realized he was going to do it.

The man's eyes glazed over and stared out at

nothing. Soren quickly erased any memory of the encounter from his mind and sent him on his way. The small spell he placed on the man's mind would lift when he turned the next corner, and he would believe that he had just been woolgathering when he realized that he didn't remember walking down the previous corridor, if he even thought of it at all.

Soren pushed the guilt he felt to the back of his mind, promising himself to do heavy penance for his deeds after he checked on his father. Since running into the Seninae shattered the spell over him, he quickly recast it before someone else came wandering down the hall and spotted him. He didn't think he could handle tampering with someone's mind a second time. The thought of doing it again made him feel nauseous.

When he reached the door to his father's chamber, before he could even reach over to grasp the door's brass handle, the sense of danger almost overwhelmed him, causing his knees to suddenly give out on him so that he slipped bonelessly to the marble floor.

Shaken, it took Soren several moments to get ahold of himself before he felt confident enough to send a Probe of Inquiry into the room, using every bit of skill he possessed to keep it shielded from detection. His probe immediately detected the presence of two people in his father's office, but when he tried to identify them, his probe suddenly ran up against a powerful shield on both their minds.

Soren could feel his heart suddenly start to race. *All right, so they have strong shields on their minds. There's nothing abnormal about that,* he rationalized.

Yet, shouldn't his probe have been able to identify them, a little suspicious voice whispered in the back of his mind. Soren swallowed against the fear that began to clench at his throat. He had to keep his wits about him.

Once again, Soren tried to identify the two people. He knew that one of them had to be his father. He could sense at least that much without the aid of his mind magic, but he might as well have been trying to probe a wall for all his probe could read either one. He immediately abandoned that approach.

Cautiously he rose to his feet and tried the latch of the door. As he suspected, it was locked. Soren bit down on a scream of frustration. He knew that something was wrong, dammit, but he couldn't very well go to his superiors without some proof other than a feeling that some wrong-doings were occurring. Without the ability of Empathy, they would just as likely laugh at him as dismiss it out of hand.

He toyed with the idea of trying to break through one of those shields, but immediately dismissed it as something only a fool would attempt. His mage abilities were not very strong.

I can't just stand here and do nothing! he thought in frustration and sent his mind-probe out again. If he couldn't penetrate the shields, at least he could examine them thoroughly.

What he discovered made his blood instantly turn cold. The shield around the Ans-domnae's mind was not his own, and among the Domni that could only mean one thing—treachery. Soren yanked back his probe with the speed of someone who discovered he had unknowingly stuck his hand into a nest of poisonous vipers and took a couple of involuntary steps away from the door.

I must bring help! Soren thought wildly as he started to race down the corridor.

However, before he could even run halfway down the hall, a blast of pure energy struck him from behind, sending him crashing to the floor before he could even yelp. His body shuddered violently with the backlash of energy released when his bodily shields shattered. He lay in a crumbled heap, too stunned to do anything other than gasp after the breath that had been brutally wrenched from his lungs.

Through eyes blurred by tears of pain, Soren saw the silhouette of a man stalking towards him like one of the great cats advancing towards its downed prey, wearing the gray robes of a Domnae.

"Fool! You thought you could hide your mind-touch from *me*!" a vaguely familiar voice sneered. "You made a grave mistake, boy. A pity that you'll never have the chance to make another."

Soren tried to lunge at the traitor, but his limbs refused to obey him. Only then did he realize that a paralysis spell had been cast over him. Strangely, that realization brought on no fear. He glared up defiantly at the advancing Domnae, blind hatred blazing in his eyes. Only when the man stepped into the bright illumination of one of the lanterns on the wall did Soren get his first good look at the Domnae. His eyes widened in recognition, and a powerful hatred he didn't know he was capable of raged through his entire being.

"You!" he managed to snarl before another burst of power from the Domnae's outstretched hand sent him into an oblivion through a wall of agony and hatred, his last thought a plea to Seni for vengeance.

***

A timid knock at the door broke through Allison's troubled thoughts as she lay sprawled on one of the couches in the sitting room, the usual spellbook opened in her lap. She turned her head towards the door and then frowned.

Who could that be at this hour? she thought worriedly as she sprang up from the couch to answer the door. *I thought only Aidric, I, and the Council were the only ones crazy enough to be up so late!*

Of course, in her case she had been waiting up for Aidric to return from his latest, but not uncommon, late-night Council meeting. Diryan and the Lord Commander had been contemplating for days now on whether or not to send a bevy of both magical and non-magical troops to the Na'aran-Mihran border. Reports from some of Diryan's spies within Mihr had stated that Roderick had been building up his army and gradually moving it towards the border in battalions as small as fifty men. They now stood camped to both the east and west of the Telek River with no signs that they planned to invade Na'ar anytime within the next few days.

Every Foreseer in Lamia, including Allison, had been consulted on the matter, yet all insisted that there would be no Mihran invasion into Na'ar in the near future. Only Penrith, the Providencen envoy, had seen a step farther, and insisted that there was a high probability that the gathering troops could merely be a distraction to trick King Diryan into sending his full forces to Na'ar's aid while he centered on his real target, which was more than likely to be the Kemosian palace. Roderick did, after all, have the aid of Mordant, who had the ability to open a portal large enough to move a great portion of Roderick's troops at a time.

However, the possibility of an attack on Na'ar could not be outright dismissed either, so now they were debating on whether or not to break the stalemate and declare open war on Mihr at first light tomorrow in order to send troops storming across the Mihran border before giving Roderick the chance to carry out his plans. If King Diryan declared war, then tonight would be the last time she would see Aidric for a long time, if ever again. It had been torture having to sit here alone in the suite, anxiously waiting for Aidric to return.

Allison opened the door with a cold lump in the pit of her stomach, afraid that whoever stood at the door was a messenger sent by Aidric to inform her that war had been declared and he was leaving for the Mihran border tonight. Her stomach clenched even tighter when she saw that her unexpected visitor was one of the king's pages.

Dear God, it can't be! she thought with horror as she stared mutely down at the expressionless adolescent.

"A message for you, Milady Golden Mage," the boy announced tonelessly, his face passive, but his eyes betraying his wariness as he handed her a scroll sealed with an unfamiliar stamp.

Numbly, Allison took the scroll from him and nodded her thanks, not trusting herself to speak without instantly breaking down in anguish. She slowly shut the door once the boy bowed and hurried away and forced herself to walk to the couch and sit before she read the scroll. With hands that shook, she broke the seal and braced herself for the words she had been dreading all night.

She had been prepared for the very worst, the news that Aidric was indeed leaving that very night to go off to war, but nothing prepared her for the news the scroll really had to report. Allison suddenly felt as though she had been slammed in the face with a sledgehammer. The letter slowly fell from her trembling hands and onto the floor with barely a sound.

"Oh God, *no!*" she whispered hoarsely. "He can't be! He *can't!* Not Soren! Not—"

Allison stared down at the coiled parchment that had fallen to the floor, her mind numb as the sentence that had suddenly turned her world upside down began running through her mind as though on continuous repeat.

"...*instructed to inform you by order of will that Domnae Soren A'ban, Brother in Divinity, was found slain...*"

Only then did her numbed mind awaken, and the wail of anguish that emerged from her lips was almost unrecognizable as human. She quickly progressed into heart-wrenching sobs that shook her entire frame, her mind focused on only one agonized thought.

I failed him. Oh God, I promised him—I promised! Now he's dead—and—and I failed him—

Allison didn't remember when she had reached for the glass of wine she had been casually sipping for her nerves only a few moments earlier, but suddenly it was in her hand, then gone in one gulp. She reached for the bottle on the end table, desperate to drown out the pain. Before she knew it, she was staring at an empty bottle in her hands, and she knew it was not enough, not enough to ease the anguish in her heart.

CHAPTER TWENTY-THREE

S ometime later—sand-marks, days, years—through a drunken haze of pain as Allison lay in a twisted heap in the center of the sitting room surrounded by four empty wine bottles, the sound of the front door opening and closing barely registered to her numbed mind. She heard someone gasp, then pounding footsteps that seemed to come from a thousand miles away. The empty bottle she clutched like a lifeline was gently pried from her left hand, followed by the scroll she fisted in her right.

Then a pair of firm arms suddenly enveloped her, and her mind didn't seem so clouded anymore. Her eyes abruptly focused, and Allison found she was staring into a pair of pale-violet eyes, glistening as if with unshed tears. Then she remembered—the messenger, the news of Soren's death, reaching for the wine bottle—and for the second time that night, lost control of herself completely. However, this time she had the comfort of a shoulder to cry on, and it made all the difference.

Sometime later, when the last of her sobs faded away and she lay exhausted in Aidric's arms, Allison lifted a head that felt as if an elephant had been dancing on it all night and looked into his surprisingly tear-stained face. Her head still swam with drunkenness, but she was still coherent enough to understand what he had done for her, and to remember the source of her pain.

"I p-promised him t-that I would g-go back to t-truthfully swear my oaths to S-Seni to him," she whispered brokenly. "I promised h-him, and now he's d-dead—and I failed him! I failed him—like I failed *her!*"

And although she had thought that she could cry no more, the flood of tears returned with that last anguished cry. Aidric said nothing, perhaps sensing that she didn't want to be comforted by words. He merely held her tightly against the warmth of his body, his hands stroking her back gently, and offered her the only thing that could possibly comfort her, his presence. As far as Allison was concerned, it was enough.

By the time her sobs died down, she was so exhausted that she clung to consciousness by only the barest of threads. She didn't remember when Aidric had risen and carried her to her room, only that she was now suddenly surrounded by a different kind of warmth and softness and a blanket was being tucked snugly all around her body.

Aidric's hand brushed a lock of sweat-dampened hair from her forehead, more a caress than a simple gesture. Then warmth began to flow within her body that soothed the ache in her head and warmed the coldness of grief and guilt in her heart.

It seemed as she drifted towards the mercy of a healer-induced sleep that Allison felt warm lips cover her mouth gently for one sweet moment, but then again, maybe she was already dreaming.

***

With a choked sigh, Aidric collapsed into the tall, leather chair behind his desk and immediately slumped over onto the wooden surface before him with his face buried in his hands. Only now did he feel free to release the floodgates on the strong torrent of tears he had kept at bay as best he could while he had seen to Allison's needs, not so much tears for the young Domnae he had known long ago as a novice, but for the woman whose soul, even in sleep, was lost in guilt and grief. There was still a considerable amount of sorrow there for Soren, but nothing that warranted the gut-wrenching sobs that now rocked his body.

Such pain—and guilt—even now it overwhelms my emotions to the brink of chaos! Seni help me, I don't understand why!

A moment later, he lifted his head up and attempted to regain control of himself—no small feat considering the emotional residue that Allison's anguish had left behind in the sitting room for his Empathy to pick up, even as tightly shielded as he was. He knew that he needed to deal with those impressions as soon as possible unless he wanted everyone who stepped through his front door to suddenly drop to their knees weeping, but right now, that was the least of his problems.

"Aidius," he groaned, hastily rubbing his stinging eyes, wistfully wishing that he had the ability to self-heal the knife-stabbing ache in his head and bone-deep weariness. "This couldn't have happened at a worse time."

A Domnae had not been murdered in the Temple's own city in well over a thousand years. He didn't believe for even a moment that the ending of that good fortune was just a tragic coincidence.

Though desperately longing for the respite of falling into his bed for his much needed and long overdue sleep, Aidric knew his bed would continue to collect dust for a bit longer. He paced the length of his study, his mind whirling with speculations and questions.

He considered the disturbing contents of the letter he had snatched from Allison's hand while she had lain in a drunken heap on his floor. It hadn't said much, just the vaguest of details of the incident, mainly that Domnae Soren had been slain and that he had wished that Allison be notified should he meet such a premature end.

Surprisingly, Aidric had felt no jealousy that Soren had left behind the type of instructions that were normally reserved for intimate acquaintances such as family, friends, or lovers after only knowing her for a few days. Maybe it was because he knew firsthand the strong effects Allison had on people. She had certainly turned *his* brain to mush the first time she had fixed those amazing green eyes on him.

Such innocence that had no business in the eyes of a woman her age...

Hastily, he shoved that thought away, knowing that he didn't dare allow his mind to go wandering down that particular, well-trampled path. He simply had too much to concern himself with at the moment to allow himself that distraction, pleasant as it was.

Aidric was also not at all surprised that the letter had been so vague. Allison was, after all, an *Outsider* and a *woman* to boot. Being a strictly all-male divine order with no exceptions, they would be more likely to confide information to Roderick than to a woman, simply because Roderick was male.

However, they seemed to have no problems whatsoever with women in the military, be it magical or non-magical, or in the Temple guard. Aidric had given up trying to understand the reasoning of the Brothers in Divinity at an early age, and their views on a woman's role in religion had always seemed annoyingly short-sighted of them. Yet, never more so than at that moment.

He needed more information than what the letter provided if he ever hoped to determine if his suspicions held any weight, or if they were merely the paranoia of a wearied mind that had just returned from a very disturbing Council session centered on talks of war to find the woman he secretly loved in a drunken heap in the middle of his floor. Domnae Soren was, after all, a friend of Allison's, and from the small threads of court gossip he had picked up during the days following Allison's return from the Temple, that friendship was widely known. Several reliable sources to the gossip scene had reported seeing them and Raya laughing together with the casual air of long-time friends as they had headed into the palace on the day of Allison's return from the Temple.

With the threat of the known, but as of yet still

unidentified, spy Roderick had lurking in the shadows of the palace hanging over his head like a wasp at his back ready to plant its stinger in him at any given moment, Aidric felt that he should leave nothing to chance, no matter how farfetched it might seem at the time.

Furthermore, it could not have escaped Roderick's attention just how easily Allison could be unsettled. Her shyness had certainly not escaped anyone's notice, and unfortunately, the knowledge of her occasional panic attacks had somehow reached the eagerly stretched ears of the gossip circles. Only Seni knew how that had happened, though Aidric had his suspicions. It was not unheard of for a palace guard to gossip with the best of them.

The murder of a friend would certainly leave her unsettled, and perhaps be the blow that shattered her delicate hold on her mental stability. Judging from the wretched condition he had found her in tonight, Allison had come damned close to the edge—*too* damned close for his peace of mind.

By now, everyone pretty much assumed that the question of her destiny would affect both Lamia and Mihr, and the Providencen priests agreed. ...*when you can get a straight answer out of them at least*, Aidric thought darkly.

Perhaps Roderick thought that if she was to be

reduced to an emotional wreck, then she couldn't possibly be a threat to Mihr and as a result, couldn't possibly be the savior of Lamia, inadvertently causing the downfall instead.

Of course, this was all merely speculation—at least until he could get a hold of certain facts.

Aidric abruptly stopped pacing and glanced over at the large sandclock that was built into the wall. *Hmm—it's two sand-marks before the first morning mark. Seninae Deman no doubt is dreaming sweet visions of pious harmony, and Seninae Vallois is still under sick-watch with heat-flu, poor soul. That leaves Seninae Jael, and unless someone managed to sneak up behind him and rap him on the head simply to get him to his bed at a decent sand-mark for once— which isn't damned bloody likely—he should still be on his knees praying for our hopeless souls. News, and more importantly, the details of a Domnae's murder, should have reached him by now. Thank Seni for small favors.*

Aidric quietly looked in on Allison to make sure she had not broken the sleep spell he had cast over her before hurrying over to the palace's southwestern wing that housed both the worshipping temple and the Senini's quarters. The palace's silent, darkened halls did nothing for his dire mood, and the steady echo of his boots on the marble floors sounded like a herd of stampeding horses crashing through the nighttime silence.

As he predicted, the old priest was indeed awake. His soft knock was immediately answered with a muffled call of invitation from within the room. Despite the great age shown by unruly white hair that had once been the color of the darkest of nights, cut in the typical short style of all the Senini, and a face with more wrinkles than Aidric's sheets on a sleepless night, the wizened Seninae that had risen from his knees from behind his prayer nook to face him showed only a vitality that Aidric would have sworn had divine origins—especially at this unholy sand-mark.

Aidric bowed his head respectfully and waited silently for the ritual acknowledgment.

"Seni's grace to you, child," Seninae Jael said, spreading his hands out in welcome. "My ears and heart, as always, are open to your woes. Tell me, Mage-general, what brings you to my door at this unlikely sand-mark?"

"Tonight I learned that a Domnae was found slain in the Temple City," Aidric replied, getting right to the point, "a young Domnae named Soren A'ban—who incidentally happens to be the son of the Ans-domnae."

Seninae Jael's eyes widened slightly in surprise, but other than that, his expression remained as serene as ever. "Indeed," he said evenly. "I did not think that any outside the Brothers in Divinity knew of this tragedy." He paused, his dark eyes boring into Aidric's as if searching for something hidden. "Perhaps we should sit?"

He gestured towards the two wooden chairs facing each other against the wall that were used during confessions. Aidric nodded, glad to relieve his aching feet. Only now was he beginning to feel the effects of his earlier pacing.

Aidric suppressed a shudder at the sense of *déjà vu* that washed over him as he took the seat he had occupied so many times in the past under equally unpleasant situations, the most prominent in his mind was the horrible few quarter-moons after Alina's betrayal when he had wished nothing more than to die.

"Now," Seninae Jael said once he had settled himself into his chair with a grace Aidric envied, "do enlighten me on how it is you have come by this information and why it has captured your interest enough to seek me out long after you should have sought your bed."

"My ward, Allison, received a letter this night informing her of the death, apparently at the instructions of the deceased," Aidric explained. "Domnae Soren was one of four mages sent here to escort her to the Temple at the High Priest's orders a little over a moon ago, and it seems they developed a friendship. The letter, however, was understandably vague in explanation, and as you may have already guessed, I have come here tonight to seek more information."

Jael's eyes narrowed. "What interest have you in this matter?" he asked warily.

Aidric had expected him to ask that question. Senini, like their Providencen brothers, guarded their secrets as devoutly as a mother guarded her children.

"A suspicion, mostly, my lord," Aidric admitted. "Domnae Soren was a friend to one who has many powerful enemies, and unless I have more information on the circumstances surrounding the murder, I cannot possibly know if my suspicions have any merit."

"Hmm," was all Seninae Jael said for a long moment, staring at Aidric as though weighing his soul in judgment. Aidric could only hold his gaze and endure in silence.

"Very well," Jael said finally an eternity later, "I shall go against my better judgment and tell you all you desire, seeing as how you are not inclined to indulge in gossip as many others here feel so thus inclined to do. I would ask that you reveal none of this to anyone other than your ward, and only if the information proves to be vital to the safety of Lamia or to your king. Agreed?"

"Yes," Aidric replied simply, struggling to keep

the eagerness out of his voice.

"The body of Domnae Soren was found in an alleyway behind a merchant's shop a quarter-moon ago by the owner," Jael began after a moment's silence. "He was dressed in his uniform, and his medallion and other ceremonial jewelry were still on his person, thus ruling out a simple mugging, of course. His mind had been totally incinerated by a mage-bolt, yet when one of the Domni probed him, he could not detect the slightest hint of a magical signature. Two other bodies were found along with his, and from the evidence, apparently Domnae Soren had been able to stave off their attack before he, himself, was overwhelmed. Their bodies reeked of Domnae Soren's magic. However, their identities are still unknown, although they have the look of Lephans.

"What we do not understand is why Domnae Soren was outside the Temple in the first place. He had not been assigned duties within the city that day. In fact, many Domni insisted that he had been in prayers that morning but then disappeared sometime during the service without notice, which should have been near to impossible."

For a Domnae, I seriously doubt that, my lord, Aidric thought dryly. *You seem to forget that I, too, trained with the Domni novices and often had snuck out of prayers with the most cunning of them! You would be surprised what the combination*

*of a powerful shielder and skilled illusionist could accomplish—
or a little touch of mind tampering for the less scrupulous!*

He suspected that Soren had used similar methods of skipping out of prayers, but there still remained the question of why? He itched to point out such observations to the old Seninae, but he held his peace. He doubted that Seninae Jael would admit to such going-ons in the Temple.

"As you well know, it is no small feat to successfully overpower a Domnae," Jael was saying, breaking into Aidric's reverie, "so it had to have been well planned out. But, the question still remains—for what purpose?"

He sighed, suddenly looking every bit of his rumored one hundred summers. Aidric remained respectfully silent while Jael frowned in contemplation, sensing that Jael had more to say.

It was a few moments before the Seninae spoke again. "Earlier, you hinted that the Golden Mage fits into this tragedy somehow. I cannot see what gain the slaying of a Domnae, even one who had befriended her as you say, the oath-breaking blasphemers hoped to achieve if it was indeed for the motive you have suggested, Mage-general. Tell me your speculations."

For the next half sand-mark, Aidric recounted his suspicions that Roderick may have been the mastermind behind the murder, and the motives of why the

Mihran king could possibly have to chance such a thing as the murder of a Domnae. Roderick had done it before, after all. Jael listened quietly for the most part, interrupting only to ask a question or to argue some point of Aidric's reasoning, but Aidric could tell by the stoniness of the old priest's expression that Jael was beginning to believe that what he speculated could possibly be true.

"Roderick is a kinslayer and oath-breaker of Seni," Aidric concluded after the last of his suspicions had been voiced. "He consorts with mages of the vilest evil that very well could conceal their dark magicks from the light of the Domni. I believe the Temple should be made aware of the possibility that their old enemy may be the culprit behind such a heinous crime. If Roderick is behind the murder and sufficient evidence is found, then all of Seni's lands could breathe a sigh of relief to have the judgment of the Temple brought down on our greatest foe at long last."

Silence fell over both of them at the conclusion of his words, broken only by the slight sound of their steady breathing and the faint flickering of the mage-flame-lit lanterns. Finally, Seninae Jael fixed his eyes bemusedly on Aidric and said, "I shall meditate the rest of the night on all you have said and confer with my brothers at first light. Go now to your rest, child, and remember well that which you have promised. I shall summon you when the time comes."

Knowing that protesting would fall on deaf ears, Aidric nodded stiffly and left the Seninae's rooms no less troubled than when he had arrived. His only consolation was that at least he could still grab a few sandmarks of sleep before he had to sort out Allison. He felt as if he had been doing major spellcasting all day without a moment's respite. He only hoped that his future talk with Allison would be more enlightening on his heart than the talk he had just had with Seninae Jael.

CHAPTER TWENTY-FOUR

A whisper of sound to his right caused Aidric to suddenly awaken out of fevered dreams he could only half remember. For a split-second, he froze, his battle senses fully alert before he realized that he was in his bed and not on the battlefield he had been dreaming about.

He turned his head towards the door and started when he saw Allison standing timidly in the doorway still dressed in her robe, her face drawn with fatigue and her eyes deeply shadowed and haunted. Her hair was still tousled from sleep, as if she had come straight to his room from her bed.

For a moment, Aidric panicked, fearing that he lay exposed in nothing but his underclothing, but then sighed in relief when he remembered that he had been so tired when he finally made it to his bed that he had just fallen into it without bothering to undress.

"I-I didn't mean to wake you," she said softly. "I felt someone touch my mind and thought it was you waking me."

Aidric awkwardly sat up, suppressing an urge to groan when his bones violently protested, and motioned for her to join him. "In a sense, I *did* wake you, but not intentionally," he replied apologetically as Allison hesitantly seated herself on the edge of his bed. "You were in no condition to fall asleep naturally..." She blushed a deep crimson at that. "...so I cast a healing-sleep spell over you that you might rest without bothersome dreams. What you felt was the spell wearing off. At any rate, I'm glad you are here. How do you feel?"

"Better," Allison said slowly, blushing even more with what he suspected was shame. Then she laughed bitterly. "Considering how I behaved last night, I don't think I could have felt any worse—or have sunk any lower."

"While I don't condone what you did to yourself, I *do* understand, Allison," Aidric said gently, wanting to comfort her in his arms but knowing that now was not the right moment. "There was a time in the past when I, myself, did as you did last night. Seni help me, but I understand only too well. I'm certain many a court gossip would be most pleased to tell you the tale of how the Mage-general drunk himself into such a stupor that the healers couldn't wake him for two days."

"*You?*" she asked, her eyes widening a little in disbelief. "B-But why?"

He smiled ruefully. "Yes, me. Despite what many others believe, I *am* as human as the next man, and as for the 'why' of it, that, little cat, is a tale best told some other time. For now, shall we concern ourselves with the exact 'why' behind your little episode last night, hmm?"

Allison cast her eyes down in shame, but she nodded her assent. "I owe that much to you," she mumbled.

Aidric shook his head in exasperation and placed his hand firmly under her chin, raising her head until she was looking directly into his eyes. "No, you don't 'owe' me anything," he stated firmly. "If there's any 'owing' of anything, then it's owed only to yourself."

Allison swallowed, against nervousness or tears, Aidric wasn't sure, and said, "I know you've read the letter. I remember at least that much."

Two tears suddenly crept from beneath her pale lashes and lazily began to make their way down cheeks that were still slightly raw from crying. This time,

Aidric didn't hesitate to take her into his arms to comfort her as she began to cry once again.

She wept softly on his shoulder for a few moments before she was able to speak again. I p-promised him, Aidric," she said shakily. "Just like—like I promised—Katherine. And I let them both down! God help me, I let them both down!"

Ah, so now the heart of this unsurpassable grief is lain bare for me to see.

"You didn't," Aidric assured her quietly, stroking her hair soothingly and feeling a little guilty at the pleasure that simple gesture gave him. "You couldn't possibly have known that Domnae Soren was to meet such an unexpected end. No one could have unless Seni deemed it necessary to gift us with the Foreknowledge of it, and that, he did not. As for your sister, I don't know what it was you promised her, but I suspect that you being brought here to this world so unexpectedly figures into your guilt, somehow. In any case, neither situation was within your control."

"But the promises were still broken, no matter that I had no choice," Allison insisted flatly. "I promised Kat that I would rescue her from her crazy father. I promised Soren that I would swear my oaths to Seni to him. I waited too long, and now it's too late to do either! I'll never see my sister or Soren again!"

Aidric could see that she would not be comforted,

so he decided to change tactics. If Allison refused to be comforted, then perhaps he could shock her out of this dire mood that had swallowed her.

After all, he mused wryly, *it worked for me.*

"That's quite enough of that," he said firmly, pulling away from her for a bit. "I've always thought more of you than this, behaving like one of those frilly court maidens who wail and pity themselves over matters which could not be helped. Wailing about failing Soren is *not* going to bring him back."

Aidric tactfully avoided mentioning her sister just yet, thinking that it would be pushing her just a little too far. After all, he didn't want her to hate him after all this was over. He had to bite back a chuckle at the look of utter astonishment on her face. Seninae Jael had told him he had looked as though he had just been horse-kicked when using a similar shock tactic on him. Allison looked more like he had just announced that she was really his long-lost sister.

Before she could lose her initial surprise and start bellowing in anger as he had, he hastily continued, "If you continue to berate yourself like this, then it will only be a matter of time before that nasty thought becomes an obsession, one that will surely end in disaster!"

"Is that all you care about?" she cried, her eyes beginning to smolder. "What my mental state will mean to your precious Lamia!"

Aidric didn't so much as flinch at the rage that was directed to him, though he certainly wanted to. "To the six hells with Lamia!" he said softly, but with as much heat behind his words as she had put behind hers. "What I'm talking about is you! What such thoughts will do to *you*! You are my ward and not only that. You are my friend, and I'll be damned first to the worst of the six hells before I allow you to destroy yourself as I once nearly destroyed myself!"

Aidric only realized that he had grabbed ahold of both Allison's arms and was gripping them tightly when she let out a little cry of pain.

He immediately released his death grip and stammered, "Allie—little cat—I'm sorry." His body still quivered with the strong emotions he was experiencing.

Allison merely looked at him soberly, not a hint of her earlier anger visible in any of her features, and rubbed her arms where he could still see the red imprints of his fingers. Left unhealed, there would definitely be bruises later. Then she sighed, and to his surprise, reached for his hands that lay limply in his lap and gave them a squeeze before releasing them.

"I understand now," she said softly, "I mean, about what that line of thinking can do to me." Right now, if a swarm of *dyani* had suddenly appeared in the room all around them, Aidric would not have been able to tear his eyes away from hers, even at the cost of his life. "Sometime, you'll tell me all about it." It was not a question.

Aidric nodded, not trusting his voice at that moment. Then wordlessly, he reached over to place both his hands over the impressions his fingers had made into her delicate skin. It hardly took any energy at all to coax the broken blood vessels to heal. She smiled thinly when he removed his hands, and she saw only her normal, pale flesh underneath. Still, neither one of them spoke.

Suddenly, Allison's smile turned wicked, and he followed her eyes as they roamed up over his disgracefully, rumpled clothes until her gaze stopped at his hair. Then, quite unexpectedly, she deliberately reached over and began to finger a strand of his hair, chuckling softly to herself as she did so. Aidric was so taken aback that he couldn't have uttered a word to save his soul.

"I don't think I've ever seen you with so much as more than one hair out of place," she said with amusement. "You're always awake and so put together by the time I manage to drag myself out of bed. Now you look as if someone tried to tie knots into your hair, while someone else was equally determined to get every last strand of hair to stand on end!"

Aidric finally got his mouth to work again after giving her his most fearsome glare. "Be glad that I'm too much of a gentleman, or else I would say the same of your hair—except I think that the knot-tier succeeded in his task!"

She stuck her tongue out at him and started to lash out at him with an equally insulting rebuke, but she got no farther than the first couple of words before they both doubled over with laughter.

"Oh, come now! I'm not all that dreadful-looking am I?" Aidric managed to gasp out between laughs.

Wiping away the tears in her eyes, Allison managed to get herself under control again before she answered, "Hardly." Then she tilted her head to the side and added shyly, "In fact, I think it suits you." There was no mockery in her tone.

However, as Aidric instinctually reached out to touch her face, she jumped up from the bed and bounded out his bedroom door, calling over her shoulder that if she hoped to make her mage lessons in enough time to learn something useful before she had to race off to her music lesson with Aren, then she had better pull herself together for the day.

Aidric could only stare at the door in bewilderment. He couldn't help thinking that once again, a crucial moment had been lost.

CHAPTER TWENTY-FIVE

B rushing a few tendrils of hair annoyingly from her eyes, Allison wearily trudged into the courtyard, wincing as the bright sunlight suddenly assaulted her eyes. She sighed, knowing that she had seen little other than the inside of Aidric's suite, much less direct sunlight, these past few quarter-moons. She figured it was high time that she made some changes.

Lessons, both mage and bardic, continued on as usual day after day without incident. They no longer seemed a heavy chore to be endured but just an everyday part of her life. She could no longer imagine her life without them, and her life before she had arrived in Lamia was swiftly becoming a painful chapter that was lived what felt like a lifetime ago, though the pain of being torn away from Kat was still as fresh as the first day.

Neither could she imagine her life without Aidric playing some part. She still agonized over that dim memory of the night she had drunken herself into a stupor when she had learned of Soren's murder, of Aidric finding her half-conscious on the floor of his sitting room, of his driving some of her drunkenness away in order for them to talk, or rather, for her to talk and he to listen before putting her to bed without a drop of scorn for her actions.

But most of all, she fretted over the dim recollection of his hands soothingly brushing across her forehead in a gesture that had felt so loving and knowing that he had just spared her from having to suffer the consequences of her idiotic behavior in the morning. As she had drifted off into that welcoming oblivion of spelled sleep, Allison especially remembered the feel of his lips on hers and not certain if that part had merely been the dream of a girl whose heart ached with loss or the gesture of a man who truly cared for her beyond friendship.

Aidric had certainly acted as though nothing so intimate had passed between them the next morning when they had talked in his bedroom, and after the humiliation of knowing Aidric had seen her at her all-time lowest, she didn't have the courage to ask him about it. Thus, the relationship between them remained the same—innocent, caring, but nothing beyond the bounds of a deep friendship. Allison supposed that she should be grateful that she had at least that, but convincing the heart that ached terribly for more was all but impossible.

With her Ti'ar language book and one of Aidric's spellbooks tucked underneath her arm, she settled herself in the soft grass beneath the shade of a clump of small trees and bushes that would keep her hidden from interruptions. Today she had been having a hard time keeping her mind on her lessons, and Allison thought that a little fresh air, sunlight, and a change of scenery might help stimulate her concentration. Today was the day that Aidric was going to test the strength of her magical shield-breaking skills, and she wanted to be absolutely sure she had the words of the incantation and their meaning down pat.

Allison lazily leaned up against the small trunk of one of the trees and opened her spellbook. It was the very book that she had first pulled off Aidric's bookshelf the day she had come to Lamia. It had been several quarter-moons after before she had remembered to ask Aidric why the pages were written in a different language than the title on the spine.

Aidric had laughed and explained that the book was a very powerful spellbook that had been penned a couple of centuries before during the silent war with Rathtyen when everyone was seeing Rathen spies in every shadow. He had said that the mages of that time had thought the best place to hide their precious spellbooks was in plain sight, thus they came up with the idea of hiding the spellbooks under the guise of peasant folklore. Allison had found the whole idea silly. If she were a spy, the first thing she would do was paw through every book she could find, regardless of the title.

She absently leafed through her spellbook until she found the correct spell, her mind still on Aidric. However, before she could even begin to study the ancient words, she sensed the presence of someone drawing near.

Before she could look up, a deep, melodic voice she did not recognize said behind her, "Milady Allison, may I have the pleasure of speaking with you?"

She glanced over her shoulder at her unexpected visitor and then groaned inwardly when she recognized the handsome, but arrogant bard, Patrym. Seeing no way out of it without being rude, she forced herself to smile politely and gestured for him to take a seat next to her.

He wasted no time in seating himself a mere few inches to her right with a grace she grudgingly envied.

He grimaced a little as he did so, probably, she reasoned, for having to sit on the bare ground and soiling his rather expensive looking *sholkie* breeches. From what she had heard of his reputation, he most certainly seemed the type.

"I noticed you staring at me at my last recital, and I've been curious to know why you didn't come to speak with me?" he announced arrogantly.

The tone in his voice made it sound as if she had been practically drooling over him, which instantly pissed her off. Allison decided to give as good as she got. If he wanted to play the court fop, then she most certainly could play the typical court maiden—with a slight adjustment.

"Staring?" she asked sweetly, widening her eyes slightly. "Oh, I must apologize then if it appeared as if I was doing so. I was merely trying to figure out where I had seen you before. Then I remembered that Aidric had pointed you out to me. He said you were one of the court's finest bards."

Well, that much was true, but she had to practically swallow her tongue to keep from laughing when she remembered what else Aidric had said about him!

"Indeed?" Patrym replied, raising an eyebrow in surprise. "What else did the Mage-general have to say about me?"

"Oh, nothing much," Allison lied. "Aidric isn't

one to gossip. In any case, I'm sorry if you thought it rude of me not to have come over to at least say hello, but I thought *you* were coming over to *us*. At least it appeared as if you were, but I guess I was mistaken."

For a split-second, Patrym appeared a little ruffled, but he recovered so quickly that had she not been paying such close attention to his changing expressions, she would have missed it.

"That had been my plan, milady," he replied smoothly, "but I was detained by a swarm of admirers. As any bard will readily tell you, once you are surrounded, it's virtually impossible to disentangle yourself from them!"

I'll bet, Allison thought wryly but schooled her face to one of indifference. Maybe if she appeared bored, then he would give her up as a hopeless cause and leave her to her studies. If he kept up this intolerable haughtiness much longer, then she knew that she would end up insulting him, and something told her that with this bard, it would not be such a good idea.

"Really?" she said noncommittally, adjusting her book on her lap and hoping he would take the hint.

Allison dared not tell him openly to go away. She had heard enough gossip from the ladies at court to know that the more you told Patrym to take a hike, the more insistent he was to win your attentions. Apparently, he believed that all women were simply playing hard to get. He didn't understand the notion that someone, heaven forbid, was not attracted to him.

Genia, one of Queen Ileanna's ladies-in-waiting, had confided in her that a couple of women had gone to his bed just so he would stop pestering them. Word was that if a woman wasn't overly exceptional in the bedroom, then he would quickly lose interest in her, and these women made sure that they were not. However, for Allison, that simply was *not* an option!

True to his reputation, Patrym didn't appear to notice her indifference in the slightest. In fact, he seemed to be doing his best to inch his way into her personal space. Any closer and he would be practically sitting in her lap. As he did, he finally noticed the spell-book in her lap and wrinkled his nose at it in obvious distaste.

"Mage-craft," he said as though he had suddenly tasted something bitter. "Such a tiresome discipline to learn and so time-consuming since you are seldom at court or even here in the courtyard. Wouldn't you rather be doing something other than learning those dreadful spells?"

Like be with you? I would rather spend a moon locked up in the same room as Aren or practice my magic to exhaustion than sit through court or in your company! Allison thought and had to bite her tongue to prevent herself from telling him just that!

Instead, she said aloud, "I *am* the *Golden Mage*, after all. I would think that you would be praying to Seni that I learn the use of my powers like everyone else. There's still the *prophecy* to consider. You don't want to wake up one day and find Lamia in ruins do you?"

There! Maybe that'll scare him off, she thought smugly, though the expression on her face was deadly serious.

Patrym paled, and was it her imagination or did he inch a little away from her? He smiled weakly and replied, "Of course not—but a little fun on the side couldn't hurt either. Your beauty shouldn't be wasted buried behind a spellbook or in war." Then inexplicably, he regained all of his earlier arrogance. "Why not come to my suite tonight, and we can start becoming better acquainted with each other? By the time morning rolls along, I do believe we shall know each other *very* well, indeed…"

Allison nearly choked at his audacity. It took all of her control to prevent herself from knocking that arrogant grin from his face—along with a few teeth.

"Do you?" she said coolly. "Well, I'm sorry to disappoint you, but I already have a prior engagement tonight."

To her further annoyance, Patrym's smile only got larger and more predatory, like a shark scenting blood in the water. "Oh, I know all about your nightly liaisons with the Mage-general. Who in Lamia has not heard of them? It's of no matter to me. Aidric was always greedy with his women, and I don't see his lifering on your finger yet! Even then I don't think I would deny myself your charms!"

Allison was so shocked at that level of matter-of-fact bluntness that she could only stare at him with open disgust, struggling to find a voice that had suddenly deserted her. Patrym, however, took advantage of her momentary astonishment to grab her arms, jerk her to him, and to crush his lips firmly against her own. For a couple of seconds, Allison was too stunned to react, and Patrym apparently took her lack of response as a good sign because he immediately tried to deepen the kiss, trying to force his tongue between her closed lips.

That suddenly got her stunned mind working again, and what happened next was something born out of sheer panic. Allison felt energy inadvertently enter and race through every channel within her body a split-second before Patrym shrieked with pain and flung her violently away from him.

Allison landed flat on her back, so she didn't immediately understand what it was she had done to him. Feeling sick, she was afraid to look, afraid that she had accidentally killed him, no matter that he had forced himself on her and she had done so in self-defense.

However, to her immense relief, she could still

hear Patrym howling in pain, so she knew that at least he was still alive. She quickly scrambled onto her feet and saw the bard dancing around before her, cradling his hands against his chest and continuing to screech in true agony at the top of his lungs. Only then did the nauseating smell of burnt flesh reach her nose, and she knew what it was she had done.

Somehow, in her panic, she had lashed out at the hands that imprisoned her arms with energy from the Mage-field and seared them. The sleeves of her arms, when she looked down at them in a kind of shock, were completely unmarked.

Feeling the bile rise to her throat, Allison grabbed her books, turned on her heel with a choked cry, and fled the horror of what she had just done, the courtyard conspicuously empty of a single soul.

***

Unconcerned with what his neighbors might think, Aidric slammed his front door shut so violently that it was a wonder that he didn't knock it off its hinges. He knew no one would dare disturb him if they even suspected that he was having a fit of temper. Not even Selwyn was a brave enough soul to venture near him when he was in a rage.

His head fell against the door as he squeezed his

eyes shut in perhaps some childish hope that if he shut them, then what he had just witnessed in the courtyard would magically cease to be true when he opened them again.

Aidric pounded his right fist on the door. *Dammit! Why did I have to see that? And why in the six hells did it have to be* him? Angry tears began to fall, but in his hurt, he hardly noticed the sudden moisture running down his face.

He had been returning to his suite from the latest Circle meeting, and as he had cut through the courtyard, he had suddenly heard voices behind one of the hedges, voices that had been all too familiar. Silently, he had stepped up to the hedges and peered over them shamelessly, fearful of what he was about to see but knowing that he had to know.

Sure enough, his worst nightmare had been confirmed at the sight of the woman he loved in a passionate embrace with a man he loathed with all his heart. All he had been able to do was turn away sharply as though the sight blinded him and hurry to his suite before they or anyone else could see him.

"*Why?*" Aidric cried over and over as if he was chanting, pounding his fist hard on the door until his skin was split and bleeding, and the pain forced him to stop.

He stared at his bloodied hand for a long time before he moved away from the door and sank into the nearest couch with all the grace of a goat, for once not caring that his clothes were wrinkling.

He wanted to blame her, his bleeding heart searching desperately for a scapegoat to hate, but he knew that she was not at fault. *If anyone is to blame, it's me*, he thought darkly. *I had my chance, on numerous occasions, but the coward that I am, I ran away from the thought of giving my heart freely to another woman after what happened with Alina.*

A sharp pain shot through his injured hand as he fisted both of them tightly. *Dammit! What did I expect? That Allison would wait for me forever to find the courage to tell her how I felt? Oh Aidius, but why did it have to be* Patrym? *Even after all she knows about him?*

Aidric miserably glanced at the sandclock and knew that she would be returning soon for her mage lesson. "Unless, of course, she decides to skip in favor of Patrym's bed," he muttered flatly. "Seni help me, how shall I ever face her again?"

CHAPTER TWENTY-SIX

A llison walked briskly down the long corridor of the Mage Hall, trembling uncontrollably, and struggling to keep tears of fright at bay. She thanked God, Seni, and every other deity she could name that there was no one around to stop her. After what had just happened between Patrym and her, she didn't think she could face anyone without losing it completely. She needed to find Aidric!

God, God, what have I done? What have I done? she thought on the brink of hysteria. By now someone must have gone to Patrym's aide, learned what she had done. *What will they do to me? Throw me in the dungeons?*

She shuddered at the thought. Aidric reluctantly

had once shown her the palace dungeons at her insistence, and the tiny, rock-walled cells, the unmistakable smell of human waste, the musty dampness, and the darkness were enough to haunt her nightmares for days after.

God, what will Aidric think? She had used her mage powers to hurt someone. The thought of him looking at her in disgust was unbearable.

Unfortunately, she reached the door to his suite only too soon, and there was nothing for her to do but enter and allow fate to handle the rest. This wasn't something she could run from. It was time to face the music.

Allison took several long, deep breaths before she felt calm enough to open the door, as neutral of an expression as she could manage plastered onto her face. Running into the suite blubbering incoherently was the last thing she needed to do. He was probably in his study. She would sit down, explain herself as quickly as she could, and maybe together they could fix this terrible mess.

She stopped short, her heart clenching painfully in renewed panic. No! She wasn't ready yet!

Aidric was already seated in the center of the room on his pile of cushions, and he even had a pile of cushions across from him for her even though she had stopped sitting during her lessons for some time now.

He turned his head slightly towards her as she stood frozen near the door.

However, that small movement alone wasn't what suddenly had her mind screeching in warning as she forced herself to walk at a normal pace to her set of cushions, all the while feeling a breath away from bolting from the suite entirely. It was the look of utter coldness in his eyes, something she had never seen directed towards her.

Equilibrium shattered and not knowing what else to do, Allison silently set her books onto the floor beside the cushions before she sank down onto them, her nerves starting to crack. She needed to tell him what she'd done, but the words lodged against the huge knot of dread that had formed in her throat under that unexpected icy gaze.

Then it hit her.

He knows, Allison thought frantically, all the blood draining out of her face so quickly that she felt lightheaded. *God help me he knows, and if he's not furious, then I don't know him at all!*

She opened her mouth and closed it several times, at a loss of what to say, but before she could utter a word, Aidric spoke in a shockingly normal tone, "I hope you've been studying the lesson I gave you or else this lesson will be harder than any you have ever endured."

Allison blinked at him stupidly. That was the last thing she expected him to say. The coldness was still in his eyes, but if he knew what she had done, why didn't he confront her with it? Did he want her to sweat over it awhile? Was this her punishment?

It took every ounce of willpower within her already fragile psyche to keep back the tears of fear and anguish that were threatening to surface, but somehow she managed to find her voice to answer him. "I studied it." She was rather surprised that her voice didn't waver once.

What the hell was she doing? Why was she going along with him as though this was just another day, another lesson? She needed to confess what she had done *now*!

Aidric nodded stiffly. "Good. We'll begin by testing just how well you have mastered this offensive attack. I'll go stand against the bookcases on the farthest wall, shielded with as many different types of magical barriers as my power allows me to hold over myself. Your assignment is to blast through as many of them as you can with a single blow from where you are seated."

Allison opened her mouth to vehemently protest, but a sharp, cold look from him made the words die on her tongue along with something deep within her heart.

"You won't mark me. The shield in which I hold closest to my body is virtually impenetrable, and I don't think even *you* have the power to break through it at this stage. We'll see how much studying you have actually done this morning." That last part he almost spat out, and that was the last confirmation she needed on whether or not he knew exactly what she had done to Patrym—and that he was furious over it.

Backed into a corner, the only chance she had to try to fix this nightmare was to do what he asked without protest. After living with him for several moons now, Allison knew that Aidric would talk about it when *Aidric* wanted to talk about it—no sooner, no later.

She watched him rise and stride stiffly across the room to his chosen position. His face was still the same mask of coldness when he turned around to face her, his arms folded as if to say "well?" Never had he seemed more intimidating, not even the first time she had opened her eyes to find him towering over her.

Allison hesitated a moment before she reached out with her mind to the Mage-field, drawing its energy to her and then channeling as much of it through her body as she could safely hold, chanting the ancient Ti'ar words softly through it all, all the while terrified that her emotions were too chaotic to be channeling at all. If she made a mistake, such a large amount of power could easily destroy her body completely.

Nevertheless, she continued until she had drawn all the power she could, recognizing with a surge of self-loathing that more than trying to appease Aidric's anger, she was doing this dangerous, stupid thing because she was more terrified of stopping and having to say what she had done aloud. Saying it out loud in front of Aidric would make it real, words that she could never take back.

Thrusting her hands forward, Allison prepared to fling the enormous power she held literally in the palm of her hands at Aidric in an all-out dagger of power, the incantation that would release and shape the power ready on her lips. Their eyes met, and all time seemed to stop.

Allison could feel her entire body begin to tremble as seconds became minutes, and the heavy silence continued on. She couldn't do it. She just couldn't bring herself to attack him, no matter the reason. What if he was wrong? What if her power *did* penetrate through his strongest shield? She didn't have to be an expert in magecraft to know that he wouldn't survive the blast.

I don't want to hurt anyone else.

The coldness in Aidric's eyes soon turned to impatience when he realized that she wasn't going to strike him. She knew he could see the power swirling in her body and the concentration of most of it in her hands.

"Why don't you cast the power forth?" he finally asked, breaking the uncomfortable silence. "What are you waiting for? I assure you that in a combat situation, your opponent won't give you this much leisure in your spellcasting. Strike me now!"

Allison shook her head firmly and whispered, "I can't."

"'Can't'?" Aidric echoed so harshly that she almost lost her control on the streams of energy when she jumped. "What do you mean you *can't*? Didn't you tell me that you studied the lessons I assigned you? Now you tell me you're unable to cast forth your spell!"

"I—" Allison began miserably, but Aidric's next words cut her off as smoothly as a knife slicing through warm butter.

"I didn't think you would ever lie to me, Allison," he spat out angrily. "What was so important today that you *had* to ignore your lessons? Or would you rather be somewhere else, is that it?" Allison flinched as he took a step towards her, his eyes threatening all kinds of violence. "That's it, isn't it? You would much rather be in your lover, Patrym's, bed, wouldn't you? The taste of his lips on your own is but a few depths old and still you are eager for more!"

Aidric stalked over to her, reaching down to roughly grab her upper arm. She cried out, despite herself. "Do it," he growled, his eyes blazing frightfully with power drawn by fury. "Cast your magic forth! *Cast it!*"

At the mention of Patrym's name, the tiny control Allison still had over her emotions snapped, and she shot to her feet, feelings of anger, hurt, and fear thundering through her until she hardly had any sense left at all.

Before she knew what she was doing, Allison tore her arm out of his iron grip and shoved him away hard. "All right, fine!" she roared as Aidric stumbled backwards. She flung her hands before her once again and released the stream of power at her hands, while in the same instant shouting, *"Ti lansani di tansou nothian!"*

It seemed as if bright, yellow fire shot out from the palms of her hands. The moment the last syllable was voiced, the two streams of energy combined as one, and before she could even blink, it struck a still-disoriented Aidric full force in his chest. She could feel the distorted ripples of power as Aidric's shields instantly shattered as he flew back across the room and slammed into one of the bookcases with bone-crushing force as though he had been caught in the blast of a bomb.

337

Not so much as a sound escaped his throat. His expression didn't even have time to change. It all happened within a blink of an eye. With horror, Allison watched his body crumble to the ground as lifelessly as a ragdoll.

For a few moments, she just stood there gaping down at his body in shock. Then a wail that could have been a match for the cries of the damned filled the room as she raced over to his body and dropped down to her knees. That was when the now-familiar smell of scorched skin reached her nose.

Allison released yet another wail of anguish, thinking that it was Patrym all over again, but this time it was a thousand times worse. This time the flesh she had scorched was that of Aidric's chest—a chest that did not rise and fall with breath.

"Dear God, *no!*" she cried. He was dead—*dead*—and she had killed him! "No! I won't let you die, dammit! I won't!"

Then before she knew what she was doing, Allison had her hands over his heart, the blistered, crisp skin revealed by the gaping hole burned into his shirt feeling alien and sickening against her hands, and she was gathering her own body's energy, allowing it to flow from her hands into Aidric's body. Aidric had not yet gotten around to teaching her the healing arts, but she had read all about the methods in her spare time.

In theory, she knew how healing was done, but she had never actually attempted a healing before. Now she would find out whether or not all that reading would pay off. Her life, her world, *everything* depended on her success.

Allison concentrated on probing Aidric's body with mental eyes and hands, searching to find every last injury, then shooting his heart full of the healing energies. She coaxed the damaged flesh her probe had detected around his heart to begin healing itself with the help of her added life-energy, willing it to start beating again with everything she had in her. As the energy flowed from her body to his, she felt herself weakening as if all her blood was draining out of her.

A few, agonizing seconds later, she was rewarded when she felt his heart begin to beat again, first irregularly, then more normalized and strongly underneath her hands. With the last of her strength, Allison lifted her hands away from Aidric's chest, had just enough time to register that his skin had also been healed of the burns without a hint of scarring, before she collapsed onto his body in a position that would have had her blushing in any other circumstance.

Wave after wave of dizziness washed over her, and a spot of darkness was already beginning to cloud her vision. Allison shut her eyes tightly, willing the threatening blackness away, and when she slowly opened them again what felt like an eternity later, a pair of dazed, pale-violet eyes were staring back at her. A rush of adrenaline suddenly surged through her, and the cloud of darkness retreated a bit from her mind.

It took her a couple of breathless moments before she realized that Aidric was alive and conscious, but when it finally all registered, she let out a cry that was half-sob and half-relief and did what seemed the most natural thing in the world to do at that moment—she kissed him.

His mental shields obliterated, she easily felt Aidric's startlement.

Allison pulled away almost immediately, horrified and embarrassed at what she had just done. The expression on Aidric's face was totally unreadable, his eyes staring up at her mutely as though he couldn't quite believe what had just happened. Even though his emotions were now slamming into her with all the power of a freight train, they were too chaotic to sort out.

Awkwardly trying to move off his chest, she struggled to make her mouth work again in order to apologize for the kiss but failed on both accounts. Her efforts merely earned her another wave of dizziness. The healing had simply left her too weak to do much more than twitch, and it was all she could do to keep the edges of blackness at bay. She also seemed to have lost her tongue completely.

Then Aidric lifted a hand weakly to her face, slowly brushing her hair back from her cheek until his hand came to rest on the back of her neck. Before she knew what was happening, he pushed her head down gently, but insistently, towards him until her lips were once again pressing against his, warm, eager lips that shockingly kissed her with so much passion that she shuddered in the ecstasy of it.

The darkness at the edges of her mind instantly vanished. It was as though his touch renewed the life-energy she had given him in the healing.

It was a long moment before they broke. It was even a longer moment before either one of them spoke, their eyes locked on one another in a kind of numbed contentment. If there was ever a time Allison had not been sure about how Aidric felt about her, the look of pure love and happiness that now radiated from his eyes told her all she needed to know even without the echo of those same emotions flowing into her curtesy of her Empathy. It was as if she had only imagined the fury that had burned within his eyes only moments earlier.

"Do you know how long I've wanted to do that?" Aidric asked softly into the silence, a wry smile touching his lips.

Allison smiled shyly down at him. "Probably not

as long as I have. If I'm being honest with myself, even though you scared me half to death at the time, I've been attracted to you ever since you placed that sleep spell over me the first time."

He managed a weak chuckle. "And all this time I thought that had you had a dagger in your hands at that time, you wouldn't have hesitated to thrust it into my heart!" He suddenly looked sheepish. "You stole my heart from the moment I first saw you in the Forest of Illusions."

"All those days living here with you, wondering, wishing, and I never did *anything*, never hinted that my feelings towards you had changed. I guess I was just afraid of your reaction. I knew you cared, Aidric, but I didn't know how much. I should have listened to Raya."

He sighed. "And I, Sel. He's been pestering me for moons to speak my true feelings. I guess I, too, was afraid. Those two have probably been pulling their hair out in frustration over us. To think that it took something like *this* to finally draw us together!" He grimaced and then added, "As terrible as I feel right now, I would have preferred the more traditional ways of courtship…"

Despite his teasing tone, Allison's heart clenched painfully. "I'm so sorry!" she cried, her voice stricken. "I almost killed you because I lost it! If it hadn't been for some miracle that I managed to figure out how to heal you, you would be dead now! You *were* dead! Even now, I have no idea just exactly what I did, but I don't care as long as it *did* work. If I had lost you—"

She shook her head and shut her eyes briefly in anguish. No, she couldn't think about that now, she couldn't allow herself to fall apart now, not when she still had something to fix. "Aidric," she began hoarsely, "about Patrym—"

Aidric shook his head slowly and placed a finger against her lips to silence her. His touch was enough to have silenced her for the rest of her life. "What happened between you and Patrym doesn't matter now," he said quietly. "It's something that happened in the past, and the past is something I, especially, have no right to begrudge anyone."

Allison's eyes widened. "But it *does* matter," she insisted urgently. "From your angry words, you must have seen what happened between us earlier, but not everything like I thought." She cast her eyes down shamefully, but she forced herself to continue. "I can't let you go on believing that I've been in Patrym's bed. Believe me when I say that I would rather sleep with your horse than go to bed with that arrogant bastard!"

"But, I saw—"

"Yes, you did," she immediately interrupted, "but it's not what you think. He *forced* himself on me, Aidric, and for a moment or two, I was simply too shocked to react. I should've expected him to try something like that, but I didn't. I didn't think even he would ever dare cross that line. Aidric, please, *please* believe me that when I did react, it was out of sheer panic."

At his puzzled look, Allison took a deep, shaky breath, then forced herself to continue, "I—he was holding my arms, and I desperately wanted him to let go. I guess when I started panicking, I managed to unconsciously draw energy from the Mage-field and somehow used it to burn his hands through the skin of my arms." She looked at him in anguish. "Even though he's scum, the last thing I wanted to do was hurt him that badly! And to make matters worse, I freaked out and ran off without trying to get him some help!"

"Serves him right," came Aidric's shocking reply. "Maybe this unfortunate accident will teach him to keep his hands to himself for a change! Although I wouldn't normally encourage such an extreme defense, you can't be placed at fault, and when Patrym runs to the king over the matter as he certainly will, Diryan, most assuredly, will say the same. I'll deal with the matter as soon as I'm able."

He hugged her more fiercely than she would have thought him capable of in his weakened state. "Now it's my turn to apologize for losing my temper in my—

jealousy. No matter what I thought you had done, I had no right to accuse you of doing anything wrong. I pray, unworthy as I am, that you'll forgive me in time."

Allison laid her head onto his chest and let out a tiny sob. "There's nothing to forgive."

If anything, they had *both* acted like idiots.

"Do you know how wonderful it feels to finally be able to hold you in my arms, to say freely, little cat, that I love you?" Aidric crooned softly into her hair.

Her heart began to race when she heard the words she had never dared to dream to hear from his lips. "I love you too, my friend, teacher, and protector," Allison whispered back and raised her lips to his to claim another kiss.

When they finally came up for air, Aidric said mischievously, "If we both weren't in such a wretched state, then I would have suggested that we go off and start proving some of those rumors circulating around the court true!"

Allison blushed furiously and tried to cover up her embarrassment by adding, "Yes, you're quite right—about the wretched state, I mean. Obviously we can't stay here on the floor all day, no matter how comfortable your chest is! Now that the excitement is over, I think I'm more than ready to go pass out in my bed, but—"

"No problem," Aidric interjected. "I'll just call in

the cavalry."

His eyes unfocused for a bit while he used thought-speech to call in whatever help he had in mind. Allison knew that they were in an awkward position, and she just prayed that whoever came to their rescue was someone they both knew. Starting a whole new batch of embarrassing court rumors wasn't something she was particularly keen to do.

"Who did you call?" she asked anxiously. "What did you tell them?"

"Sel," he replied. "And Maldon. They're the only two that are in the palace at the moment whom I can trust to keep this behind their teeth. Nothing good would come of the kingdom learning of this accident. They're also bringing a couple of healers with them. Seni knows what it was you did to yourself in order to heal me or for that matter, what you did to *me*, and I would feel better once a healer looks at us both. I imagine they'll arrive here fairly quickly since I only told them that we met with an unfortunate accident during your mage lesson."

"Aidric! You didn't! They must be frantic!"

"I did," he said with a small chuckle. "I couldn't resist repaying the favor for all the times they extended the same courtesy to me."

Before Allison could retort, Selwyn, Maldon, and

considerably more than the two healers Aidric had requested came barging into the suite, all simultaneously demanding to know what had happened. There were several gasps when they spotted them lying in a crumbled heap on the floor. They all nearly fell over each other in their haste to reach them, arguing furiously over who would examine them first.

Aidric flashed them a murderous look and gathered all of his strength to utter a single word, "*Enough!*"

He then laid his head back down onto the floor in the following silence and closed his eyes wearily for a moment before opening them again and fixing the group surrounding them with a hard look.

"Please," Aidric said quietly, "I asked you to keep your voices down, and yet you all come bursting in here bellowing at the top of your lungs! And Sel—" He raised an inquiring eyebrow at the redhead. "Did I not say only *two* healers?"

"They insisted on bringing more," Selwyn replied defensively.

"I apologize, Milord Mage-general," one of the healers said, a homely brown-haired man that looked to be in his mid-thirties, "but Lord Selwyn sounded rather agitated, and I thought the situation might warrant a few more healers."

"No matter, Dallan," Aidric said with a sigh, closing his eyes again. "Both of us are simply too weak to rise from the floor. I would ask that you get us into our beds before you examine us. Then I'll gladly explain what has happened."

***

Diryan stared expressionlessly at the bard before him, wishing not for the first time that he had been born a peasant. When Lord Garai, one of the Circle representatives to the bards, had stormed angrily into his study after he had been announced, he never in a million years would have guessed the grievance Garai had reported.

He would be damned before he allowed the man or Ion to see how much the news had disturbed him. Damn the woman! The kingdom was already wary of her as it was even though she hadn't done a single thing besides showing her presence to warrant their distrust. If word of what she had done to Patrym spread among the gossips, it would only be a matter of time before the villagers were at the palace gates demanding her blood.

There was no doubt in his mind that Allison *had* done harm to Patrym, although the majority of the young bard's story rang false. No matter the reasons, the damage had been done, and Diryan knew that he had to do everything in his power to bury the truth of the matter from the public. However, he first had to obtain the girl's version of the incident.

"Ion, thought-speak the Mage-general," Diryan commanded. "Inform him that I request his presence and that of his ward immediately." He turned to Garai. "Bard Garai, is Patrym able to come here before me as well to support his claim?"

"The damage to his hands was minimal," Garai admitted, "though the greater damage was to his mental state. He is understandably deeply shaken by the incident, and I don't believe it wise for him to encounter the Golden Mage so soon."

Diryan nodded. He had expected as much. He started to speak again, but Ion's urgent voice froze the words on his lips.

"Your Highness, the Mage-general informs me that neither he nor his ward are able to answer your summons. It seems as if they met with an accident during the Golden Mage's lessoning, and both are now confined to their beds at Healer Dallan's order."

Diryan sucked in his breath. Damn! He did not need this now. What next?

"What has happened?" he asked more sharply than he intended.

"The Mage-general gave no details, 'Highness, though he did say that he knows the nature of your summons," Ion reported.

That didn't surprise the king in the least. "Then I must go to him. Bard Garai, remain here until I return. After I have the girl's story, I shall return to proclaim my judgment. Ion, bespeak my councilors, and inform them that our meeting will be postponed for a sand-mark."

Both men bowed their heads in accession as Diryan rose and hurried out of the Royal Wing to the Mage Hall, his guards falling into step a few handspans behind him. Only then did his hard expression melt into a frown of worry as he wondered exactly what had happened in Aidric's suite. Was it a coincidence that these two accidents had occurred within the same sand-mark? The king did not believe so.

Diryan was met at Aidric's door by Healer Dallan, no doubt on his way back to the Healer's Hall. Dallan bowed respectfully before he said, "Both the Mage-general and the Lady Allison are faring quite well despite the circumstances, Your Majesty. The Lady Allison sleeps now, but Lord Aidric is, not surprisingly, alert. If I have your leave, I must return to the Hall."

He nodded his permission, and Dallan bowed again before taking his leave. The king wasted no time in going to Aidric. Aidric sat weakly in bed, his skin a bit paler than usual, but otherwise, he appeared surprisingly unharmed.

"Tell me," Diryan said simply as he took a seat

next to Aidric's bed.

Aidric fixed him with those eyes that unnerved, although for the first time, Diryan couldn't read the expression that lay within. There was something different there, something important, but for the life of him, Diryan couldn't put his finger on it.

"It was an accident," Aidric said, a ghost of a smile touching his lips. "The blame rests entirely on my head. I intentionally pushed her over the edge, but that's a tale better told later. I believe it's Patrym whom you came here to discuss."

"Yes, Patrym," Diryan said sternly. "I trust the Lady Allison has confessed her actions to you?"

"Patrym brought his injury on himself," Aidric said calmly. "He attempted to force his attentions where they were not wanted. She panicked. It was an accident, no more."

"Garai came to me with Patrym's claim," Diryan said, watching Aidric's expression closely. "According to Patrym, Allison made him believe that his attentions were welcome."

There was a flash of anger in his eyes, but when Aidric spoke, his voice remained calm. "You know better than that, Diryan."

"Yes, I am well aware of Patrym's infamous reputation. He has had his own fair share of claims against him, but Aidric, that still doesn't change the fact that

Allison used her magic to harm a citizen."

"Can you blame her?" Aidric scoffed. "You know as well as I that Allison has a timid nature. She isn't prone to such rash acts of violence. She simply panicked and lost control. Seni knows it's happened before. What Patrym did was assault, and it's not the first time he has done it. It should've been *she* who brought grievance to you. I feel he received the punishment he deserved."

"Perhaps yes," Diryan agreed cautiously, "but I fear the kingdom will not see it as you do, lad. Already, Garai demands that she be heavily reprimanded before the public."

"For defending herself?" Aidric asked incredulously. "He believes the bastard's tale?"

"You forget. Patrym was once his ward and apprentice, but whether or not Garai believes Patrym is not the issue here. People are still wary of the Lady Allison, lad. What do you believe will occur once it becomes publicly known that the Golden Mage seared the hands of a bard? It's a fate some bards say is worse than a slow and painful death. As eagerly as tongues wag in this court, you can well imagine what twisted tales will reach the ears of the villagers. Before the sand-mark is out, word will be that she has murdered him!"

The king saw the abrupt flash of understanding in

Aidric's eyes, followed by a look of determination so fervent that Diryan was slightly taken aback.

"Then no soul other than those involved will know of the incident," Aidric vowed.

The king agitatedly ran his hand through his hair. "It's not that simple," he said with a sigh. "It occurred in the courtyard. Seni knows how many witnessed it. Even the king cannot thwart all gossip, mores the pity."

"No," Aidric agreed reluctantly, his brows furrowed, but then, his lips abruptly stretched into a malicious smile. Diryan didn't in the least bit like the diabolical gleam in Aidric's eyes that accompanied that smile. "Only Seni, Himself, could possibly accomplish such a feat, yes, but perhaps we can use the inevitable gossip to our advantage."

"How so?" Diryan asked warily.

"Patrym is very proud," Aidric said. "He revels in his reputation as a womanizer almost as much as in his reputation as one of the finest bards in Lamia. Said where the right ears can hear, the news that a maiden, whether the Golden Mage or some unknown mage, seared his hands because of his unwanted attentions will cause the people to see the situation in a new light. I'm not the only soul in the palace who can't stand the sight of the insufferable man."

"Remind me to never cross you, lad," Diryan said

dryly. "You have all too cunning a mind, and if the situation wasn't as serious as it is, I know where I would tell you to stick such a suggestion. I know I would be wasting my breath by forbidding you to do such a thing, so I'll not even bother. I only warn you to be careful, Aidric, for said within earshot of the *wrong* ears could be more dangerous than you realize— especially one particular pair of ears."

By the uneasiness in his eyes, it was clear that Aidric needed no further explanation.

CHAPTER TWENTY-SEVEN

Allison looked up from the book she was reading at the whisper of sound she heard in the direction of her bedroom door. She instantly smiled brightly when she saw Aidric, dressed in his navy blue robe, standing in the doorway. She was happy to see that he was strong enough to rise from his bed. After lying in bed all day under the healer's strict orders, she had been more than ready herself to get out of bed and had thought to use the excuse of seeing how Aidric was doing. It seemed Aidric had thought to do the same.

She wondered if the healers had told him about what she had done to him. The four healers who had attended to her were, to say the least, shocked when she had attempted to explain what she had done to

Aidric to restart his heart and heal the terrible wound in his chest. They had told her that they had never heard of such a thing.

As far as they could tell, she had used a large portion of her life-force to bring Aidric back to life, an act that had come closer to killing her than she had realized. Had she used just a little more of her life-energy in her healing... It was something Allison didn't want to think about and hoped that Aidric wouldn't bring it up now.

"How do you feel?" Aidric asked, still standing in the threshold.

"About a thousand times better," Allison assured him. "In fact, I was just about to go ask you the same. It looks like I wasn't the only one tired of bed."

"Well—" he said with a shrug, suddenly seeming nervous.

For a while, he just stared at her, wearing the most peculiar expression on his face, and belatedly, Allison realized that she was wearing nothing but her nightgown—her very thin and snugly fitting nightgown that hid nothing. She felt her face begin to flush, but she forced herself not to reach for the robe that was thrown carelessly over the chair next to her bed or even to lift the blankets resting over her lap higher.

"Allison," Aidric said suddenly, a bit urgently, the intensity of his stare multiplying exponentially. She looked at him expectantly, saying nothing. "I—I mean—would you—dammit! Why can't I find the words I seek?" he cried frustratingly.

Suddenly he crossed the length of the room in two swift, long strides and fell to his knees at her bedside, leaving her to stare at him with slowly widening eyes. Then before she knew what was happening, Allison suddenly found herself enveloped in his strong arms, and his warm lips were pressing urgently onto her own with a desperation and hunger that stunned her.

Even so, she melted into his arms willingly, parting her lips in an invitation for a deeper kiss. Aidric shivered—with pleasure or relief she wasn't sure—at her eager response, and his kisses at once became less urgent and desperate and more gentle, sensual, until he had her moaning against his lips with pleasure.

Sometime later—depths, sand-marks, years— Aidric broke the kiss, but he didn't immediately pull away from her. Instead, he bent closer to her ear and whispered huskily, "Come."

He rose to his feet and held out his hand to her. Allison eyed it mutely with an expression as though she had never seen a hand before. Then she raised her eyes to his and saw the unvoiced question in them. Her eyes widened a little when she realized what he was asking, what he had tried and failed to ask with words before, and she swallowed nervously at the lump that had abruptly formed in her throat.

Deep down, she knew this moment had been inevitable from the instant she had turned and saw him standing in her door. One of the many things gossiping with the queen's ladies-in-waiting and the ladies at court had taught her was that to the Lamians, jumping into bed with someone was as common as kissing.

Shockingly, Allison suddenly found herself accepting his proffered hand before she had even consciously decided to do it, and Aidric slowly coaxed her from the bed to her feet. He had to take her other hand to steady her as she swayed, abruptly feeling a wave of weakness wash over her that had nothing to do with any lingering ill effects from the healing she had done earlier. Allison shuddered in anticipation at the mischievous smile he directed at her.

Aidric wordlessly led her out of her room, down the hall, and into his own bedroom. Allison bemusedly wondered why they had not just stayed in her room as he closed the door behind them and dimmed the lights with a single thought until the lanterns held only tiny flames that were little more than sparks. After that, when Aidric drew her into his arms and his lips found hers again, there was no more room for thought. Only later would she learn from an amused Raya that Lamian propriety forbade a man to take a woman in her own bed.

As Allison felt Aidric gently tugging the sleeves of her nightgown away from her shoulders and slowly down her arms, she seemed to awaken from her swoon as if someone had suddenly slapped her across the face and began to realize the severity of the situation. Half of her mind screamed at her in reproach, asking if she knew what the hell she was doing, and the other half still under Aidric's spell promptly told the reasoning half to shut up.

I know what I'm doing, she thought stubbornly, though a hint of doubt was already creeping into her mind.

Oh, do you? the reasoning half sneered mockingly.

Allison chose to ignore that last thought. She had never given to a man what she was about to give to Aidric, and she wondered just how much was because she had not felt right about it or because she still hadn't gotten over her stepfather's brainwashing she had endured as a child. Well, whatever her reasons were in the past, nothing had ever felt more right than now when she was in Aidric's arms, and she wasn't about to let that small bit of doubt hold her back any longer.

With trembling fingers that seemed to have lost all dexterity, Allison untied his robe, and Aidric gracefully slipped it off without breaking their kiss, allowing it to fall to his feet. As she suspected, he was gloriously nude beneath the robe.

Hesitantly, she ran her hands over his body, awkwardly at first, in contrast to his skilled exploration of hers, feeling the finely-toned muscles of his chest and upper arms with a thrill of excitement running through her.

Aidric groaned against her lips as his hands almost feverishly explored her body in the most delightful ways, and with some embarrassment, Allison abruptly realized that she felt the result of his passion quite clearly against her belly. Then, in the next instant, Aidric had whisked her off her feet, and she was suddenly enveloped in the softness of the blankets of his bed.

In the back of her mind, Allison vaguely remembered her outburst to Keldan the day of her first music lesson when she had told him quite fervently that she wouldn't jump into Aidric's bed at the first crook of his finger. She could not help smiling at the thought. Well, he had crooked, and lo and behold, she had followed without much, if any, real hesitation.

Hypocrite, her voice of reason whispered sardonically.

As Aidric loomed over her, an iridescent shadow in the darkness of the room, Allison began to tremble, suddenly recalling every story her girlfriends had told her of their first times and the one thing that was true for each of them—the inevitable pain. She stiffened involuntarily at Aidric's touch and gazed up at him with frightened eyes. She could just see his face in the darkness and saw the sudden look of understanding flash across his eyes, followed by a look something akin to shock, and then an immense joy that instantly transformed his face into that of an angel.

He tenderly smoothed the hair from her face and said softly, "You're an innocent, aren't you?"

She nodded, not trusting her voice. She was at once grateful for the darkness that hid her flaming cheeks.

Aidric chuckled softly, though it was with delight and not mockery. "You can't even begin to imagine what it means to me to be the first man to show you love in this manner, to touch you as no other has ever touched you." He bent down and brushed a tender kiss across her swollen lips. "There is nothing to fear, my beloved, my little cat. I could never do anything to harm you."

Then there were no more words as he proceeded to show her that there was indeed nothing to fear, rousing such incredible sensations in her that she soon forgot the sharp pain of that first penetration and lost herself completely to the pleasure.

Sand-marks later, when she finally drifted off to

sleep, her body pleasantly exhausted and wrapped contentedly in Aidric's arms, Allison realized that with this last act of defiance to her stepfather, she had finally left behind that old life full of insecurity and hatred and was at last truly a part of Lamia. She knew, without a doubt, that from then on, she would never fear the eyes of a crowd again.

CHAPTER TWENTY-EIGHT

A lthough darkness had fallen over Lamia a couple of sand-marks earlier, the skies above the palace glowed with an illumination twice as bright as the brightest sunlight. Thunder growled menacingly in booms that seemed to shake the very foundation of the world.

Perched on his horse at the edge of the palace grounds, Galen wildly looked up into the thrones and flinched when he saw spider webs of blue lightning spinning themselves at unholy speeds across the cloudless, night sky. His horse's eyes rolled back wildly as it screamed and began to dance around in fear, causing him to fight to both calm the animal and stay in his saddle.

What in Seni's name is happening? Galen thought frantically as he struggled to drive his horse closer to the palace gates.

He could already see the green mage-flames licking some of the palace's buildings. Clouds of smoke also rose eerily to the sky, uncannily resembling the swarm of the hellish *dyani* sans the teeth, swirling and writhing with unholy life in the typical *dyani* manner. Human screams pierced the night, sounding even more deafening than the sonic booms of the thunder.

The palace gates stood unguarded and wide open, the once strong iron of its thick bars now melted and twisted grotesquely. Four bodies, presumably some of the guards, lay strewn a few handspans from their posts as if they were ragdolls tossed carelessly onto the ground by a child throwing a tantrum, uniforms mostly burned away and their bodies blackened and partially consumed beyond recognition.

As Galen raced towards the chaos, several sections of the palace collapsed into large piles of rubble and flames, the marble portions seemingly shattering in the intense heat. The sound was deafening, the sounds of the earth cracking open. Distantly, he wondered how the flames were managing to spread and consume everything so rapidly, especially when marble didn't so much burn as expand and explode. But then he had reached the edge of the palace stables, and there was no more time for thought.

Galen vaulted from the back of his horse without even bothering to wait for his mount to stop. He hit the ground running and practically flew around the corner of the riding field and then abruptly stopped in stunned disbelief at the scene that presented itself before him. A sea of burning bodies littered the palace lawns as far as the eye could see. Both soldiers and civilians lay in smoldering heaps, positioned in the last throes of their death, each unnaturally twisted body more ghastly than the first. The stench of charred flesh invaded his nostrils almost immediately, and it was all he could do not to fall to his knees retching.

Only one thought gave him the strength to wade through that field of carnage—his wife and children. Galen forced himself not to look down at the many faces at his feet twisted in eternal grimaces of agony, not to see the glazed eyes still widened in terror. He dared not, lest he began to recognize those unfortunate souls who would never again see the light of day.

"Milyn!" Galen shouted despairingly into the smoky gloom before him as he picked his way through the maze of bodies towards the Mage Hall in his search for his family, coughing and frantically gasping for breath through the smoke that seemed to reach down his throat with scorching claws to rip out his lungs. The stench of burning bodies was unbearable.

"Sashan! Tage! Sandria! Where are you?"

Then, as if Seni, Himself, had reached down His mighty hand to banish the horrors around him, the smoke suddenly parted, the stench of death left his nostrils, and his beloved family was racing towards him. Galen had only enough time to call out his wife's name in joyous relief before a lightning bolt abruptly struck the ground between his family and him. The world around him dissolved into a white hot blaze as Galen belatedly attempted to shield his eyes from the blast with a forearm. Only when his back slammed into the ground did he realize that the blast had knocked him from his feet.

When his vision cleared an eternity later and he was able to breathe again, Galen was greeted with the very scene he had ridden his horse near to foundering to prevent. His family lay in a crumbled heap where they had fallen—and through the swirls of thick smoke behind them stepped the Golden Mage.

Her form glowed a preternatural green, as though she had somehow become the mage-flames she had cast, and she was dressed in robes of black and gold— *Roderick's colors.* Her unbound hair flew wildly in the fierce wind that seemed to have manifested from nowhere, causing her to appear even more menacing, but what truly froze Galen's blood with terror was the fierce green eyes that held no hint of madness but all the cruelty of the world.

She smiled slightly, a gesture that made her look more demon than human, and raised her hands. Although impossible for any without the gift of Innersight, an ability he did not possess, Galen could clearly see the energy flowing through her body to gather, uncast, at her outstretched hands.

"*No!*" Galen roared, his voice dripping with both horror and anguish.

He tried to rise from the ground, but with a strangled cry, he realized that the demonspawn had left him unable to move, his back broken in the fall. As if the scene unfolded before him in slow motion, Galen helplessly watched the power leave the Golden Mage's hands, the golden energy mockingly beautiful, and even more slowly, he watched that power engulf his wife's body and ignite until she was no more than a thrashing shape of green flames.

The shriek that was ripped from Milyn's throat was inhuman, the wail of the souls of the damned given a brief vision of the thrones that forever lay beyond their reach. Then, one by one, Galen was forced to watch the bodies of his children burst into flames and hear their agonized pleas to him for salvation as the mage-flames slowly, unmercifully, consumed them alive.

He could not close his eyes.

Soon their screams were drowned out by his own howl full of rage and agony, but still the sound of a woman's cruel laughter reached his ears, taunting, enjoying his pain—

***

Galen abruptly shot up in his bed, tears leaking from his eyes, and a scream still emerging from his lips. He immediately clamped down on his cry when he realized that he was in his bedroom and not on that lawn of unholy death. His body and sheets looked as though someone had doused him with a whole bathing tub of water. The smell of burning flesh still lingered keenly in his nose.

Frantically, he reached over for Milyn in order to reassure himself that she was safe. When his hand just kept on reaching into empty air, he panicked and jumped out of bed, racing for the door without bothering to grab a robe to cover his half-nude body. He had to find them! He had to get to the king! He had to warn him about *her*!

However, before he could dash through the front door, he finally fully awakened and realized that it had all been a dream, the same dream he had dreamed a dozen times before, but with a new twist. He also remembered that his wife was still occupied with the outbreak of heat flu in Peri. He breathed a shaky sigh of relief, and slowly trudged his way over to the children's bedroom to reassure himself that they were really safe.

Aidius! Galen thought shakily. *I haven't had that dream for a couple of moons now. Nor has it ever seemed so real before. Damn it all! I could smell the burning flesh! I could never do that before! I have never actually seen the demonspawn—*

He shuddered, feeling the tears beginning to gather in his eyes again, and brutally forced the vision of his family engulfed in mage-flames from his mind.

Silently, Galen opened the door to his children's room and slipped inside. Three, unmoving lumps occupied the three beds against the far wall, apparently undisturbed by his cries during the nightmare—if it was indeed a nightmare.

He soundlessly walked over to the bed of his eldest son, Sashan, and stood for a long moment, just watching the rhythmic rising and falling of the boy's chest. Although eleven summers old, in sleep Sashan looked as innocent as a newborn babe. In the hands of the Golden Mage, Sashan *would* be as helpless as a newborn babe!

His body lay in a crumbled heap before Galen. The bodies of his mother, brother, and sister lay sprawled just a few paces away from him—then their bodies were suddenly engulfed in flames. He could see the look of pure agony in his son's fright-ened, blue eyes, pleading for the salvation that Galen was help-less to give him or the others.

Galen shook himself out the memory. *I cannot allow this to come to pass!*

He abruptly turned on his heel and stalked out of the room, not even bothering to shut the children's bedroom door behind him, heading straight for his study and the sheathed dagger forged by a magesmith that he secretly kept hidden away in a panel in his bookcase that not even Milyn knew existed. The panel, itself, hidden behind a series of old books he seldom consulted anymore, appeared innocently enough to be the circle of growth rings roughly the size of two fists from the tree used to construct the bookshelves. The slightly lighter rings concealed rather cleverly the out-line cracks of the panel.

Galen pressed the three, slightly raised imperfec-tions in the wood along the rings in the proscribed or-der that would trigger the springs to open the panel. The little circle of rings immediately popped open, re-vealing the small compartment, about two handspans across, that housed the dagger that was illegal to all but non-magical troops.

If anyone had even suspected him of having such a weapon in his possession, his neck would have been in a noose faster than he could have opened his mouth to explain its presence, especially since he had acquired it precisely for the illegal use he was about to put it to.

Carefully, Galen removed the sheathed dagger from the compartment, closed the panel, and re-shelved the books he had removed. Then just as carefully, he sent a Probe of Inquiry into the dagger to check that the spell that had been forged into the blade had not faded after lying unused for two years.

The strong energies that could only be derived from a Mage-field immediately greeted his probe, and he felt his shoulders sag a bit in relief. The spell was still intact and as strong as the day it had been forged into the blade.

When used on a normal adversary without any mage gifts, the dagger was simply that—a dagger, but when used against a mage with powerful shielding, the spell forged in the blade turned it from an ordinary dagger into a powerful weapon that could ruffle the calm of the most powerful of mages since it was the only weapon capable of instantly penetrating a mage's magical shields, no matter their number or strength. Its only flaw was that each dagger could only be used once.

Each kingdom that possessed a Mage-field had at least one magesmith employed by the crown. Only the Lord Commander could legally commission magically forged weaponry from the magesmith, and he, only if he bore the monarch's signed and sealed permission.

Galen had come into possession of his spelled dagger by means that he would have normally shied away from if he had not believed that the future safety of his family and the rest of the kingdom would depend upon his having such a weapon in his possession. Plagued by terrible dreams, he had traveled to Sarim where it was rumored that an old hermit living deep within the Vearean Mountains had the knowledge of magically forging such weapons.

After a half-moon of careful inquiries, he had finally been directed to a hidden mountain path leading to the old man's abode. Galen was, to say the least, shocked to discover that no such hermit existed but only a cleverly hidden smithy of illegally forged magical weapons. Despite his misgivings, Galen had shelled out the demanded one thousand gold coins for the dagger he now held in his hands, and tonight, if all went well, he was about to prove that it was worth its monstrous price.

All mages traditionally cast shields around their persons while they slept. He saw no reason why an apprentice-mage should not do the same. In any case, whether the demonspawn had a shield about her or not, the dagger would not fail to do its job.

Clutching the hilt of the dagger so tightly that his knuckles turned white, Galen headed determinedly out of his suite without bothering to properly clothe himself and to the door of the Mage-general's suite, which he knew awaited him unlocked.

***

A whisper of sound abruptly awakened Allison from pleasant dreams of Aidric and her walking hand in hand under a star-speckled sky and kissing underneath the glow of a full moon. As she sleepily regarded the darkened room around her, wondering what had awakened her, she nearly panicked when she realized that she wasn't in her own bedroom, then blushing, remembered that she had not retired to her own bed that night.

She glanced over to her left and saw Aidric hastily pulling on a pair of breeches and knew that it was his abrupt absence beside her that had awakened her. But wasn't it still the middle of the night? Allison didn't think that she had been asleep all that long. A squinting glance at the sandclock confirmed that the first sun was still a few sand-marks away from rising.

"Aidric?" she said softly, gathering the blankets around her chest as she sat up.

He started, then turned to face her, his face wearing a troubled expression, but it immediately melted away into a warm smile. At the sight of his bared, well-muscled chest, Allison couldn't help blushing when she felt a tinge of desire and remembered the lovemaking they had shared only a few sand-marks earlier.

"I'm sorry, my beloved," Aidric said ruefully. "I didn't mean to wake you, but Ion just bespoke me that I'm needed in the Council Room immediately."

"Trouble?" she asked with a frown, afraid that he was going to be sent away on a tour of duty just when they had discovered their love for one another.

He nodded as he reached for the shirt he had lain on the bed. "Someone attempted to cross over the border illegally from Na'ar. The Shield was heavily tampered with, and based on the evidence of the probe that the border guards performed, it wasn't a minor mage that did the tampering. The mage covered his or her tracks too well. Diryan suspects that it was another one of Roderick's attempts to bring the Shield down."

His eyes darkened. "Perhaps it was even he who did the tampering, or Mordant. Anyhow, Ion didn't give me all the details, but I suspect I'll be in my saddle heading for the border within the sand-mark. In cases such as these, a mind-prober is needed, and in that, I'm second to none. I'll bespeak you if I'm to be sent off, but in the meantime, I want you to try to get some more sleep. Even if you don't have mage lessons in the morning, Keldan assuredly will still be eagerly awaiting you." He grinned wickedly. "We weren't exactly early to sleep even though we were early to bed!"

Then before she could even think to blush, Aidric bent over to kiss her tenderly before straightening to finish lacing his shirt.

"As much as I would rather be in my bed with you in my arms, I'm afraid that duty calls."

"There's always tomorrow night," Allison said brazenly, miraculously refraining from blushing again.

Aidric chuckled softly and planted one more kiss firmly onto her lips before grabbing his cloak from the back of a chair and swiftly heading out the door.

For a long while, Allison merely lay in bed, already missing the feel of Aidric's body next to hers and thinking that she would never be able to fall asleep again, but before long, she was once again swept off into an array of pleasant dreams.

CHAPTER TWENTY-NINE

The Mage Hall was deathly silent as Galen cautiously groped his way down the darkened corridor towards Aidric's suite, his bare feet making not even a whisper of sound on the cold, marble floor. Beads of sweat formed on his forehead and began to stream down his face once he reached his destination.

He winced as the door creaked loudly when he slowly pushed it open, the sound echoing monstrously loud throughout the corridors behind him. He froze for an instant and held his breath, feeling his pulse beating fearfully in his ears. When he heard no sounds of stirring from within, he stepped into the suite, wincing yet another time as the door whined shrilly again as he shut it behind him.

Damn it, you would think he would oil his hinges once in a while, Galen thought, annoyed, and then had to restrain himself from laughing hysterically at such a mundane thought when he had such an unpleasant task ahead of him.

Soundlessly, Galen crept across the sitting room and stepped through the arch into the hall. He had visited Aidric's suite on numerous occasions, therefore he was very familiar with the layout of the place. The demonspawn would be sleeping in the spare bedroom to the right. The door to her room was wide open, and he thanked Seni that he wouldn't have to risk awakening her with yet another creaky door.

In the almost absolute darkness of the room, the Golden Mage was just a massive lump in the center of her large bed. She didn't even stir when Galen stepped into her room and hastened over to her bedside, not even when he tripped over some unknown object on the floor and a tiny curse slipped from his lips.

As Galen stared down at the slumbering lump on the bed in sudden uncertainty, his mind filled with the horrifying visions of the dreams he suffered for almost three years now, dreams that surely must be Foresight dreams and almost guaranteed the agonizing death of his family and thousands of other innocent Lamians.

An uncontrollable rage suddenly filled his mind

when he thought about the king allowing this murdering spawn of the six hells to continue living despite his dire warnings of disaster and death.

Am I the only one who isn't a blind fool? Galen thought furiously. *Do they not see? King Diryan says that it's Seni's will to allow her to live, but is it also His will for me to idly sit here with the knowledge* He *has gifted to me through my dreams and do nothing? Milyn, Sashan, Tage, little Sandria—she will slaughter them all like livestock while I'm condemned to lie helpless listening to her sadistic laughter intermingled with my family's screams! Those horrors will never come to pass! She will die!* Die*!*

Clutching the spelled dagger so tightly that his hands violently trembled, Galen raised the weapon and brutally plunged it into the chest of the demonspawn without a moment's hesitation or thought for the consequences of his actions.

There was no bright flash when the dagger penetrated her shield; there was no scream of agony.

As he drew the dagger back from the lump, Galen gaped down at the bloodless dagger in his hands in disbelief. Then, for the first time, he really *looked* at the unmoving lump on the bed and realized that what he had taken for the Golden Mage was in fact a pile of blankets. Grinding his teeth so roughly that his jaw began to ache, he threw down the dagger onto the bed in disgust and grabbed the knot of blankets, flinging them against the far wall in a blind rage.

The demonspawn has tricked me! When I find her, I'll cut the black heart out of her chest and shove it down her throat until she chokes on her own vileness!

He stalked out of the room, forgetting his earlier stealth as he searched first the bathing room and then Aidric's study. When his search turned up nothing, Galen finally turned to Aidric's bedroom, and upon seeing the single slumbering shape in Aidric's bed that was undeniably female, that unique blonde hair spread out wildly on her pillow, his rage became even greater.

The rumors are true! She's seduced the Mage-general! It's only a matter of time before she corrupts him to help her in her cruelty! This time she won't escape Seni's judgment!

Nearly incoherent with rage, Galen didn't even pause to wonder why Aidric wasn't also in the bed as he approached Allison with murder in his eyes, his mind intent on his solitary task of assassination. He raised the dagger over her heart, certain that this time the job would be done.

***

Danger!

Allison woke up all at once, her eyes immediately flying open as her mage senses alerted her to an alien presence in the room, one with deadly intentions. The nightmarish sight that greeted her was the sight of a dagger that reeked of Mage-field energy positioned directly above her heart in the process of stabbing down and two eyes looking down at her that held no sanity.

Before she could cry out in horror, sure that she was a couple of seconds away from death, there was a bright flash of white light. It illuminated the face of the owner of the maddened eyes for a split-second, which was then followed by a backlash of tremendous power that rocked her senses as she both physically and mentally felt the shields around her body shatter. Then miraculously, the blade suddenly stopped a mere inch above her heart, quivering as though it struggled to cut through an unseen barrier.

As she starred up at her would-be murderer with eyes widened in shock, a name flashed through her numbed mind. *Galen.*

Galen, the mind-mage she had felt staring at her several times over the course of the last few moons, the man who had seemed nervous and a little afraid every time she had run into him. Allison vaguely remembered that first encounter with him as she had sat talking with Raya in the courtyard. She knew he had been watching her that day, and she could have kicked herself for not realizing the possibly danger. Now she was about to pay for her carelessness with her life.

In his madness, the shields on Galen's mind were

down and a tidal wave of thoughts, images, and emotions flooded into her mind. She saw all the dreams of chaos and death involving her, the infinite sea of burning bodies, the smoke and emerald mage-flames destroying Lamia's palace, dreams she, herself, had shared. She felt the intolerable amount of fear he harbored in his soul, but most of all, she felt the soul-wrenching agony and rage he experienced when the glowing apparition that bore her face murdered his family in cold blood before his very eyes.

She felt the conflict within him now, on whether or not her death was truly justified, that what had stopped him at the last second from plunging his blade into her heart was the look of blatant fear in her eyes that didn't even remotely resemble the cruel gaze of the thing in his dreams. He had carried the fear of these dreams for years now, enough to allow the seed of obsession to fully grow and to implant the thorns it had spawned painfully into his soul.

Galen was not a murderer.

He was not her enemy but a frightened man driven over the brink into madness by his horrifying visions of carnage, doing what he felt was right to save the lives of his loved ones and those he was sworn to protect. Tears began to swell in her eyes and then to stream down her face, tears of fear and heartache for the man that stared down at her with eyes that mirrored the conflict within his soul. Never good with words, they were now her only hope for salvation.

With an effort, Allison found her voice and pleaded softly, "Galen, please don't hurt me! Dreams—they're only dreams! Let's talk about this. You don't have to do this!"

For what seemed like an eternity doubled, they stared fixedly into each other's eyes, Galen's still swirling between reason and madness. Allison hardly dared to breathe, terrified that any movement from her would cause him to plunge that dagger into her chest.

What could she do? It was impossible for her to channel enough energy for a defensive spell in the split-second he would need to stab her. God, where was Aidric?

To her horror, Allison saw the wild glint abruptly return to Galen's eyes and instantly knew that madness had triumphed over reason.

A scream rose in her throat, and at the same time, Aidric's voice, sounding like a voice from the heavens, said softly, "Galen, don't."

At the sound of Aidric's voice, Galen snarled like a rabid beast and lunged at Aidric with the dagger. Allison didn't even have time to scream before a flash of power illuminated the space between the two men, and Galen was suddenly crashing against the far wall.

She distinctly heard the clatter of metal as the dagger fell to the floor. A moan sounded out into the silence, followed by the sounds of weeping.

Then darkness of the room was illuminated as a mage-flame abruptly appeared in the lantern suspended in the middle of the ceiling.

Trembling, Allison warily sat up in the bed, wrapping the blankets around her to hide her nakedness. Her eyes fell on the dagger lying on the floor beside a now-sobbing Galen, and she shuddered, suddenly feeling sick. Aidric immediately rushed to her side.

"Are you all right?" Aidric asked anxiously, helping her to rise from the bed and hugging her fiercely against his body. She was surprised to find that he was also trembling.

"He didn't hurt me," she said tremulously. "Aidric, he didn't know what he was doing. He thought—"

"I know," Aidric interrupted as he held her head to his chest, his fingers running gently through her hair along her scalp in an effort to sooth her. "I saw his mind, and I felt his pain."

They turned as one and looked down at the weeping form on the floor. On a whim, Allison pulled away from Aidric and walked over to the mind-mage. She knelt down and after a couple of false starts, hesitantly placed a comforting arm around his shoulders.

Galen jumped at her touch and raised his tear-stained face from behind his hands. His eyes widened when he saw that it was Allison.

He instantly began weeping again and babbled between sobs, "Seni help me, what have I done? What have I done? I'm a beast! A murderer! A traitor to all that Lamia stands for! Summon the guards, Mage-general! Summon the guards so they can take me to my judgment!"

Allison felt Aidric kneel beside her. He too placed a hand comfortingly on Galen's shoulder.

"That won't be necessary," Aidric said firmly, fixing his eyes on Allison who didn't hesitate to nod.

"But—but—I defied the king's wishes!" Galen sputtered, staring at Aidric as if the Mage-general had gone over the deep end as well. "I tried to *murder* your *ward*! I attacked *you*!"

"But you didn't harm either one of us," Aidric said quietly. "That's what is important. Allison and I understand why you were driven to do this. We, too, have had dreams of chaos and death, but they aren't the *only* dreams we have had. Many of us who share the Foresight gift, including Seer Penrith, have also had visions of Roderick's downfall and peace returning to the land and the lands around us. Mind you, it's a peace that will not last long, but any peace, however short-lived, is better than having never experienced any at all."

Aidric glanced over at Allison, and their eyes met. She understood only too well what lay between the lines of what he had said. If everything turned out the way everyone hoped, there would be peace, yes, but the prophecy the Natian Six had left to the world was already unfolding all around them, unbeknownst to all but a select few who were forbidden to speak of it.

"I've been a greater fool than the fools I accused everyone, including the king, of being," Galen said bitterly, refusing the hand Aidric offered him as he rose stiffly to his feet. He glanced down at his half-clad body, his bare feet, and laughed humorlessly. "I look the madman, don't I? I deserve the dungeons, the shackles, for the evil I tried to commit."

"Nonsense," Aidric said firmly. "Go home to your family, Galen. Your children are young, indeed, and they need you. Who am I to deny them their father, their security? Let's all do our best to forget the madness of tonight. I only ask that you give me your solemn oath before the ears of Seni that you will never try to murder Allison again."

Galen lowered his eyes in shame. "You will have it. I don't know what I have ever done to deserve your forgiveness, but I swear to you, Mage-general—and to you, M-Milady Allison—that I'm deeply sorry for what I have done tonight. I swear to you both on all I hold sacred that I shall never, no matter what I may believe, conspire to do ill to the lady again, and may Seni strike me dead if I should ever violate my oath!"

Aidric nodded his satisfaction. Allison was surprised that Aidric had accepted Galen's oath so quickly, but she had learned long ago that Aidric never accepted anything on a whim. He truly believed that Galen was sincere. Glancing down at the dagger that had almost ended her life, she wished she could be just as certain.

As if sensing where her eyes roamed, Aidric slowly bent down and retrieved the dagger. Galen paled when he saw it.

"As for this," Aidric said, frowning down at the thing as if the mere act of touching it made him want to puke, "I'll deal with it properly. I don't even want to know where or how it was obtained, but unless you fancy your neck in a hangman's noose, I suggest that you not try to obtain a second."

"I shall not," was all Galen said. He couldn't look at either of them, his entire demeanor radiating shame.

Allison, on the other hand, looked at them both in confusion. She eyed the dagger more closely. The weapon appeared ordinary enough. In fact, it looked a lot like the daggers all Lamian soldiers were issued. Aidric, himself, owned one very similar to it, so she didn't understand what had just passed between the two men. Were mind-mages forbidden any type of weaponry? If so, it just didn't make sense.

Aidric held the dagger horizontally between his two hands, and the hair on her arms immediately began to stand on end as Allison felt him channeling energy from the Mage-field. The dagger began to glow a brilliant gold, followed by a blinding flash that caused her eyes to burn and tear. A burst of heat also brushed her cheeks. When her vision cleared, the dagger was gone.

Wordlessly, Aidric waved Galen to leave, and the older man was only too happy to obey. Only when she heard the front door clicking shut did Allison lose the calm front she had presented and immediately fell back into Aidric's arms.

"I was so scared!" Allison sobbed, her voice muffled against his chest. "I woke up just as he was swinging the dagger down, and I thought I was dead for sure! Oh God, he would have killed me if you hadn't showed up!"

"But I did come," Aidric crooned softly, stroking her back soothingly, "and now it's over."

For a long time he stood there holding her as she cried softly, until there were no more tears and she stopped shaking. She closed her eyes as he carefully wiped away the stray tears still on her cheeks and gently touched his lips to hers.

"I didn't expect you back so soon," Allison said quietly, raising her gaze to his incredible pale-violet eyes. "I figured you would've been well on your way to the border by now. What happened?"

"Before I answer that, are you certain that you're all right?" Aidric asked, his eyes shadowed with concern.

"I just want to forget that tonight ever happened."

"Not all of it, I hope," he said gruffly.

Allison refused to blush. "No, not all of it."

Aidric released her almost reluctantly and said with an unexpected hint of humor, "I suggest that you put on a robe, little cat, before I tell you of the troubles on the border. You are much too distracting as you are!"

It was then that Allison realized that while she had cried in Aidric's arms, she had forgotten the blankets she had hastily wrapped around herself and that they now lay in a pile at her feet. She let out an undignified squeak and dived for the robe that Aidric had shucked off earlier while he laughed heartily behind her.

"You could've told me earlier!" she said accusingly, belting the robe securely at her waist.

"That I could," he agreed, his voice sounding not in the least bit apologetic.

"Have you no shame?" she demanded in exasperation.

"None," he answered cheerfully, "although you have enough modesty for the both of us."

He seated himself on the edge of the bed and patted the space beside him. Muttering to herself, Allison trudged over to the bed and plopped herself wearily down beside him. Aidric snaked an arm around her waist, and she automatically leaned against him. Just that simple gesture made her feel incredibly cherished. It did a lot to start cleansing the remaining terror of literally coming within an inch of being murdered from her soul that she had been unable to completely force from her mind.

"So?" she prompted.

"Believe it or not, the tampering at the border was nothing more than a young, headstrong apprentice-mage from Lepha with far too much spare time that was trying to prove the strength of his mage powers to his cronies by attempting to be the first mage to ever crack Lamia's Shield. He was powerful enough to cover his magical tracks well, I'll give the braggart that, but he obviously isn't too bright."

"They came all the way here just so one of them could puff out his chest a bit?" Allison asked incredulously.

"Well said. According to him and several of the young men that accompanied him, the boy constructed a portal to bring them all to the edge of our border from Lepha. Seni knows how the whelp managed to accomplish that. The power required to travel the distance he boasts would stretch even my abilities a little. I suspect that he used several portals to reach his final destination and was too thickheaded to admit it.

"Anyway, he had no sense to flee after his attempt failed. Instead, he intended to rest a few sand-marks before beginning a second attempt. Although his shields allowed him to escape the detection of one of the border guard's probes, they weren't strong enough to escape mine. I alerted the border guards to their position, and within a few depths, they were captured. They should arrive here at the palace for the king's judgment within a day."

"What will happen to them?" Allison asked.

Aidric chuckled. "More than likely, they'll receive the fright of their lives. Normally, the offense of tampering with the Shield carries a penalty of being stripped of your mage powers."

Allison's eyes widened. "You can do that?"

"Not I," Aidric replied with a laugh. "Only the High Priest has the knowledge or the power to carry out such a sentence without actually killing the accused. If any other made the attempt, then the mind of the accused would be destroyed."

"Is that what's going to happen to those apprentices?"

"Not likely. There really was no ill intended towards Lamia—at least not consciously. The lad knew the consequences that Lamia would suffer should he have, by some miracle, succeeded, for the only mage who could possibly recast the shield spell is many centuries in his grave. Unfortunately, this type of boastful tampering occurs quite frequently.

"What Diryan will likely do is inform them of the possibility that their mage powers will be stripped from them. Then, they'll be sent to the dungeons while the king and Council 'deliberate' over their punishment. When they've been left to stew long enough, half a day at the longest, they'll be brought before Diryan again to hear his decision. They'll probably be heavily fined and sent back to their mentors. By the time their mentors finish with them, I'm sure they'll wish that Diryan *had* chosen to strip them of their mage abilities. As you know, a mentor is responsible for all debts of their wards."

"I think that given the choice, I would rather rot away in the dungeons if I were in their shoes," Allison said.

"Yes, I suppose you would," Aidric said with a chuckle, "given how everyone must have warned you about my infamous temper, but my temper really isn't as horrid as everyone believes, is it?"

"Worse," she said solemnly, then ducked as Aidric tried to swat her with a pillow.

Before long she managed to arm herself with her own pillow despite Aidric's blows, and they were engaged in an all-out pillow fight that ended with them hopelessly tangled in the blankets surrounded by piles of feathers.

"How old are we?" Allison asked breathlessly between laughs.

"Two," Aidric replied promptly, "but pillow fights are for all ages, so does it matter?"

"It does when the fight takes place so early in the morning. We must be mad!"

"Speak for yourself," he said fiercely, and then silenced any further remark from her with a kiss that quickly led to other things that would have made her blush if her mind hadn't suddenly turned to mush.

CHAPTER THIRTY

Later, as Allison lay comfortably in Aidric's arms, a question nagged in her mind, one that she hadn't had the courage to ask in the past. Now that they knew each other quite intimately, she felt the need to know the answer even more.

"Aidric, who is Alina?" she asked tentatively into the silence.

He instantly stiffened, and for one tense moment, she was afraid that she had overstepped a boundary that should've never been breached. However, after a few beats of strained silence, his body relaxed again, and he let out a sigh unmistakably full of pain.

"Where did you learn of that name?" Aidric asked quietly.

"I've—heard it whispered among the young nobles and some of the servants a few times," she answered just as softly.

"It figures," Aidric said bitterly. "It seems that lot has nothing better to do than to gossip about other people's woes and personal lives."

"They said that she was your lover," Allison forced herself to say, the word "lover" rolling off her tongue as if she had suddenly tasted something vile. "Knowing how much the truth can be stretched among gossips, I didn't know whether to believe them or not. Was she?"

"Yes," he breathed so softly that she almost didn't hear him.

"Raya mentioned to me once that you had been hurt in the past when I first confided my love for you to her, but she said that it wasn't her place to talk about it. She said that if I wanted any details then I would have to ask you myself, so Aidric, now I'm asking. Will you tell me about her?"

Aidric sighed heavily again, as if resigning himself to some unpleasant fate, and said, "I suppose that it's something that you need to know. I've never spoken of that time to anyone except Seninae Jael, and only those directly involved know what actually occurred. In fact, I've been trying my damnedest to forget that she even existed."

He paused for a moment, as if gathering his thoughts, and then continued, "She was the woman that betrayed me, and damn near destroyed my life. She was the daughter of a Na'aran duke, fostered to Lamia's palace as one of Ileanna's ladies-in-waiting. It was there, a little over a year after her arrival, in the queen's chamber that I met her, a pretty, raven-haired girl that immediately stole my heart. My duties had made any relationships near to impossible, and I had been long without a partner. The fool that I was, I was quite taken with the girl, and within a quarter-moon, we became lovers. After a half-moon, she had me completely under her spell, and I was more than willing to offer her my life-ring."

"A life-ring?" Allison asked in confusion, trying to ignore the tightness in her chest at the thought of Aidric sleeping with someone else.

"Ah, I forget that you don't know of such things, though I'm a bit surprised Raya has never mentioned them to you. Let me explain." Was it her imagination, or did he seem relieved to have an excuse to stall the rest of his story? "Each male throughout all Seni's lands visits the primary temple of his kingdom on his fifteenth birthing day to create his life-ring. The ring, itself, is ordinary enough, constructed by the jeweler of the boy's choice, but the gemstone, a flawless crystal, is another matter entirely. At the temple, a member of the Domni order holding the title of Lansha-dom-nae takes a drop of the boy's blood and magically melds it into the crystal until the once clear stone is stained to a hue that is a couple of shades lighter than blood-red. The bride's ring is made during the bond-age ceremony when the two rings are bonded together by the Lansha-domnae, and the couple are spiritually sealed to one another through the magical bonding of their blood through these life-rings.

"Now, under Seni's law, we are only allowed to marry once since this bond can't be broken, even in the death of a spouse, so you can well imagine the im-portance of the step I planned to take with her. If for some reason down the line a couple finds that they are no longer compatible, there is nothing to be done but to endure the situation as best as possible, for should either one betray their spouse, the spell binding their souls together will strike the guilty one dead."

Allison was completely taken aback. "Isn't that a little harsh?"

"Perhaps," he replied thoughtfully, "but with such a price to pay for infidelity, at least one will go into a marriage with some promise of stability when we can only expect an unstable life during this time of war. So you must understand why my offering her my life-ring was a decision that I would've had to live with, come good or ill, for the rest of my life should she have accepted my proposal."

"But she didn't accept your life-ring, did she?" Allison said gently. "You wouldn't be here with me, alive and well, if she had."

"Oh, she accepted it all right," Aidric growled, and in the darkness of the room, she could just make out a grimace on his face. "Indeed, she was only too delighted with this sudden show of my emotional vulnerability. Now, I know what you're thinking, that she betrayed me by accepting my life-ring and then at the last depth refused to marry me. I really wish that it had been that straightforward. I would've been upset, yes, but such a common rejection would never have been enough to nearly destroy my life. In time, I would have recovered and perhaps have even forgiven her, but as I said, it wasn't that simple. Her betrayal was more severe than any of us could've ever imagined, for you see, she was one of Roderick's sycophants."

Allison sucked in a sharp breath. No wonder they had kept the incident such a well-guarded secret! If such a thing had been made known to the general population, then everyone would have begun to look for Roderick's hounds in every shadow—every person who behaved a little strangely would have immediately fallen under suspicion. It would have been the chaos that Roderick dreamed of and in the end, weakened Lamia at its core.

Aidric's arm tightened around her waist. "She betrayed all of us, Lamia, her family, and her kingdom, all to gain the praise of a filthy tyrant. As we were able to learn later on when she was put to the question, she was to have killed me in my bed the very night that I proposed to her. Then she was to take up with one of the twins and do the same to him. Keldan and Aren are only as powerful as they are when they cast their magic in concert. If one were to be disposed of, then the other would have powers no greater than say, Maldon's. With Lamia's most powerful mages put out of commission, then it would've been only a matter of time until he managed to force Diryan into either abandoning our allies or surrendering Lamia to his rule."

"The king would do that?" Allison asked incredulously, finding it hard to imagine the hard-cored man she knew surrendering to anybody, much less to his most hated enemy.

"If he has no other alternative, then yes, he must," Aidric replied grimly. "Many centuries ago, Miron, then the king of Lamia, signed a treaty—witnessed and blessed by the Horae—with Na'ar, Kemos, Oleria, Sersia, and Sonon, those surrounding kingdoms that don't possess a Mage-field within their borders. The treaty promised them protection by Lamia's forces, both magical and non-magical, in exchange for not only funds but also all their citizens with mage potential being sent to Lamia to help supplement those forces, and the treaty remains virtually unchanged to this day. Roderick, of course, is very familiar with this treaty, and he hopes to force Diryan to surrender by capturing either an entire village or even the palace of either Na'ar or Kemos and threatening its demise should Diryan refuse him his demands. Based on this treaty, Diryan can't legally abandon those people to such a tragic fate without bringing down the wrath of the Temple on Lamia."

"But wouldn't surrendering to Roderick be just as bad?"

"No, and both Diryan and Roderick are fully aware of that. Even though living under Roderick's hand would most certainly impoverish all but a few of his selected favorites as he has done to the people of his own kingdom, under Seni's law, any type of living is still considered better than death."

"There doesn't seem to be much logic in that," Allison commented dryly. "I'd rather die than live no better than a slave under that bastard's boot."

"Believe me, little cat, if you just stop to think about it for a bit, the logic is there, and the Brothers in Divinity would be quick to point that out to you. Life is a gift from Seni, and to forfeit such a gift, such as in suicide or because of pride in power, is considered the greatest blasphemy against Seni that mankind can commit. Since Diryan, through the treaty, is sworn to protect these kingdoms, it would be considered pride in power if he should refuse Roderick his demands and allow Roderick to slaughter thousands of people when he has the means to prevent it."

"I see," Allison said, but she really didn't.

Apparently, the concept of separating church from state didn't exist here. Maybe it was time to start focusing her studies on other areas besides magecraft and music, especially since she was a pretty big cog in the kingdom's political machine. After all, if an entire *kingdom* could be surrendered to stop an act of genocide...

"Anyhow, it seems I've strayed from my initial tale," Aidric said, pulling her away from the terrifying direction her thoughts were heading in. "Al—" He swallowed hard. "Forgive me, but I still can't bear to say her name—*she* was only too happy to accept my life-ring. I had just handed my worst enemy the key to my soul on a silver platter. Through her, Roderick could've manipulated my mind as easily as it is to channel since through the magic of my life-ring, my mind can never be shielded from the mind of my chosen life-partner once the bonding ceremony has been performed."

Why does everything have to deal with absolutes in this world? Allison thought in exasperation. *Oath-taking, marriage, religion, treaties—where are all the shades of gray? Whatever happened to compromise? It almost as if everyone's going out of their way to borrow trouble by being so inflexible.*

However, that was a discussion best left for later when Aidric wasn't so upset.

"And what about before the bonding ceremony?" she asked.

"By the mere act of wearing my life-ring, it automatically allowed me to penetrate any bodily or mental shields around her, no matter the castor. However, that particular fact foolishly slipped her mind, and that night while she lay beside me in my bed, she made the mistake of thought-speaking Roderick. I heard every traitorous word."

He paused for a moment, and Allison sensed that whatever it was that he had to say next wasn't very easy to reveal. She felt the conflict within him, and her empathic senses were picking up frightening amounts of rage beneath all the feelings of betrayal and anguish.

"Aidric, you don't have to—"

"When I—" he cut her off sharply. "—when I overheard her bespeaking Roderick, I—went mad. Because of the life-ring, she immediately realized that she was discovered and tried to stab me with a dagger very similar to the one Galen tried to use on you tonight."

Ah, so that explained his peculiar look when he had held Galen's spelled dagger in his hands. It must have brought back painful memories that he would have just as soon left buried in the past.

"However, I had the advantage of rage over her, and my offensive instincts were much faster than hers. I had her flying across the room and pinned helplessly to the floor with a paralysis spell before she could even raise the spelled dagger that she had pulled from beneath her pillow. My rage had been sensed by every empath in the palace, including Selwyn, and they came running. I would've torn her to shreds with my bare hands had they not appeared in time to restrain me. In the end, it took seven mages, among them Keldan, Aren, Raya, and Maldon, to subdue me.

"The next morning she was questioned, then tried by the Circle. I watched her dangle from the end of a noose until her body no longer twitched and then left the gallows with the intention of ending my life."

The empty smile that stretched his lips was the most heartbreaking thing Allison had ever seen, and she was at a loss of how to make it go away. The only thing she *could* do was hug his middle more tightly and silently remind him that he *did* have people that loved him very much, that he didn't have to feel so alone anymore.

"I was just so tired of it all, tired of all the betrayals, tired of Roderick's dagger always at my throat." His words just kept coming in rapid bursts, as though he knew he needed to get them out but wanting it all over as quickly as possible just the same. "It was Selwyn and Keldan who stopped me. They sent me to Seninae Jael, and it was he who helped me pick up the pieces of my life. For that, I'm forever in his debt no matter what he says!"

They both lay together in silence for a long while after Aidric finished his story, each lost in their own thoughts. Allison couldn't imagine what she would've done had someone betrayed her the way Alina had betrayed Aidric. She couldn't help feeling an intense hatred for the woman whom she thankfully never knew that had driven Aidric so close to the brink of self-destruction.

Finally, she said into the silence, "I'm surprised that you weren't suspicious of *me* considering all you've been through. Everyone else seemed to think Roderick had sent me at first. Gaelle certainly did."

"Gaelle is a pig-headed bitch whose nose is dangerously close to touching one of the suns," Aidric said dryly. "Besides, any fool knows that the hue of your hair couldn't have been the result of an illusion. Seni simply doesn't allow that to be possible. Plus, you forget that I probed your mind, and the only sinister thing I found there was your innocence."

"You Lamians must be very unbelievably naughty if you think that *I'm* the epitome of innocence!" Allison retorted with a laugh, relieved that he sounded more like his usual self.

"Ah, but are you not a Lamian also?"

She lifted herself up until her lips brushed against Aidric's ear and whispered, "Well, after tonight, I suppose I am."

EPILOGUE

Three moons passed without incident after that initial night of terror and revelation. Galen continued to hold true to his word, and although he made no move to harm Allison, he did go out of his way to avoid her presence. Whether it was because of fear or embarrassment, neither Allison nor Aidric was certain, but Aidric assured her that the oath the man had sworn to them was a powerful one, an oath that would put his soul in jeopardy should he ever choose to violate it. Given how seriously everyone seemed to take their spiritual beliefs, Allison didn't expect any more trouble from that direction—one less thing that she had to worry about.

Day in and day out, Allison worked hard at her mage and bardic lessons, her powers growing swiftly daily. Now, the full scope of her mage powers was almost a match for Aidric's. In some areas, her powers even exceeded his, such as in shield penetration, and he believed that in time, they would all exceed his magical threshold beyond anyone's imagination.

The only spells she had yet to attempt were the portal spell and her extraordinary gift of Soulwalking. Of the former, Aidric told her that she would be ready for her first attempt within the next half-moon, and the latter, she was simply afraid to even try, refusing to do it no matter how much Aidric insisted that she must. The thought of walking the lands in her spirit form while her body lay death-like elsewhere unnerved her to no end.

Allison was terrified of being lost in that spirit plane between life and death forever should something happen to her body while she didn't occupy it. Eventually, she knew that the time would come when she could no longer run from that particular ability, but until that inevitable time came, she comforted herself by refusing to even acknowledge that she could do something that was essentially astral-projection.

On a happier note, not only did her mage powers seem to strengthen more with every passing day, but her emotional bond to Aidric did as well. They both seemed more alive now than ever, and their closest friends were quick to point that out. Their relationship was predictably the hottest subject among the gossip circles of the palace and even in the villages.

Now and then, Allison heard the whispered speculation amongst the huddled groups of nobles in the courtyard of how much longer it would be before Aidric offered her his life-ring. Even the servants could be found whispering their own speculations in the shadows of the palace corridors. Raya had told her that there was even a betting pool going around concerning the date Aidric would propose to her, and she didn't know whether to be irritated or to laugh.

The prospect of such a proposal excited her. Allison wanted nothing more than to become Aidric's wife, but hell would freeze over before she ever brought it up, herself. She still wasn't sure how much Aidric had really healed over that Alina affair even though he often insisted that particular tragedy was all in the past. It may very well be years before he felt secure enough with her to offer her, literally, a part of his soul for all eternity. She would wait a hundred years for him if that's what he needed.

All in all, everything seemed perfect to her—maybe *too* perfect. Her lessons were going well, and her relationship with Aidric was as strong as ever and growing stronger every day. Her friendships to Raya, Selwyn, Queen Ileanna and all her ladies, and the rest of Aidric's friends deepened. In fact, few people these days, except the exceptionally stubborn, scarcely looked at her askance or anxiously shied away from her presence because of who she was. Most simply took her presence at court for granted. Aidric had been totally right that the Lamians would quickly see her as just another mage out of dozens at court. Allison had never been happier.

Even that insufferable bastard, Patrym, had left the palace a few quarter-moons after the incident in the courtyard, forfeiting his Lamian citizenship. A few eyebrows had risen when King Diryan had granted Patrym's forfeiture without delay and little comment, but no one had dared to question the king's motives. King Diryan Lasha was not known as an impulsive man, and trusting to their king's reasoning had thus far earned the kingdom nothing but prosperity.

Not surprisingly, word of what Allison had done to Patrym had spread like a wildfire across dry brush in the court circles, although more often than not, the mage who had seared him was not her. Soon, the tale had been twisted so severely that nobody could swear which version was the truth. Many even had scoffed at Patrym when he had sworn that the Golden Mage had caused his injury. Apparently, his arrogant reputation and his inclination towards exaggeration didn't in the least bit help with the validity of his story. *Of course* only the Golden Mage could have done such a thing to him…

Thoroughly shamed, Patrym had chosen to leave rather than live as a lesser man than he had once been. It was rumored that he had gone as far as Lepha. Allison wasn't the only one at court happy to see him go. She suspected that Aidric had lent a hand in spreading so much disinformation. However, when she had confronted him about it, Aidric had merely smiled and said nothing, which for Aidric, was no answer at all.

Shockingly, even Roderick seemed to be behaving himself. There had been no more surprise attacks of villages ever since the Mihran troops had been driven from both Kemos and Na'ar, nor had there been any more attempts to bring down Lamia's Shield. Although this sudden non-action from Mihr's monarch allowed the citizens of Lamia to breathe a sigh of relief, it only worried the king and his councilors more.

This quiet was so unlike Roderick that Diryan figured this was merely the calm before the storm. He was already receiving very disturbing reports of Roderick building up his army and recruiting new mages from Bar'taiver and Rathtyen—a land infamously known to spawn an obscene amount of power-hungry mages with the morals of demons.

Then one morning in early fall, as was only inevitable, everything suddenly went to hell. It started during Allison's early morning mage lesson when Aidric was abruptly called away to King Diryan's study. Lord Ion had bespoken him, but had offered no details, only that the matter was urgent.

Allison feared the worse. She knew that things had been all too entirely quiet down in Mihr and how much that fact seemed to upset Aidric, the king, his councilors, and the Circle. Had Roderick finally made his major play? Would this be the final conflict that would push Diryan to declare open war on Mihr? Would Aidric be sent to lead his magical troops today? Would *she* be sent to the battle lines? These questions and many more whirled around in her mind as she sat in the sitting room anxiously waiting for Aidric to return, an opened spellbook lying ignored across her knees.

Allison was a bundle of nerves by the time Aidric returned about a sand-mark later, wearing a scowl on his face and barely controlled anger flashing in his eyes.

"Is it Roderick?" Allison immediately demanded, wincing inwardly at the shrillness of her voice. "Has he attacked another village?"

Aidric shook his head. "It's something just as bad, I fear. The Ans-domnae is dead."

"Soren's father?" she exclaimed, her eyes widening a little in surprise. "Was he murdered?"

Allison was relieved when Aidric shook his head,

though by his slight hesitation, it was clear that he had his doubts. "According to the High Priest, he died innocently enough. The official story is that he was devastated that the son he had held in such high regard had met such a terrible, pointless end, and he simply lost the will to live. Plausible as it's happened more than once in the past, but I knew the Ans-domnae personally. He was a hardened man, one who seemed to have no feelings other than those he showed for his vocation.

"Although I'm certain that he loved Soren in his own way, I don't believe that even the death of his eldest son would have shattered him to that degree. It was Seni whom he held most dear in his heart, and I don't believe that he would shirk his sworn duty to Him on account of a mortal, son or no."

"So you think that he was secretly murdered and made to look like he pined himself away with grief?" Allison ventured, horrified at the thought. "Is such a thing even possible?"

"Perhaps," Aidric replied bemusedly as he gazed out of the window into the garden. "Such things have been done before, mostly by a monarch's offspring that is tired of waiting for his or her crown. It's not beyond a mage to tamper so severely with someone's mind. I can do it myself, and easily, but I've never had a good enough reason to actually do it without the threat of it weighing heavily on my soul."

"But who would want Soren and his father dead?" Allison asked, shaking her head.

"Ah, that is the question, isn't it?" Aidric answered, turning to face her again, his lips stretched in a bitter smile. "Who would stand to gain the most from the death of the Ans-domnae? That question, I believe, answers itself by who was just appointed the new Ans-domnae—none other than our dear Domnae Eban."

Allison started at the name. "*Eban?* But how—" She cut herself off in mid-sentence as she suddenly understood what Aidric was insinuating. "You think that Eban's the murderer…" she said quietly.

A memory suddenly flashed in her mind, one she had hoped to bury forever. *A corridor black as pitch—reaching out to grasp the handle of her door—something slamming into her body with the force of a sledge hammer—a frightened boy's words. "Eban—ne—Ans-domnae—vartunor! Vartunor!"*

Could that novice, Ren, have Foreseen Eban's promotion and the Ans-domnae's death? Is that what he had been doing when he had done something unauthorized with his magic that night? Had he been trying to force his mind to see more through the use of his mage powers, or had he actually been trying to stop Eban from doing whatever he had seen?

Don't be stupid, she chided herself. *You're grasping at straws. For all I know, that novice shouting Eban's and the Ans-domnae's names was pure coincidence.*

She quickly focused her attention on Aidric again, determined not to think about it again. The last thing she needed to do was stick her nose into a potential nest of vipers.

"Diryan believes that I'm seeing shadows where there are none," Aidric was saying, "but yes, I believe that Eban is responsible. I've always suspected him to have had some part in Domnae Soren's murder, although before now, it was a draw between Eban and Roderick. However, my opinion holds no weight since everyone believes me biased on the matter because of my past with the bloody bastard, but I assure you, as I have assured the king on numerous occasions, I know Eban's mind better than any other. He showed me a part of himself those many years ago, a stain I doubt any other has seen and lived to reveal. Eban and Roderick could have been born brothers, for they share a very similar greed for power and the same sadistic means of obtaining it!"

"But what power has he really gained?" Allison asked in puzzlement. "Didn't you tell me that the Ans-domnae only lords over the rest of the Domni, and in a sense, acts as a sort of messenger between the High Priest's will to the Domni?"

"Yes, and he can't order the Domni to do his bidding on anything major without the express permission of the High Priest. However, the Ans-domnae does have a certain privilege that not even the Ansseninae has—the ear of the High Priest, for the Ans-domnae also acts as the High Priest's chief advisor."

"Oh," she said faintly, feeling the blood beginning to drain from her cheeks. Suddenly she understood only too well what Eban had in mind.

Aidric nodded in satisfaction at her response and added, "It's true that Eban can't ever scheme to proclaim himself the High Priest. Only Seni may decide who holds that office, and He would never ordain such a vile piece of filth to hold the highest seat of power in all His lands. The mark of Seni on the brow of the High Priest cannot be faked. That being said, as Ans-domnae, Eban *does* legally have the ear of the High Priest now, a boy young enough and naïve enough to be manipulated by the bastard until the lad is no more than a puppet, his strings in the hands of a man as evil as Roderick!"

"Then why don't *you* seek an audience with the High Priest and tell him everything you've just told me?" Allison asked with a frown. "I know he's young, but he can't possibly be naïve enough to not see reason when it hits him directly in the head! There must be a good reason why Seni chose him for such an important seat of power, after all."

Her question seemed to agitate him even more. "I do not," Aidric answered quietly, turning his face away from her, "because I *cannot.*"

That wasn't the answer Allison had been expecting. She had thought that he would recite one of those seemingly infinite, divine laws of Seni that prevented him from leveling such an accusation, no matter how true, on an Ans-domnae or other such nonsense. The Brothers in Divinity, after all, were supposedly answerable only to Seni and themselves.

She folded her arms over her chest in exasperation. "Why not?"

Aidric was silent for a few moments before he finally lifted his gaze to meet her puzzled one. He sighed and then said with a hint of weariness in his voice, "I have my reasons, Allison. Once again, it boils down to that last quarter-moon I spent as a novice in the Temple, and I've told you that what occurred during that time I can't ever reveal to you. I've sworn to myself never to reveal that secret I've buried so carefully in the darkest depths of my soul, and never shall I forswear it!"

Allison flinched at the fervor in his voice, if not in a little fear at the smoldering rage that lay beneath those words. *What are you hiding, Aidric? What could have possibly happened to you that's so terrible that you refuse to talk about it even to me after all we've shared?*

"Aidric," she began carefully, "you've carried this burden on your soul for so long. Why do you insist on suffering more than you have to? I can tell that this secret of yours is eating away at you, and the pain that it's causing will only get worse as time goes on. I love you, Aidric, and you know that I'm always here for you as you've always been there for me every time I've fallen apart. I hate to know that you're suffering like this."

"Allison, please," Aidric said so quietly that it was almost inaudible, "I *cannot.* Don't ask this of me."

Though distressed, Allison nodded reluctantly, knowing that for now, that was all she could do.

***

His food had grown cold long ago, but Roderick hardly noticed. Lost in his memories and thoughts of his latest dream featuring the mysterious voice, his grumbling stomach was the last thing on his mind. This dream had been more disturbing than all the others combined. It was of a different landscape than all the others, different, yet somehow the same. Even his point of view had changed. Roderick no longer found himself experiencing the action of the dream, but merely observing it from a god's eye point-of-view.

The world had fallen into night, yet Roderick could see the faces of his army and the silhouettes of the enemy army clearly as though it had been day. He could even see the blue and silver colors of the Lamian uniforms, and the black and gold of his own army's. However, he didn't once think this new night vision strange. It had felt natural, as if he'd had this ability to see as clearly in the dark as an owl since birth.

Then his eyes had fallen onto the figure of a silver-haired man dressed in black and gold robes positioned directly before the Mihran army. Roderick scarcely had to think about wanting a closer view of the man's face before he found himself looking directly into the face of an old man—his own face! It had been a blow as violent as a mage blast to the chest.

Roderick had immediately returned to his more distant point-of-view of the battle, shaken more than he had ever been in his life. He was *old*! He was still at war with Lamia! How could that be?

As the battle horns blew, and the battle began and progressed, it became appallingly clear which side would emerge the victor. The Mihran troops were being slaughtered as if they were merely annoying insects to the Lamians to be smashed between their fingers. *No*! It couldn't be!

No matter how hard Roderick struggled to intervene, it was clear that his role this time was merely as an observer. Helpless for the first time in his life, Roderick had watched his own army annihilated and Aidric, as young in appearance as he was now, sear the older Roderick to ashes.

And that mysterious voice, the voice he had not heard since he had attempted to capture the Golden Mage in Kal, had spoken suddenly as he had watched his own body burning to ash, *"Would you have it so, Mihran king?"*

Roderick had awakened still cursing Aidric's name, the voice echoing mockingly in his sleep-muddled mind.

At first, the dream had infuriated him, but now he understood its warning. He had been silent too long. He had allowed the Lamians to breathe easily perhaps too long. Now it was time to show all of Seni's World his power. His time of waiting was over.

ABOUT THE AUTHOR

C.G. Garcia lives in a small West Texas town whose claim to fame is having the world's largest Rattlesnake Round-Up. She has a degree in computer science, but due to life's twisted sense of humor, ended up working in a pharmacy. A lifelong lover of all things fantasy, science fiction, paranormal and romance, she is also the author of the *Fractured Multiverse* urban fantasy/science fantasy series and the *Old Souls* epic fantasy series.

THE LAST STONE CAST
The Golden Mage Book Three

With her bond to Aidric now stronger than ever, Allison feels that she has at last become a part of Lamia and is experiencing a measure of happiness despite the loss of Soren. However, after several moons of quiet, King Diryan's spies bring news of a monstrous Mihran army marching towards Kemos, one of Lamia's allied kingdoms, forcing the king to declare war on Mihr that very day. With the powers that be still unwilling to allow her to go beyond the Shield out of fear of the prophecy she still has yet to fulfill, Allison watches Aidric and her friends go off to war, feeling idle and useless. However, fate will not be denied, and soon Allison finds herself in the awful position of being forced to make a decision everyone, including herself, had prayed she would never have to make.

www.ingramcontent.com/pod-product-compliance
Lightning Source LLC
Chambersburg PA
CBHW031415240626
47154CB00001B/42